Praise f

WATC

the

GUARD

"Clever plotting and
vate this novel into a first-rate romantic thriller. Revisiting this world will be a great pleasure."

—*Romantic Times BOOKreviews*

"Jenna Black has crafted a fine story with *Watchers in the Night*. She supplies deft handling of plot, characters, and genre, and I enjoyed the novel tremendously. I see many more fascinating novels coming from this author in the future!"

—Heather Graham, *New York Times* and *USA Today* bestselling author

"You'll want to bare your throat to Jenna Black's enthralling heroes. This cleverly plotted romantic tale will leave you hungry for more!"

—Sabrina Jeffries, *New York Times* bestselling author of *One Night With a Prince*

"Mystery, magic, and vampires! In *Watchers in the Night,* Jenna Black has created a fresh and fascinating vampire universe. What more could any lover of the paranormal ask for?"

—Lori Handeland

"Jenna Black's *Watchers in the Night* is sexy, suspenseful, and what a great read! Vampire Gray James hits the top of my Hot-O-Meter from the moment he comes back from the dead to save his girlfriend, Carolyn Mathers—who just happens to be a kick-ass PI able to take care of herself. Just the right mix of mystery, vampires, romance, great characters, and underworld shenanigans to keep me happy. I can't wait to see what happens next in the world of the Guardians!"

—Tess Mallory

TOR PARANORMAL ROMANCE BOOKS
BY JENNA BLACK

Watchers in the Night
Secrets in the Shadows
Shadows on the Soul
Hungers of the Heart

Hungers of the Heart

Jenna Black

tor paranormal romance

A TOM DOHERTY ASSOCIATES BOOK
NEW YORK

HUNGERS OF THE HEART

A Tor Book
Published by Tom Doherty Associates, LLC
175 Fifth Avenue
New York, NY 10010

www.tor-forge.com

ISBN-13: 978-0-7653-5718-2
ISBN-10: 0-7653-5718-6

First Edition: May 2008

Printed in the United States of America

0 9 8 7 6 5 4 3 2 1

For Dan, the prince who
kissed me awake

My first big thank you goes to my new editor, Heather Osborn, who faced the daunting task of having to edit this book the minute she walked in the door. Thanks as usual to my agent, Miriam Kriss, who helped tame my butterflies even if she can't eradicate them. Thanks to Sandy, the Researching Dragon, who helped find the answers to some of my "weird writer questions." And last, I'd like to thank the Heart of Carolina Romance writers, for being such an overwhelmingly supportive group. You're the best!

Hungers of the Heart

Prologue

From the moment he entered the meeting hall in Eli's mansion by the Delaware River, Drake knew this was going to be one of those nights. All it had taken was one look at the smug malice in Fletcher's expression. The pup was going to make another attempt to get Drake tossed out. It seemed to have become his pet project, though so far all he'd managed to do was escalate the tension between Drake and the others.

Anticipation made Drake's fangs descend. He curled his lip in silent threat, but Fletcher ignored him, and no one else noticed. Drake stood in his usual place—a corner that left a good six feet between him and the nearest Guardian. He might be the Guardians' ally, but never would he be mistaken for a true member of their happy little family.

As usual, Fletch waited until the meeting was all but adjourned before he pounced.

"I have another vampire kill I want to tell you about," Fletch said just as the other Guardians had started to rise from their chairs.

All voices in the room died, and everyone took their seats again as Fletcher strode to the middle of the room.

"Fletcher . . ." Eli said in a warning tone, looking up from his traditional seat by the fireplace.

Drake ground his teeth. Eli might admonish Fletcher for speaking, but he never seemed to *stop* him. And anything Drake said would only increase the chance of violence.

"This one's different, Eli," Fletcher said. "You need to know about it."

And Eli, damn him, didn't argue. Drake pushed away from the wall he'd been leaning against, standing up straight and glaring at the son of a bitch who'd been making his life miserable for months on end. He bared his fangs for all to see. Maybe a little violence was just what he needed.

Fletcher wouldn't be the first Guardian Drake had ever killed, but he would be the first one Drake *enjoyed* killing.

Fletcher boldly met his eyes, all but daring Drake to cross the short distance between them and start something. Drake itched to do just that, but doubted Eli would allow it. The overwhelming power of Eli's glamour would keep them apart no matter how badly they wanted to beat the hell out of each other. Of course, once they left the meeting it would be a different story. Fletch and some of his cronies had jumped Drake once before. Perhaps it was time for Drake to return the favor. . . .

Fletch bared his own fangs in response. "No, Killer. This time, *you're* the one who's gone too far." He reached into his shirt pocket and pulled out a folded sheet of newspaper, partially unfolding it to display a photograph. "Recognize him?" he asked, moving closer so Drake could get a good look.

Almost against his will, Drake's gaze locked on the photograph. As usual with newspaper photos, it was grainy and indistinct. The face was that of a youngish black man, smiling at the camera. Drake didn't recognize the face, but the guy must have been one of his kills. This was Fletcher's usual MO in his quest to make trouble for Drake: show the Guardians photos of the victims and families, reminding them that although Drake only killed scumbags, those scumbags were still human beings.

If Drake had killed the man, surely he should recognize the picture. But no memory stirred. When had Drake become so inured to his kills that he couldn't even recognize the face of a recent victim?

Fletcher must have read his hesitation and the reason behind it, for his face twisted in disgust and he snorted. "You're as likely to recognize him as a mortal is to recognize the cow his steak came from."

"Fletcher . . ." Eli said again, his voice a little sharper.

Fletcher's eyes bored into Drake's. "Give me one more minute, Eli," he said, unfolding the newspaper all the way. "This story's got a hell of a punch line."

The headline that was revealed when Fletcher unfolded the newspaper struck Drake like a fist in the face.

"Undercover Cop Found Slain in Alley."

Shock and dismay stole his voice, and he could do nothing but stand there and stare at the picture of the smiling mortal, and at the damning headline.

"Should I tell you about his widow and their kids?" Fletcher asked.

A denial wanted to crawl up Drake's throat, but the truth was he had no idea if he was guilty or not. For a long, long time he'd been at peace with his nature. He couldn't help his need to kill, but he could appease his conscience by killing people the world was better off without. He'd never considered the possibility of an undercover cop.

The silence in the room was an oppressive weight. Not even Drake's few allies among the Guardians could come to his defense this time.

Was Fletcher telling the truth?

"I don't recognize him," Drake said, but his voice sounded shaky, not his own. "You're just making this up, trying to stir up trouble."

"Like hell I am! I saw you kill him. And now I have proof positive that you're no different than the filthy, soulless Killers we destroy."

Drake was the Guardians' one exception to the rule that any vampire who was addicted to the kill had to die. Well, except for Gabriel, Eli's son, but that was because Gabriel didn't live in Philadelphia, in their territory. From the condemning silence that draped the room, he suspected that exception wouldn't apply much longer.

"That's enough, Fletcher," Eli said, breaking the silence. "You've made your point. The meeting is adjourned. Drake, I'd like you to stay behind."

Drake nodded, but didn't look in Eli's direction. He didn't even consider making a run for it. Even if he somehow escaped the assembled Guardians, he couldn't escape Eli's glamour. Besides, he didn't really think Eli was going to kill him, though he knew that's what Fletcher and many of the other Guardians expected.

He nearly jumped out of his skin when Gray James, the only other member of the Guardians ever to have fed on a kill, clapped him on the shoulder, a hint of support. Gray had been forced into his single kill by his maker, but had managed to avoid becoming addicted. When Drake had been changed, more than a century ago, his maker hadn't forced him to kill—he'd just neglected to mention that Drake had any choice in the matter.

Of course, given who Drake had been before he'd been turned, he hadn't been as troubled by the killing as perhaps he should have been.

After Gray made the first move, a handful of the other Guardians made their own silent demonstrations of support. But most of them either ignored him or regarded him with undisguised loathing.

After the last Guardian was gone, Drake waited for Eli to pass judgment, every instinct in his body telling him he wouldn't like that judgment one bit. At least the room hadn't gone cold like it did when Eli was really, really pissed.

"Did you do it?" Eli finally asked, his voice carefully neutral.

Drake sighed heavily, but it did nothing to relieve his tension. All these years, he'd convinced himself that he was a Killer with a conscience, that he was somehow better, more worthy of life than other Killers. Had he been lying to himself all along? "I don't know. I don't recognize him, but that doesn't necessarily mean I didn't kill him." He scrubbed a hand through his hair. Just how much did Fletch hate him, anyway? Enough to lie about this?

Probably. In Fletcher's black-and-white view of the world, all Killers were evil and had to be destroyed. If making up a story like this was the only way to get Drake killed, or at least kicked out of the city, then he might feel it was his duty.

But even if this was a lie, the very fact that it was possible was highly . . . disturbing.

"Sit down," Eli said.

Drake didn't like the tone of Eli's voice, or the look on his face. He had a feeling that Fletcher was going to get his wish.

He'd allowed himself to become complacent during the decades he'd worked for Eli. But he, more than anyone, should have known that nothing ever lasts.

"Gabriel's been after me for months to come to Baltimore," Drake said, staying on his feet. That was a slight exaggeration. Gabriel, a fellow Killer and a born vampire of immense power, had invited Drake to join his fledgling Guardian organization in his home city of Baltimore, but the invitation had only been offered once. Still, Drake was certain he'd be welcome there. Of course, it would mean working for an unstable hard-ass with a cruel streak a mile wide. Somehow, he didn't think Gabriel would make quite the benevolent leader that Eli did.

"I see," Eli replied. The fact that he didn't insist Drake sit down as ordered suggested he was already letting go. "And you'd like to take him up on his offer?"

Drake gritted his teeth. No, he didn't want to. Philadelphia had been his adopted home for more than a century, and though the Guardians had never accepted him, he'd felt . . . comfortable here. Working for Gabriel would be anything but comfortable. Hell, Drake wasn't even sure he'd manage to live very long with Gabriel as a boss. However, if he was going to be kicked out anyway, he might as well salvage what little dignity he could manage.

"You don't really need me in Philadelphia anymore," he said, forcing the words out. Now that Eli had learned how to create an avatar, an illusory version of himself that was capable of leaving the grounds of his mansion even though he couldn't leave in body, he was no longer so badly in need of Drake's strength. Guardians would forever be the underdogs against Killers, whose strength, both psychic and physical, was significantly greater. But Eli was one hell of an ace in the hole.

Another long and uncomfortable silence draped the room. Drake couldn't help hoping that Eli would ask him to stay, but wasn't surprised when he didn't.

"It might be best for all involved if you joined Gabriel in Baltimore," Eli said softly. "I'm sure that if you really did kill this man, it was under the assumption that he was just another criminal. And as you know, I'm in no position to throw stones. But I'm not sure that Fletcher and his friends won't eventually take things into their own hands if you stay."

Drake's anger spiked. "Don't play games with me, Eli. We both know that if you ordered him to behave, he would. If you want me gone, be man enough to say it."

Eli merely raised one gray eyebrow and regarded him with mild condescension. "If I wanted you gone, I'd say so. And I don't know where you get the idea that my authority is so unshakable it could survive anything. Provoke him enough, and Fletcher will risk the consequences of disobeying me. If you have an offer from Gabriel, I think it will be better for everyone if you take it."

Drake still thought Eli was being a hypocrite, but the man was more than a thousand years old. Once he took a stance, there was no budging him.

"Fine. I guess this is goodbye, then." Drake did his best to hide his pain under a stony façade.

Eli slowly rose from his seat. He had wiped all expression from his face, an infuriating trick of his. "I suppose it is." He reached out his hand for Drake to shake.

Drake wanted to turn his back and get the hell out of there immediately, but he forced himself to shake Eli's hand. Memories of other goodbyes hammered at the walls of his mind, but he savagely forced them away. There was no one better than he at keeping the past locked in the past where it belonged.

Of course, Eli being Eli, he wouldn't just shake hands. He held on when Drake tried to pull away.

"You're still one of the good guys," Eli said. "Even if you killed this man. I hope you realize that."

Drake wasn't so sure. Once upon a time, he had most assuredly *not* been one of the good guys. Maybe he'd never really changed.

"Uh-huh," Drake grunted, meeting Eli's gaze once more.

Eli gave him a sad smile. "You're too angry with me to talk right now, I know, but if you ever need anything, you know my number." He finally released Drake's hand.

Without another word, Drake turned his back and walked away.

1

DRAKE HAD BEEN living in Baltimore for almost a month, and he still hadn't fully moved in to his new house. The place had belonged to a fledgling Killer Gabriel had dispatched when he'd taken over as Master of Baltimore, and no one had set foot in it since its owner's death. So far, Drake had spent most of his time cleaning out the detritus of six months' neglect and repairing the worst of the damages. It appeared the former occupant hadn't been much of a handyman. Or a housekeeper.

Tonight's task was to get rid of the hideous peeling wallpaper in the first-floor bathroom. He'd feared he'd have to steam it off—a tedious and time-consuming process—but when he started pulling at one of the strips, it tore away easily from the wall. Unfortunately, the wall beneath the wallpaper was painted a dreadful shade of puke green. Drake was beginning to hate this damn house.

He'd just torn off the last strip of wallpaper—along with a big patch of the ugly green paint—when his doorbell rang. He stuffed the wallpaper into the trash, then tried to rinse some of the sticky, pasty mess off his hands as the doorbell rang again, repeatedly. A quick psychic survey told him there was a vampire on his doorstep. He hoped it wasn't Gabriel—he was feeling too surly right now to keep his tongue under control, and Gabriel usually rubbed him the wrong way within the first five minutes of any conversation.

His hands were still sticky, and he would probably have to use Lava soap to get all the paste off, but whoever was ringing the bell didn't seem eager to wait.

Drake exited the bathroom and headed for the front door, realizing it couldn't be Gabriel. If Gabriel wanted in this badly, he would have used his telekinetic powers to unlock the door. The doorbell was now accompanied by the sound of a fist hammering against the wood.

"I'm coming!" Drake shouted as he hurried through the living room, temper flaring. He doubted whoever was at the door could hear over the constant ringing and banging.

He didn't bother looking through the peephole, instead flinging the door open as soon as he'd unlocked the last lock.

The temper that had been simmering in his chest died down instantly when he saw Jezebel, Gabriel's fledgling and lady-love, standing on his doorstep with red-rimmed eyes and tear tracks on her cheeks. Now that she wasn't pounding on the door anymore, her arms were crossed over her chest and her shoulders hunched in what looked like a defensive position. She looked small and miserable and frightened, and foreboding buzzed through Drake's body. He quickly stepped aside to let her in.

"What's wrong?" he asked.

Jez stood in the foyer and shivered. "Gabriel's missing."

Drake frowned, then took her by the arm and guided her into the living room. She didn't seem capable of moving on her own, and her eyes were distant, as if only a fraction of her attention was focused in this room. He had to press down on her shoulders to get her to sit on the couch. Then he took a seat next to her.

"What do you mean, missing?" he asked.

She blinked, and her eyes finally focused on his face. She shivered again. "I mean I can't find him anywhere, and when I try to communicate with him, I get nothing."

By some quirk of Gabriel's unusual birth, his bond with Jezebel was much closer than the usual bond between a master and fledgling. They were able to sense each other's emotions to some extent, and they were able to communicate telepathically.

"I can still . . . feel him. He's alive. But I can't reach him." She looked at Drake with wide, frightened eyes. "What can that mean?"

"Maybe he's blocking you for some reason." Drake could well imagine Gabriel trying to block her out if he was doing something she wouldn't like. But Jezebel shook her head.

"This feels different."

"Did he have any plans for the day that you know of?" Another of the many differences between Gabriel and "normal" vampires was his ability to tolerate the sunlight. Most vampires grew progressively more tolerant as they aged, but Gabriel had been able to travel about as freely as a mortal man since puberty.

A tear leaked from Jezebel's eye and she wiped it away with the back of her hand. "Not that he told me. He came to bed with me this morning, and when I woke up at sunset, he was gone." She sniffed loudly, then swallowed back tears. "We have to find him."

"I assume you tried calling his cell?"

She gave him a look of pure annoyance. "Of course I did."

He made a placating gesture with one hand. "I was just making sure. You looked pretty distraught when I first opened the door." She still looked miserable and frightened, but she wasn't much of a weeper. When the initial shock wore off, she would leap into action with reckless abandon. It was the "reckless" part that worried him.

"If someone's hurt him," she said, "I'll kill them."

Jez wasn't a Killer. In fact, as far as Drake knew, she'd never killed anyone, mortal or vampire. But the look in her eyes said she meant what she said.

"Let's not jump to conclusions just yet," he counseled. "Gabriel's damn hard to hurt. I'm sure there's a perfectly good reason you can't reach him right now. He'll probably be in touch soon. It's only been, what, forty minutes or so since sunset? Maybe time got away from him and he hasn't realized you're awake yet."

But Jez shook her head. "If he were planning to go out, he would have told me. *Especially* if he was going so far away we couldn't communicate."

Drake wasn't so sure. Gabriel was an autocratic, controlling bastard, and though there was no question he loved Jez, Drake could think of any number of reasons why he'd neglect to share his plans with her.

Jez skewered him with a piercing stare. "Did he tell *you* he was planning to be away?"

The thought was laughable—Gabriel wasn't big on sharing. "He didn't mention anything."

Jez looked suspicious. "I'd better not find out this is some kind of male conspiracy to protect my delicate sensibilities."

Drake couldn't help smiling. "You won't. I swear, he didn't confide in me. But I still think it's too early to get upset. I'm sure he wouldn't intentionally worry you like this, but he's as capable of making a mistake as the next man. Why don't we head back to your place and wait to see if we hear from him?"

She leapt to her feet with an impatient grunt. "I can't just sit around and *wait*!" She started toward the door, but Drake cut her off before she reached it. She was more on edge than he'd realized, because she actually lowered her fangs and growled at him. "Get out of my way, Drake."

He kept his voice low and soothing. "Hold on a minute. You can't just go dashing off by yourself without a plan."

"Watch me," she snapped, trying to dodge around him.

If Gabriel really was in some kind of trouble, then Jez was clearly no match for the enemy. And whether Gabriel was in trouble or not, if Drake let her rush into danger, Gabriel would kill him. He once again blocked her path, this time grabbing her arms to hold her still.

Her eyes practically glowed with fury. "Let go."

Of course, if he manhandled Jez in an attempt to keep her here, Gabriel would probably object to that, too.

"Please, Jezebel," he said, trying to imbue his voice with all the calming, soothing qualities Eli always did. "Let's go back to your house first and make certain he hasn't called and left a message. If he hasn't, we'll go looking for him together."

Without some clue as to where he might have gone, it would be a fruitless search, but perhaps it would appease Jezebel long enough for her good sense to return. Drake let go of her arms while holding her gaze.

Her fangs withdrew as he watched, but there was still an unmistakable glint of anger in her eyes. "All right," she agreed, her voice clipped and brusque. "But don't get in my way again. Understand?"

"Sure," Drake agreed. He hoped it wouldn't come to that, but he'd do whatever he needed to do to keep her safe while Gabriel was gone.

With one more warning glare, Jez stepped around him and jerked his front door open.

* * *

AS LUCK WOULD have it, they didn't have to set foot in the house that Gabriel and Jez occupied to get their first inkling of what might have happened to him.

Drake didn't recognize the couple who were sitting on the steps leading up to the columned doorway of the palatial Federal Hill house. But from the way Jezebel gasped, he thought he could venture a guess as to their identity.

The woman was a petite, dark-haired beauty with a pale complexion. The V-neck of her clingy burgundy sweater revealed a great expanse of what would have been cleavage had she not had the breasts of a teenage boy. Sitting one step behind her was a sullen-looking young man in an expensive Italian suit, his shirt unbuttoned to display as much of his chest as the woman's.

The woman stood up gracefully despite a pair of stiletto heels that added four inches to her height. Her companion remained sitting, his eyes now fixed on Jezebel. The smile on his face was best described as unwholesome. He ran his tongue suggestively over his full lips.

Jezebel ignored the man, instead coming to a stop with her legs shoulder width apart, her arms akimbo.

Drake stepped up beside her in silent support, keeping an eye on the dangerous-looking male.

The woman smiled, an incongruously sweet expression on her face. "Why, Jezebel dear, is there a new man in your life?" She gave Drake a mocking once-over, then nodded in approval. "I must commend your taste." Her English held a trace of an accent, though Drake couldn't place it. German, perhaps?

"Get the hell away from my house, Brigitte. And get your boy toy off my stairs." Jezebel sounded deceptively calm, but every nuance of her stance radiated tension.

Brigitte raised one eyebrow. "Or what?" She looked at Drake again. "Your new boyfriend might be nice to look at, but he's no match for me or Henri."

Henri had dragged his eyes away from Jezebel and was now staring at Drake. The expression on his face didn't change, as if he lusted after both of them equally, though from what Drake understood of him, it wasn't necessarily lust for sex that put that eerie gleam in his eyes.

Other than Gabriel, Brigitte was the only born vampire Drake had ever heard of. Younger than Gabriel by a full two centuries, she was nevertheless more practiced at manipulating the unique bond between a born vampire and his or her fledgling, and Henri was almost as old as she. Together, they were a formidable force, especially considering the weakened state Gabriel remained in ever since he'd rescued Jezebel from some kind of psychic Purgatory. His incredibly powerful glamour wasn't reliable these days, and Drake could imagine him falling prey to Brigitte and Henri if they caught him when his glamour failed.

Jez was practically vibrating with tension and fury. With Gabriel around, she'd always been the voice of reason, the antidote to his fierce and erratic temper. Drake had almost forgotten she had a temper of her own. And her control over it was fraying.

Brigitte giggled, a sound that grated on Drake's nerves.

"Do you think she's going to attack me, Henri?" she asked her fledgling, who finally rose and came to stand at her shoulder.

"Oh, I do hope so." Henri's accent was much stronger than his maker's, and obviously French.

Brigitte giggled again. "Behave, dearest. I have a strong suspicion Gabriel would be unable to forgive us any harm we did to his little plaything."

Henri raised one corner of his mouth in a sneer. "That would be tragic."

Brigitte's brow furrowed in annoyance and she glanced at him briefly. Henri lowered his head but didn't apologize or take the words back.

"What have you done with Gabriel?" Jezebel demanded.

"Don't worry, he's fine. In fact, I've done him something of a favor, as I intend to explain. Would you be so kind as to invite us into your lovely home?"

"When Hell freezes over."

Brigitte's smile remained sweet and innocuous. "You can invite us in, or we can force our way in." She swept both Jez and Drake with a contemptuous glance. "The two of *you* certainly aren't going to stop us."

Jez didn't look like she was about to see reason, so Drake quickly spoke up.

"Let's hear what they have to say," he suggested. "You know we need to, whether we want to or not."

The look Jezebel shot him was not in the least bit friendly, but he didn't care. She had to know they were outmatched. Besides, they couldn't let Brigitte leave without telling them what she'd done with Gabriel.

With a grunt of disgust, Jez pushed past Brigitte, giving Henri a wide berth as she stomped up the stairs and shoved her key in the lock. Drake had never seen anyone unlock a door with so much fury before. Brigitte and Henri shared a condescending, amused smile, then linked arms and followed Jez into the house.

Feeling like an afterthought, Drake brought up the rear.

The house that Jez and Gabriel shared had belonged to Gabriel's mother when she'd been the Master of Baltimore. Which meant it was palatial in scale and decor. The marble foyer with its grand staircase and carved mahogany balustrade was enough to awe the average American, but neither Brigitte nor Henri spared a glance at their surroundings. No doubt the old and powerful vampires of Europe—so much older and more powerful than almost any in the New World—lived in homes that were *literally* palaces.

Jez guided her unwanted visitors into the "receiving room," a converted drawing room decorated with the opulence and excess of Versailles, complete with a gilt ceiling. It was Gabriel's mother who had decorated the place, but Gabriel hadn't seen fit to change anything. To say the room was over the top was an understatement, but it did at least catch Brigitte's attention. She examined the genuine Louis XV furniture and the dark, brooding oil paintings that adorned the walls and smiled.

"How very interesting," she murmured. "Somehow, I can't picture Gabriel in his sexy black leather fitting in here."

Both Jez and Henri visibly took exception to the implication that Brigitte thought of Gabriel as "sexy," but she didn't give them time to object before she took a seat on the edge of one of those lovely antique sofas and spoke again.

"As you've obviously guessed, I have Gabriel."

Henri took up a post standing behind Brigitte, both his hands lying lightly on the back of the sofa. Once again, however, his unnerving attention was fixed on Jez, his eyes locked at chest level. Jez was far too distracted to notice, and she took her own seat to the right of Gabriel's seat of honor—an incongruous-looking twentieth-century Stickley chair at the head of the room.

Drake hesitated, not sure where he should sit, and Brigitte looked distinctly amused. His usual seat was to the left of Gabriel's, but he didn't like the symbolism of leaving the seat of power empty.

Knowing it was going to piss Jez off big time, Drake nonetheless dropped into Gabriel's chair.

Brigitte smiled in what looked like satisfaction, and Jez glared at him in outrage.

"I see *someone's* tired of playing second banana," Brigitte said.

Drake managed a casual shrug, though internally he squirmed in discomfort. He'd been "second banana," as she termed it, his entire life. It was a role he was accustomed to, felt comfortable in. But there was no such thing as a vampire democracy. With Gabriel gone, someone had to take charge. Being more than a century older than the next oldest of Gabriel's Guardians, that task fell to Drake.

"I'm not one for delusions of grandeur," he said with what he hoped was nonchalance. "But I'm the second in command, so if Gabriel's not here, I'm in charge."

Brigitte's smile only deepened. "Maybe you'll find the position suits you. Maybe you wouldn't be terribly disappointed if Gabriel remained gone for a good long time."

Jez shot to her feet, but before she got more than a squeak out of her mouth, Drake seized her with his glamour. "Sit down, Jezebel," he said, then used his glamour to enforce that order. She glared at him even more fiercely, but he knew he was doing the right thing. With Gabriel in danger, she was going to be far too emotional to play nice with Brigitte.

Brigitte laughed. "What an impressive display," she mocked. "Did you see that, Henri? He was able to subdue a baby fledgling."

Henri touched his tongue to his lips again. "I'm *very* impressed."

"Are you going to waste more time playing games, or will you get to the point?" Drake asked, keeping his hold on Jez while pretending to ignore her.

Brigitte shot him one of her terribly sincere-looking fake smiles. "If you know anything about me, Jonathan, you should know that playing games is one of my favorite activities."

Drake was startled enough that he lost his hold on Jez.

"Jonathan?" Jez asked, curiosity temporarily replacing anger.

Brigitte looked at Jez and raised one shapely brow. "You sound surprised, dear. Did you not know the identity of your sweetheart's second-in-command?"

"My name's Drake!" he snapped while mentally he did his best to regroup. How the hell had she learned his name? Even Eli hadn't known it.

"Indeed," Brigitte agreed. "*Jonathan* Drake. Mother, Eloise Stewart. Father, Connor Drake. Born a bastard in New York in 1872. Shall I continue?"

It simply wasn't possible for her to know this. The only people who knew his true identity were in New York. The mortals among them were long dead, and considering the dreadful violence of the neighborhood where he'd once lived, it had seemed likely the vampires who'd known him would also be dead by now. Apparently, that wasn't the case.

Dammit. In the space of a few heartbeats, he'd allowed himself to lose total control of the conversation—and of himself.

What did it matter if Brigitte knew his full name? And what did it matter how she'd learned it? *Pull yourself together,* he commanded himself.

He reached out with his glamour once more and captured Jez, then ruthlessly shoved aside all the questions and doubts that hammered at him.

"Tell me what you've done with Gabriel and what you want."

Brigitte pouted. "You're no fun."

"I'm devastated to hear that."

She laughed with what might have been her first hint of genuine humor. "I can see it breaks your heart. But I'm sure you'll provide entertainment eventually."

"And you're beginning to bore the hell out of me. Where is Gabriel?"

"He's safe," she said once again. "You might not appreciate my methods, but I do have his best interests at heart. I need him, and he's no good to me dead."

Brigitte was under the misguided impression that because she and Gabriel were both born vampires they were somehow soul mates, or at least natural allies. And Brigitte desperately needed an ally. In the Old World, born vampires were slaughtered at birth. Gabriel had managed to live only because Eli had kept him hidden and then fled to the New World when his existence became known. Brigitte was allowed to live because her mother was one of *Les Vieux,* the oldest and most powerful vampires in all of the Old

World. Like Eli, *Les Vieux* were physically bound to their homes but could create illusory avatars of themselves that could travel the length and breadth of the territories they controlled. Being illusions, these avatars were indestructible.

According to Gabriel, Brigitte's mother planned to keep her alive only as long as her power remained manageable. But Brigitte had grown powerful enough that she feared for her life and had thus fled to America. She had some vision of teaming up with Gabriel and storming the castles of the Old World when they were old and powerful enough to destroy *Les Vieux*. The fact that Gabriel wanted nothing to do with her didn't seem to have sunk in. Or perhaps it was her supreme arrogance that convinced her that one day, she would win him over.

Drake felt his hold on Jez weakening despite his superior strength. He flicked his gaze in her direction, willing her to hold still and keep quiet even as he let her go. He hoped she had enough functioning brain cells to realize she only amused her adversary by her too-obvious reactions.

"Tell me exactly what you're keeping Gabriel safe from," Drake demanded, and Jez stayed silent.

Brigitte lost her perpetual smile, her eyes suddenly grave. "My mother is sending a delegation to America. They plan to capture me and take me back home. And, since they know Gabriel's here, they'll want to take care of him, too. Only him they'll just kill."

Jez made a low growling sound in the back of her throat. "And how do they know Gabriel's here?"

Brigitte covered her mouth with her hand, her eyes widening in mock distress as she gasped. "Oh, dear. I think I may have let that slip last time I talked to Mother."

Drake restrained Jez with glamour once more, knowing she wouldn't be able to keep silent in the face of that revelation.

"Why would you do that?" Drake asked. "If you have his best interests at heart, as you claim."

She rolled her eyes. "I have my own best interests at heart first." She looked over her shoulder at Henri. "Why are the pretty ones always so stupid?"

Henri tore his eyes away from Jezebel's chest and met his maker's gaze. "You are pretty, and you are not stupid."

She fluttered a hand at her chest. "You're such a charmer!"

He snorted, then went back to his examination of Jez's breasts. It was really beginning to get on Drake's nerves.

"One would think you'd never seen breasts before," Drake said, knowing he should keep his mouth shut but unable to resist. He made a show of glancing at Brigitte's nonexistent cleavage. "Then again, maybe you haven't."

Twin spots of color warmed her cheeks, though Henri didn't acknowledge the taunt with anything more than a dirty look. However, he stopped staring.

"Are you *ever* going to get to the point?" Drake asked.

Her cheeks still rosy, Brigitte answered in a flat

voice. "The point is I have Gabriel somewhere safe, where my mother's delegation can't get to him. And, coincidentally, where he can't help my mother's delegation get to *me*. Their plane should be arriving in Baltimore any moment now, and they will most definitely want to speak to Gabriel. Naturally, they will promise to leave him alive, but they'll be lying. And they'll think *you're* lying if you tell them you don't know where he is. The good news is their antiquated rules of engagement will insist they defeat the local master before harming his people or hunting in his territory. The bad news is if they get desperate enough, they'll ignore the rules.

"I want you to know that whatever they might promise or whatever they might threaten, you don't want them to catch me. Because, you see, if they do, then you'll never find out where I've hidden Gabriel. Let me assure you, he won't be escaping from where I've put him. Do you have any idea how long it would take a vampire of his age to die of starvation?" She shuddered theatrically. "Not a good way to go."

Jez's eyes widened in distress, though Drake's glamour wouldn't allow her a more dramatic display.

Drake shook his head. "What do you want of us? What will it take to get Gabriel back?"

Brigitte smiled. "I don't expect you to take on the delegation. They are well out of your league. But any efforts you can make to hamper them will go a long way toward assuring Gabriel's safety.

"You'll get Gabriel back when the delegation has been defeated, one way or another." She gave him a sly look. "Unless you decide that seat feels comfortable, in which case I would be happy to negotiate alternate terms."

He felt Jez's eyes on him but didn't dignify Brigitte's statement with a reply.

With a satisfied smirk, Brigitte rose, and Henri hurried around to the front of the sofa to offer his arm, which she took.

"We'll see ourselves out," she said, and allowed Henri to steer her toward the door. Then she pulled up. "Oh, wait!" she cried. "I almost forgot." She disengaged her arm from Henri's, then fished a folded piece of paper from her pocket. She held the paper out to Drake.

"This is for you," she said, her eyes glittering with some expression he couldn't interpret.

When he didn't take it, she let the paper fall to his lap. With a satisfied little sigh, she returned to Henri and allowed him to escort her to the front door.

2

IT HAD BEEN almost three months since the *Seigneur* had called her to his bed. Faith had begun to hope he'd tired of her. Though that wouldn't necessarily be a good thing. With his attention came a heavy dose of protection. Protection that she, as an orphan—a vampire whose maker was dead—badly needed.

She stood outside the door of his hotel room, hand poised to knock, but couldn't quite get herself to do it. They had checked in less than an hour ago. He'd barely given her time to unpack before calling down to her room and demanding she come to him.

Why this sudden interest, when for three months he'd barely acknowledged her existence? She flattened her hand against the door and closed her eyes. It could be merely the stress of their unwanted mission. Or of having to leave his home territory, something that was anathema to a vampire of his age.

Or, it could have something to do with the fact that her sister, Lily, had come home from boarding school for an extended visit. Dread tightened her chest. Lily was only sixteen, a relatively normal mortal teenager. But there was no denying that she was blossoming, her body filling out nicely from the gawky angles of her childhood. And Faith had caught the *Seigneur* giving the girl a thorough once-over on the plane.

For all his many faults, the *Seigneur* was not a pedophile. During his mortal life, his own daughter had been raped and murdered at the age of ten, and he abhorred any hint of violence against children. He'd taken surprisingly good care of Lily, keeping her away from his vampires as best he could. But he'd lived his mortal life six hundred years ago. Perhaps his definition of an adult and Faith's were not the same.

She blinked back tears and took a deep, steadying breath. It was Faith he'd commanded to his bed, not Lily. Lily was safe, at least for now. But dear God, she had to get her out of his reach, and soon.

If only she had the faintest clue how to do it.

The door swung open as she stood hesitating.

There was no denying that Armand Durant was an impressive specimen of manhood. He'd been in his early forties when he'd been turned, but in that annoying way that men had, he looked distinguished rather than past his prime. Thick salt-and-pepper hair framed an elegant, aristocratic face, and his eyes were a startling sapphire blue.

She lowered her gaze to the floor. "*Seigneur*," she

said in greeting. He always made her feel like she should curtsy in his presence.

He swung the door open wide, stepping aside to make room. "Please do come in, *ma petite*," he said, as always imbuing his words with amused condescension.

She swallowed hard and moved past him. No matter how many times she'd served him in his bed, she'd never get used to it, never get used to the knowledge that her body was not her own anymore, that she would forever be subject to another's will.

As befitted a man of his station, he'd rented a grand suite. The decor was reminiscent of the opulence of his manor house in Rouen. Out of habit, she did a quick psychic scan. There were three vampires in the room across the hall. A lone vampire occupied another room a little ways down the hall. That would be Charles Giroux, Armand's right-hand man. Elsewhere on the floor, she sensed the presence of mortals, some of them no doubt part of the *Seigneur*'s entourage, but some of them ordinary guests. And in the room that adjoined Armand's, there was a solitary mortal presence.

Faith's heart clutched with panic. He had denied her request to let her share a room with Lily. She'd never expected him to grant it—he knew perfectly well that if he gave her the opportunity, she'd grab her sister and make a run for it.

Armand laughed softly. "Ah, now I understand why you've been so quiet lately. You fear I have designs on your dear sister."

She met his eyes, trying to be brave while still properly subservient. "She's just a child, *Seigneur*."

He smiled at her. "I am aware of that. I have put her in the adjoining room for her own protection. No one would dare trouble her there. You know as well as I that not all members of our merry band can be trusted. But come. I have neglected you shamefully all these months."

He was wearing an antique brocade dressing gown that would have looked effeminate on a modern man. On him, it looked terribly sophisticated. Unfortunately, it didn't conceal much—there was an unmistakable tent forming.

Faith's throat tightened as he approached. With her eyes lowered, she couldn't help seeing the evidence of his arousal; but if she raised her gaze, she might find herself trapped by his eyes, and that would be even worse. Her pulse throbbed rapidly in her throat.

Of course, Armand was never content to let her hide from him. He lifted her chin with his finger, meeting her gaze as the familiar crease of puzzlement formed between his brows. His finger traced down her throat, lingering over her frantic pulse. He wasn't delusional enough to think her pulse raced with desire.

He shook his head. "Have I ever hurt you?" he asked softly. "In bed, I mean," he quickly amended.

It was true that the only time he'd caused her any physical pain was when he'd beaten her for allowing her sometimes sharp tongue to get away from her. His damned glamour made sure that her body enjoyed everything he did to her in bed, and for all his capacity for brutality, he was a surprisingly gentle lover. But nothing she could ever say would make him understand that what he did to her was still rape.

A tear leaked out of her eye. She couldn't help it. After three months of blessed freedom, this new summons stung somewhere deep inside. And the thought that he might turn his attentions to Lily . . . She shuddered. In Lily's eyes, her "Uncle Armand" practically walked on water. Faith couldn't imagine how dreadful the disillusionment and betrayal would be if he forced her to his bed.

Armand caressed the single tear away with the pad of his thumb. She felt the touch of his glamour in her mind, softening the edges of her distress—for now. His lips came down on hers, and her mouth opened against her will, granting access to his tongue. His fangs had descended, their needle-sharp points pricking her lips.

"Yes," he murmured against her lips as he ground his erection into her belly, "I have definitely neglected you too long."

God, how she hated him right now, even as she obeyed the demands of his glamour and slid down his body till she was on her knees before him.

For the first time in years, she tried to fight free of the glamour, even knowing it was useless. She was a fledgling, and he was a *Seigneur*. She couldn't hope to win.

A cry of frustration escaped her as she reached out to part his robe, her mouth opening despite her every effort. As she'd guessed, his erection was at full mast already, an intimidating weapon. Her cry turned to a whimper as the tip of him brushed her lips.

And then, to her utter shock, he released her from his glamour. She scrambled away from him, landing on her butt with an undignified thump, her breath sawing frantically in and out of her chest. She closed her eyes, trying to calm herself once more, trying to think.

Before she could form a coherent thought, he'd come up behind her, hauling her to her feet, his arms wrapped around her, trapping her own arms by her sides, his lips caressing her ear.

"Why do you fight it?" he whispered. "You know I will pleasure you. Why must you make it a battle?"

She sucked in a deep breath and let it out slowly. The damnable thing was, he really and truly didn't understand. She'd been with him long enough to know that although he was brutal when he thought it necessary, he wasn't wantonly cruel. If he understood what he was doing to her, if she could somehow get through to him, then he wouldn't do it. But the bastard just wasn't capable of that kind of empathy. Either that, or she wasn't eloquent enough to explain it.

When she didn't answer, he let out a little sigh. Then, his glamour slammed into her full force, stealing the last vestige of her free will.

* * *

DRAKE STARED AT the folded piece of paper Brigitte had dropped on his lap. He didn't want to open it.

"Aren't you going to read it?" Jez asked. He had no doubt she was still angry with him, but she'd put the anger aside for now.

Setting his jaw grimly, he unfolded the paper. There was nothing written there but a phone number with a 212 area code, a terse *Call me,* and the letter *P* as a signature. But it was enough. *More* than enough.

He crumpled the paper into a tight wad and shoved it in his pants pocket.

"Well?" Jez prompted.

He shook his head. "None of your business," he said, more sharply than he meant to.

Her eyes narrowed, and with uncanny instinct she homed in on just the topic to make him squirm the most. "Jonathan, eh?"

He grimaced. No one had called him Jonathan except his mother. To everyone else, he'd been Johnnie. Johnnie Drake—the bogeyman who'd come to get you if you crossed the man who held his leash. "I haven't gone by that name for more than a century. It's best you wipe it from your memory." As he'd tried to wipe it from his.

"Why?"

Because I said so. "Because it's irrelevant."

Jez shrugged. "Brigitte seemed to think it was important."

"It was only important as a tool to show off her knowledge."

"If it turns out to be important and you don't tell me, Gabriel will kick your ass when he gets back."

"It's not important," he repeated. As far as he was

concerned, Brigitte digging up his real name was nothing more than a parlor trick. Either that, or a petty torment. "I have a past, just like everyone else. But I've left that past far behind, and it has no bearing on the current situation."

Again, Jez shrugged. "I'll just have to take your word for that, I suppose."

He could see from the look in her eye that she was practically dying of curiosity, but she managed to swallow it. For now. "So what happens when we hear from this delegation?" she asked instead.

He thought about that for a long moment. If what he'd heard about the European vampires was true, then he was practically a fledgling in comparison. Gabriel's Guardians would be seriously outmatched, and thanks to Brigitte they'd be in a precarious position from the very start.

"We stall and hope Brigitte can get rid of them, I suppose," he said.

Jez blinked at him. "We're going to count on *Brigitte* to get us out of this mess? Are you crazy?"

"Believe me, I'm open to suggestions if you've got any."

"All right, how about we find Gabriel and get him back? Or was Brigitte right and you kind of like sitting in that chair?"

Drake restrained a surge of temper. He met her glare with one of his own. "I haven't the faintest desire to be the Master of Baltimore," he told her, and it was the God's honest truth. He'd never wanted to be a leader, never wanted that kind of power—or that kind of responsibility. "But until Gabriel gets back, that's what I am."

Jez's face turned mutinous, but he continued before she could voice her opinion. "This delegation of theirs will assume I'm in charge because I'm the oldest and strongest." This wasn't saying much, considering that the only members of Gabriel's Guardians not currently in the room were a pair of fledglings even younger than Jez. "We don't want them to see us as a bunch of leaderless rabble. That would just make us seem even weaker than we already are."

"I'll put up with you taking Gabriel's place for the time being," Jezebel said. "But we sure as hell better get him back soon, and I have no intention of just waiting around for Brigitte to solve all our problems."

Once again, he reminded himself that her temper was brittle due to her worry about Gabriel. In some ways, he couldn't blame her. But his temper wasn't much better at the moment, and it took a concerted effort to reel it back in before he said or did something that he would regret.

"Let's at least see what this delegation has to say," he said, pleased at how even his tone sounded. "Until we've heard from them, we can't even begin to plan how to deal with them. It's not like Brigitte gave us much information. We don't even know how many of them there are."

As if on cue, the phone rang. They both turned to stare at it. Jez let it ring three times before she picked up.

After her curt greeting, she listened for a while. The caller spoke so softly, and Drake was just far enough away, that he couldn't make out the words.

"I'm afraid Gabriel's not available right now," Jez said, her face growing paler. The caller started to say something else, but Jez interrupted. "One moment." The caller was still talking when she lowered the phone from her ear, crossed the room, and shoved it at Drake.

"If you're standing in for Gabriel, then *you* deal with this," she said.

He took the phone. "Who is this?" he demanded.

The caller fell silent for a moment, then quickly recovered. "I wish to speak with the Master of Baltimore." It was a male voice, speaking English with a strong French accent.

"I am acting Master of Baltimore," Drake said, the words sounding awkward in his own ears. "Whom do I have the pleasure of addressing?"

Another hesitation. "You are not Gabriel Cromwell."

Drake wondered how Gabriel would take to being assigned Eli's surname. "I will ask one more time, who am I speaking to?" Perhaps he was setting a confrontational tone a little earlier than necessary, but if he was going to be Master of Baltimore, he had to act the part.

"I am Charles Giroux. I speak for the *Seigneur*, Armand Durant."

"He can't speak for himself?"

"If your master cannot speak for himself, then the *Seigneur* cannot, either."

Touché. "What do you want with the Master of Baltimore?" Drake asked, even though he knew the answer.

"That is not a question to be answered over the phone."

"Very well, then." Drake looked at his watch. "The *Seigneur* is welcome to visit tonight at . . . shall we say, midnight?" He stood a good chance of annoying his adversary with his attitude, but better to put on an annoying show of arrogance than to appear weak. "He may bring with him one other representative from your delegation, but no more."

Another moment of silence. Then, "Our *delegation*?" Giroux asked.

"Brigitte told us you were coming. Just as she no doubt told you where to find us."

Giroux muttered something that was most likely a curse. "Trust me on this, *Monsieur* . . ."

"Just call me Drake, and skip the *Monsieur* part."

"Drake. You do not wish to be involved in Brigitte's game."

No, I don't, Drake silently agreed. "I'm afraid she's already involved me. Will your *Seigneur* be available for a midnight appointment?"

"I feel certain that can be arranged. Tell me your address."

He'd won Giroux's agreement too easily, but he could hardly complain about it. Wondering how ugly this meeting might become, he gave the *Seigneur*'s lieutenant the address.

* * *

LIKE A MORTAL man, Armand tended to fall asleep after sex. As soon as Faith heard his breaths come slow and even, she slipped out of the bed and hastily dressed. She stared at him for a moment before she left. He was so secure in his power that it never occurred to him to think of her as a threat. And yet just now, naked and fast asleep in his bed, he was so vulnerable. If she could just get her hands on a gun, she could put the muzzle to his head and pull the trigger. She thought she could do that, although she'd never killed anyone. But to escape him, and to get Lily out of his clutches, she would happily do that and worse.

Unfortunately, killing Armand wouldn't solve her problems. She was by far the least powerful vampire in his entourage. She was younger than most of them, and her maker, under the mad delusion that this would somehow make his betrayal all better, had informed her that she could survive on animal blood as long as she never once gave in to the temptation to kill a human. When Armand had killed her maker for creating an unauthorized fledgling, he'd allowed her to continue feeding on animal blood—supposedly to protect her delicate sensibilities, but she wasn't at all sure his motives were so pure. As long as she didn't feed on the kill, she would always remain weaker than those around her, no matter how old she became. And she would always need Armand's protection.

Of course, even if she escaped Armand's entourage, where would she go? Her home before she'd been turned was a tiny town in rural Virginia. She couldn't go back there, not without someone finding out her secret. No doubt everyone thought both she and Lily were dead, and she had no idea how she'd explain their long absence.

She couldn't stay anywhere near a vampire-occupied territory, but when she'd left the U.S. for her fateful vacation in France, she hadn't even known vampires existed. How could she know which territories were claimed and which weren't?

Despair made her feet and her heart heavy as she slipped quietly out of the room.

Her mood went from despair to terror when the door to the opposite room opened and Marie stepped out, scowling. A voluptuous, red-haired beauty, Marie had been a high-class hooker—though Faith found the term an oxymoron—before she'd caught Armand's eye and he'd decided to reserve her special skills for himself. He'd been availing himself of those special skills frequently over the last three months, and as far as Faith was concerned, Marie was welcome to him.

Unfortunately, she was also a jealous, mean-spirited bitch who saw Faith as her competition.

Marie sniffed the air pointedly, her beaklike nose wrinkling at what she smelled. There was no concealing the scent of sex from a vampire.

"Well, well," Marie purred as she came closer.

"Looks like someone's been able to wheedle her way back into the *Seigneur*'s bed."

Faith couldn't help taking a step backward, even though she knew retreating tweaked Marie's predatory instincts. In a lightning-fast move, Marie rushed her, grabbing her shoulders and shoving her up against the wall. Faith's heart was in her throat as Marie leaned into her personal space until they were almost nose to nose.

"Armand will be angry with you if you hurt me," she reminded the bitch. Marie snarled, baring her fangs, but aside from the crushing grip on Faith's shoulders, she offered no other violence.

Marie had "warned" Faith away from Armand once before, stabbing her three times with a kitchen knife. The wounds would have killed a mortal—they merely hurt like hell for Faith. When Armand found out what Marie had done, he'd locked her in a dungeon cell for an entire week, taking her out once a night for a public whipping. Faith hated Marie almost as much as Marie hated her, but she still had nightmares about those agonized screams.

After the last of the whippings, Armand had taken Marie back into his bed as if nothing had happened. And Marie hadn't dared mess with Faith since. The look on her face suggested her self-restraint was being sorely tested.

"You keep your filthy hands off the *Seigneur,*" Marie hissed. "He's mine! If I find you in his bed again, I'll find a way to make you pay, and he'll never know I had anything to do with it."

Faith wanted to scream at the injustice of it. "I'd give anything to keep my 'filthy hands' off him, if only he would let me."

Marie backhanded her, one swift, almost casual blow that left Faith seeing stars and tasting blood. "You'd better find a way, or I will kill you."

Faith bit her tongue to keep from saying anything. If she told Armand that Marie had hit her, Marie would be punished again. But Faith wasn't sure she could bear to watch what he would do to her for this. A second punishment for the same infraction might not kill her, but Marie might very well wish it would.

Of course, Marie was destined to die eventually anyway. Armand had a famously short attention span where women were concerned, and Faith imagined Marie would not take it well at all when he became bored with her and put her aside. She wasn't smart enough to control her rage indefinitely.

Satisfied that she had made her point, Marie shoved Faith down the hallway toward the elevators. Faith just barely managed to keep her feet. She felt hostile eyes on her until the moment the elevator doors closed behind her.

* * *

ARMAND PROPPED HIMSELF up on one elbow, listening, sure Marie would not dare to defy him. He winced when he heard what sounded suspiciously like a slap, then slid his legs out of bed. Perhaps bringing both Marie and Faith with him had been a miscalculation. But he'd wanted Marie for his bed, and Faith and Lily were far too weak and vulnerable to be left at home without his protection.

No, the miscalculation had been taking Faith to his bed as soon as they arrived, flaunting it in Marie's face. He'd meant to remind the little whore how easily she could be replaced, but he should have known better.

He pulled on his dressing gown and strode toward the door. Marie had restrained herself and allowed Faith to leave, but he'd heard her threat. Apparently, she would need a different sort of lesson, though he would need to be careful how he administered it in this crowded hotel. It wouldn't do to leave bloodstains in the room, nor could he allow the mortal patrons to hear her screams.

He was almost to the door when his cell phone rang. His shoulders tensed and he stopped in his tracks. He'd been expecting a call, but not so soon. He'd thought *La Vieille* would at least want to give him time to gather a little information first.

Cursing under his breath, Armand let Marie go and promised himself he would deal with her later. He picked up the phone on the third ring, bracing himself for a most unpleasant conversation.

"I see you have made it to America without incident," *La Vieille* said without any sort of formal greeting. Her voice was eerily similar to her daughter's, but whereas Brigitte's tone was almost always playful, no matter what she was saying, *La Vieille*'s raised the hairs on the back of his neck with its menace. He didn't think that was a trick of the mind, either. Her power seemed to travel over the phone lines, which was disconcerting to say the least.

"Yes, Your Excellency," he murmured, fighting the reflex to drop to one knee and lower his head. It was a courtesy she demanded when he spoke to her avatar in person, but surely even *she* couldn't see him from across the ocean.

"And have you arranged a meeting with the so-called Master?"

Armand faltered, then cursed himself for a fool. "Not yet, Your Excellency. We've only just arrived." He closed his eyes, knowing full well what was coming.

"Your plane touched down exactly two hours and twenty-five minutes ago. That, my dear *Seigneur,* is not my definition of 'just arrived.' "

Of course the pilot of their private jet would have reported their arrival immediately, and of course *La Vieille* would have expected him to begin the search for her daughter the moment he set foot on American soil. She was not known for her patience, and she already held him in high disfavor. After all, Brigitte had fled the country on his watch. The fact that it was the *Maître de Paris* who had allowed her to leave rather than himself did not in any way mitigate his guilt in her eyes.

"I beg your pardon," he responded, hoping his voice betrayed no fear. "I will make contact as soon as we hang up."

"Hmm." It was at best a noncommittal sound, and

she did not dismiss him, so Armand stayed on the line. "You do understand what's at stake, do you not, *Seigneur*?"

His fist clenched around the phone. She rarely lowered herself to making direct threats. But then, she didn't need to. "Yes, Your Excellency," he said, and this time he knew his fear shone through. If he failed, every punishment he'd ever inflicted on his own people would pale in comparison to what *La Vieille* would do to him.

Armand knew that some of his people, mostly those underlings who had tasted his displeasure, considered him evil. But having not met *La Vieille du Nord,* they couldn't possibly comprehend what the face of true evil looked like. In his youth, he'd been a good Christian, and he'd pictured the devil as a twisted, hideous creature with a horned head and cloven hooves. Now he knew better. The devil possessed a sweetly smiling face with hair the palest of blond and cheeks perpetually rosy from a fresh kill. And the ancient dungeons that lay hidden in the depths below her castle in Lille were Hell itself.

"No, Armand," *La Vieille* purred. "I don't think you do. I'm sure you understand what *your* fate would be, but I don't think you realize the . . . magnitude of my displeasure."

But he'd known what to expect from her from the moment he ascended to the rank of *Seigneur* and she'd given him a tour of those dreaded dungeons. It wasn't just *his* life that was at stake. It was the lives of every one of his fledglings, and of every one of the lesser vampires and mortals who served him. That knowledge had guided his choice of traveling companions. He couldn't protect all his people, but if he failed, he hoped his personal favorites would be able to disappear into the wilds of America and escape *La Vieille*'s wrath.

"Do you think you're being clever, *Seigneur*?" *La Vieille* asked.

"Excuse me?"

"Do you think I don't know which of your people are your favorites?"

Armand's heart clutched in sudden panic. It had never occurred to him that *La Vieille* would anticipate his strategy.

"You fought side by side with Charles during the battle of Agincourt," *La Vieille* continued. "When years later you found him dying on yet another battlefield, you turned him to save his life. And though he is almost as powerful as you, he has remained by your side for all these years, never striving to become a *Seigneur*, or even a *Maître*. A more dedicated and loyal friend there never was. Of course, if you hadn't hoped to protect him, you'd have left him at home to rule in your stead while you were gone.

"And why on earth would you bring a girl like Faith, who I know has not graced your bed for many months now? She is a weakling—hardly an asset to your mission. Unless she means something to you personally, that is."

La Vieille was indeed the devil incarnate.

"Perhaps I should thank you," the devil continued,

"for making it so easy for me to know how to hurt you. Not only will I make you watch as those you care about receive a preview of what you will suffer, I'll make you do it to them yourself. And don't for a moment believe they can escape my wrath through distance. I have made arrangements to make sure all of you return to me in the event of your failure."

Armand's knees weakened and he hastily sat. He'd never been squeamish about inflicting pain on his subjects when they deserved it. But he made quite certain that they knew what was expected of them and what the price for disobedience would be. Even while punishing someone he felt some affection for, he remained free of guilt because they had been warned and therefore deserved it. *La Vieille* didn't care who deserved what.

"*Now* I think you understand what's at stake," she finished in triumph. "Bring my daughter to me. Alive. And bring me the head of this so-called Master of Baltimore."

The phone clicked and went dead. Armand snapped his phone shut, then lowered his head into his hands. He would succeed. He *had* to succeed. The alternative was unimaginable.

There came a tentative knock on the door from the adjoining room.

"Uncle Armand?" Lily asked. "May I come in?"

Armand raised his head from his hands. He could not deal with a fragile mortal child right now. His nerves were too raw. He'd never let her see those sides of him that might . . . disturb her. No doubt

Faith had told her dreadful stories, but Lily was young and impressionable enough to doubt her sister's word.

"Uncle Armand?" Lily asked, more demandingly.

"Not now!" he snapped, then winced at his tone of voice. Yes, it was definitely best to keep the girl away just now.

He felt her hover by the door, no doubt distressed and hurt by his brusqueness. His temper simmered, his fangs descending against his will. If she disobeyed him, she was apt to learn that not all of Faith's stories were fabrications.

Luckily for everyone, she was a relatively obedient child for a modern teenager and wisely left him alone.

3

DRAKE HAD DEBATED whether to summon Eric and Harry, the other two members of the Baltimore Guardians, to the house for the meeting with the delegation. On the one hand, he preferred to have the delegation outnumbered. On the other hand, Eric and Harry were so young and untried that they were barely stronger than mortals.

Gabriel and Jez had found Eric's maker squatting in Baltimore when they had returned from Gabriel's aborted revenge quest in Philadelphia. Gabriel had made quick work of the Killer, but had discovered Eric locked up in a basement, just coming around from having been turned. When it became clear that Eric was an unwilling fledgling who had not yet killed—and had no desire to kill—Gabriel and Jez had taken him on as the first member of their Guardians.

Harry was a different, more difficult story. He'd

been a friend of Jez's during her mortal life, when both of them had suffered from HIV and then AIDS. When she returned to Baltimore and found her old friend was finally succumbing to the disease, she'd known the only way to save his life was to transform him. Because Gabriel and Jez couldn't be sure they wouldn't create the same intimate bond they shared with one another if they transformed Harry, they'd nominated Eric for the task.

It hadn't proved as happy a compromise as they'd expected. Vampires as a general rule were solitary predators and tended to grate on each others' nerves. Usually, only a master and his or her fledglings managed to get along without killing one another. Trying to get two masters to work together effectively was a daunting task, and though Eric knew he'd never come out on top in a fight with Gabriel, he always seemed to be in danger of exploding.

They were hardly an impressive entourage, but they were all Drake had.

So it was that all four of Gabriel's Guardians were gathered in the receiving room at 12:15 when the doorbell rang. Drake had expected the delegation to arrive late. He'd even expected them to ignore his request that only two members show up. What he hadn't expected was to do a psychic scan and discover six vampires and five mortals on his doorstep.

"Damn," he muttered. He'd never thought he'd actually miss Gabriel. But he felt like an imposter, sitting in Gabriel's chair, pretending to be the Master of Baltimore in the face of such overwhelming odds.

The bell rang a second time, and Harry cleared his throat. "Should I let them in?"

Drake sighed—silently, he hoped—and nodded. "I suppose you should."

"Jesus!" Eric exclaimed, suddenly leaping to his feet. "There are eleven people out there."

Jez gasped, and Harry hesitated, looking at Drake with wide eyes.

Drake sat up a little straighter in his chair and tried to dispel any hint of uncertainty from his body language. "I know how many of them there are," he said. "Let them in."

Harry looked dubious, but headed for the front door anyway.

"Sit down, Eric," Drake said, and Eric, too, obeyed.

"This sucks," Jez muttered, and Drake couldn't help agreeing.

Moments later, Harry returned, leading the European horde. He quicky distanced himself from them and took a seat beside Eric. Drake had arranged the chairs so that his Guardians could sit close by him at the head of the room, with the delegation sitting an appreciable distance away. Of course, he hadn't been expecting eleven people, so there weren't enough seats for everyone.

It became apparent which of those people was the *Seigneur* the moment he walked into the room. Drake wasn't old enough to read auras and gauge the age of other vampires, but he didn't need to. The *Seigneur* carried himself like a leader, confidence and strength oozing from his every pore. If his bearing hadn't been enough to identify him, the way the others acted around him would have given him away. They walked in a loose ring around him, like bodyguards protecting a VIP, and they watched him constantly for cues. It was a kind of deference—inspired by fear as much as by respect—that Drake recognized all too well.

The note that Brigitte had delivered, and that was still crumpled in his pocket, reminded him once again of his youth and of his first years as a vampire. Even back then, he'd never aspired to be a leader, but he'd had plenty of experience with the concept of ruling by intimidation. Enough to recognize it when he saw it.

The *Seigneur* must have given some sort of cue, but Drake didn't see it. His entourage parted to let him step to the fore, then fanned out in a semicircle behind him like a herd of trained circus horses.

Drake couldn't compete in power, or in numbers. All he had was attitude, and he knew better than to act intimidated.

He looked everyone over slowly, identifying which were vampires and which were mortal. He started when he realized the teenage girl who stood near the back was a mortal. She was a pretty brunette, with wide dark eyes and questionable taste in clothing. She was the only one in the party who didn't look like she'd just come from a fashion shoot. She also couldn't be more than fifteen or sixteen years old, and Drake couldn't for the life of him figure out what she was doing in the entourage of a Killer.

The *Seigneur* was sizing up Drake and the Guardians, too, so silence reigned for perhaps two minutes. It was the *Seigneur* who finally broke that silence.

"In my country," he said, his accent far less pronounced than that of his lieutenant, "it is customary for the host to stand when greeting his guests."

Drake remained seated. "In my country, it is customary to arrive with only those people who have been invited. I believe I invited you and one other. I count considerably more in your party."

Some members of the entourage grumbled at that, but the *Seigneur* shot a look over his shoulder and they fell silent. He strode forward a few more steps, his entourage hanging back. Drake leaned back in his chair as if perfectly at ease. He even met the *Seigneur*'s eyes, though he was sure the Killer was more than old enough to overcome him with glamour.

"It is my understanding," the *Seigneur* said, "that in America people are more blunt than I am accustomed to in my own land. So I will be blunt. You are outmatched. You would be outmatched even if there were only two of us." He spared a glance for Eric, Harry, and Jez, and his lips curled into a condescending smile. "Even the weakest of my vampires could defeat these fledglings, and most of them are powerful enough to defeat you, too."

He had no idea how old any of these vampires were, but he knew enough to realize that a man didn't rise to become *Seigneur* until he was *much* older than Drake. "I'm aware of that. But I figure if wholesale slaughter were your plan, you wouldn't have bothered with the charade of a meeting. I presume you want something from me?"

The *Seigneur*'s expression did not change, but a chair suddenly slid from its place across the room to rest behind him, and he sat down. It was a demonstration of power that would have been more impressive if Drake hadn't seen Gabriel and Eli in action. The entourage drifted a little closer, and the *Seigneur* crossed his legs and steepled his fingers.

"I do not wish to be rude," the *Seigneur* said, "but my business is with the Master of Baltimore, not with his second-in-command."

And yet, he'd just pulled up a chair to talk. "According to Brigitte, your business with him involves killing him. You can't be terribly surprised not to find him waiting for you."

The *Seigneur* made a dismissive hand gesture. "Not a word that comes from her mouth can be trusted. One might suspect she is attempting to ensure we do not form an alliance against her."

Drake regarded him with infinite skepticism. "So you're telling me you have no intention of killing Gabriel?"

The *Seigneur*'s expression remained bland. "Unless he's planning to cross the ocean to invade our territory, he is no concern of ours."

Rarely would Drake trust Brigitte's word in anything, but he suspected that in this one matter, her word was more reliable than the *Seigneur*'s. "Even if I believed you, I doubt Gabriel would."

The *Seigneur* arched an eyebrow. "Your master is a coward, perhaps?"

Jez started to object. Without turning around to face her, Drake used his glamour to keep her quiet.

Drake put on a condescending smile. "He isn't a coward by any stretch of the imagination. But he isn't a fool, either."

"I tire of this game. Tell him that if he refuses to see me, there will be . . . consequences."

Drake really hated to admit that Gabriel wasn't around, that the Guardians were completely vulnerable. But if the *Seigneur* was going to kill the Guardians to punish Gabriel for not showing up, then Drake figured he had no alternative.

"I'd be happy to convey your message. If I knew where he was."

Once again, the *Seigneur* raised an eyebrow, his face a mask of polite curiosity.

"Brigitte has apparently captured him," Drake said. "She was concerned that he might help you find her. We don't know exactly what she's done with him. All we know is that he's alive."

The *Seigneur* laughed. "You expect me to believe that Brigitte has the power to capture a born vampire of his age? *I* am capable of overpowering her. I am not a born vampire, and I am not that much older than Gabriel."

Well, Brigitte had warned Drake he wouldn't be believed. "Do you really think she'd let anyone in your country see how powerful she's become? If you overpowered her, then it's because she allowed you to."

The *Seigneur*'s brow darkened at that. "Even if that's true, Gabriel is still considerably older than she is. I cannot believe she could capture him."

Drake shrugged. "Believe what you will. I'm telling the truth. I'm told it has something to do with the age of her fledgling and her skill at manipulating their bond. But even if that weren't the case, she could have used that tranquilizer your people have developed." Until Gabriel's battle with his mother and her henchman, they'd thought there was no such thing as a tranquilizer that could work on a vampire. Although *tranquilizer* was a misnomer. The drug worked by creating so much pain even a vampire of Gabriel's enormous power lost all his strength and couldn't concentrate enough to use his glamour.

The *Seigneur*'s stare was piercing, but Drake refused to squirm under it. Finally, the Frenchman smiled faintly. "It may be that you are telling the truth," he conceded. "Then again, it may not. I will give you the benefit of the doubt, as long as you provide me and my party with hospitality for the duration of our stay in your lovely city."

"Hospitality?" Drake asked, though he had a sinking feeling he knew exactly what the *Seigneur* meant.

"I will require rooms for myself and my entourage. From what I've seen of this house, you don't have space for all of us to have separate rooms, but I will require separate accommodations for myself, Charles, and the child." He held out a hand without looking back. "Come here, Lily."

The girl Drake had noticed before came forward, smiling. One of the *Seigneur*'s vampires, a short and slender woman with hair so dark it was almost black, took a step forward also, reaching out to the girl. Drake thought there was a family resemblance between the two. Lily slipped by her, rolling her eyes.

Lily took the *Seigneur*'s outstretched hand and practically bounced to his side. His expression lightened, and the smile he showed her seemed genuine. He held the girl's hand, then looked at Drake. "Will you guarantee this child's safety in your home?"

Drake was momentarily at a loss. It wasn't as if he'd agreed that the *Seigneur* and his party could stay at the house. Hell, it wasn't even his house. Then again, it wasn't like he had much of a choice when the *Seigneur* could use his refusal as an excuse to kill them all.

Lily gave him a little extra time to think as she rolled her eyes again and said in exasperation, "Will you *please* stop calling me a child, Uncle Armand?" Her accent was pure American, with a hint of a southern drawl, making Drake even more curious how she'd come to be mixed up with these European vampires.

Armand laughed and patted her hand. "I'm six

hundred years old, *ma petite*. I'm tempted to call *them* children, too." He jerked a thumb toward the Guardians. Lily heaved a long-suffering sigh, but didn't argue. Armand turned his attention back to Drake.

"I ask again, will you guarantee her safety?"

"Of course," Drake said. Behind him, Jez made an indignant noise in the back of her throat. He turned slightly so he could see her. Her face was flushed red, her eyes narrowed as she glared at him, but she didn't say anything. She might not like any of this, but she understood as well as he that they were not in a strong bargaining position.

"And will you guarantee the safety of my people?" Drake asked in return, though he doubted a guarantee would mean much.

Armand nodded. "Naturally. As long as I don't find out you're lying to me about your master's situation." He looked at Lily. She met his eyes and smiled. Then her eyes went strangely blank, and the *Seigneur* continued. "Now, if I were to discover you or your master aiding Brigitte in eluding us, not only will the guarantee be revoked, but I will kill you all." He took a moment to give each of them a chilling stare. Meanwhile, Lily continued to gaze vacantly into space. "Are we understood?"

No one answered, but then no one had to. Apparently satisfied that his threat had been taken seriously, the *Seigneur* released Lily from his glamour.

"We are all weary from traveling," he said. "We will

pack our belongings and return before morning. Will that be ample time for you to prepare our rooms?"

Drake wondered what the *Seigneur* would do if he said no. Instead he just nodded and wondered just how bad a disaster this was going to become.

4

ARMAND DIDN'T LOWER himself to such menial chores as packing or unpacking his own belongings, so he ordered his valet to take care of it while he accompanied Faith to her room, one floor down from his own. She didn't know what he wanted from her, but she doubted it was anything good. His presence made her nervous enough that she had to insert the card key three times before the door would open. Armand stood in the entryway while she grabbed her suitcase and started packing.

"Did you find this *Drake* attractive?" he asked.

Faith dropped the suitcase on the bed, looking at the *Seigneur* in astonishment. "What?"

The corners of his eyes crinkled with humor. "It is not a difficult question."

She stared at him, trying to fathom what he wanted—without any success.

The humor drained from his eyes, and the corners

of his mouth tightened in annoyance. "Come now! I'm not going to fly into a rage if you say yes, if that's what you're worrying about."

No, Armand Durant was not the sort to fly into rages. He could be terrifying and deadly, but whatever emotions he had, he kept locked up tightly inside him. Even when he inflicted the most terrible punishments, he always seemed calm and removed.

Still not knowing what he wanted, she decided to answer honestly. "A woman would have to be dead not to find him attractive." The acting Master of Baltimore had been badly outmatched, and yet he'd still managed to ooze confidence. That in itself would have made him attractive enough, but when she added the handsome face with its full, sensual lips, the intelligence that shone through his dark eyes, and one very fine body displayed under a tight black T-shirt and supple-looking black leather pants, he became definite fantasy fodder.

Armand laughed. "And a man would have to be dead not to feel the same about you. And don't tell me you think vampires are dead."

She blushed and lowered her gaze, not sure why she was responding to his flattery. It wasn't as if he hadn't told her before that he thought she was beautiful, and it wasn't as if it mattered.

"What's your point?" she asked, pulling open a drawer and digging out a handful of clothes.

Armand came farther into the room, sitting on the edge of the bed and watching her as she packed. "If Brigitte is to be believed—which, naturally, may be doubtful—these Baltimore vampires subsist on animal blood, just like you do."

Faith froze, still bent over the suitcase. Her hands had tightened on the handful of clothes, and she hastily put them down and stood straight. She met his gaze and couldn't think of a single thing to say.

He smiled at her, though the look in his eyes was too calculating to make the smile entirely genuine. "I know you've wanted to escape from me from the moment we met. And I also know that even if you managed to spirit yourself and your sister away, you would have nowhere to go." His gaze sharpened. "Or maybe you would."

Faith swallowed hard. "What do you mean?" Her heart fluttered in her throat.

"I must admit to a certain amount of skepticism about the Master of Baltimore's whereabouts."

Faith frowned at the non sequitur. "I don't understand."

"In all likelihood, he is hiding somewhere nearby."

She still didn't get it. "And?"

Armand's smile became condescending. "And it's highly likely that his people, particularly his lieutenant, know *where*. A woman of your obvious charms might be able to—how shall I say it?—lower his guard?"

Faith slammed the suitcase shut, too furious to control herself. "You unbelievable bastard! You can force me to your bed all you want, but that doesn't make me a whore!"

With a flick of his hand—and no change in

expression—Armand used his telekinesis to send her flying across the room until she slammed into the wall. The impact knocked the wind out of her, and she slid down, clutching her ribs as if that would somehow force her lungs to inflate once more.

"Don't forget your place," Armand said quietly. He rose from the bed and came toward her.

Faith braced herself, cursing her lack of control. She knew better than to talk back to the *Seigneur*. Within the first month of living with him in his manor, she'd learned—painfully—to swallow every protest that wanted to rise to her lips. Sometimes it felt like cowardice. Other times it just felt like common sense.

When Armand reached down and dragged her to her feet, she fully expected him to beat her. Being a vampire—even a young one who fed on animal blood—she could endure a lot of abuse and be completely healed within an hour at the most, so she reminded herself that it would be over soon. That reminder was all that had gotten her through the first hellish month with him, but she was out of practice now, and fear threatened to overwhelm her.

But he didn't hit her again, instead raising her chin with his finger so she was forced to meet his eyes. "If you were to learn from him Gabriel's whereabouts, and if your information were to lead us to fulfill our mission, then I would set both you and Lily free."

Her eyes widened, the blood drained from her face, and she could have sworn her heart stopped beating. She stared up at him with horror and hope battling in her chest.

"You will have to be subtle," Armand continued. "You don't want him knowing that you've betrayed him, or you will lose your safe haven. But I will do my best to ensure that he doesn't know the source of my information."

She blinked and shook her head, shaking free of the finger that held her chin. "Why would you do this?" she whispered. She knew she was of no particular use to him now that he had Marie for his bed—this evening's interlude being an exception to the rule. But in Armand's view of the world, she *belonged* to him, as did Lily, and he was not one to willingly give away his possessions.

He stroked the back of his fingers over her cheek. "Perhaps because I am not as heartless as you believe me to be."

She narrowed her eyes at him. "No, that's not it." Unlike some other *Seigneurs* she'd met, Armand did have a certain sense of *noblesse oblige* and considered himself responsible for the well-being of his people. But that was merely because he felt it necessary to take good care of his belongings, not because he actually had a heart, not because he actually cared.

He shrugged. "Does it matter why I would release you?"

She lowered her gaze; then, when that wasn't enough, closed her eyes. She knew nothing about these Baltimore vampires. Had no reason to care about them whatsoever. If betraying them could win her freedom—and more importantly, Lily's freedom—then she would be a fool not to seize the opportunity.

No matter how sleazy it might make her feel. And no matter what the *Seigneur*'s true motivations might be.

"I didn't think so," Armand said, though she hadn't given him her answer out loud. "Finish packing. We will meet in the lobby in thirty minutes."

Faith nodded without opening her eyes.

* * *

GABRIEL AND JEZ'S house had plenty of room to accommodate the European delegation, though most of the rooms hadn't been used since Gabriel had dethroned his mother as Master of Baltimore. Drake, Eric, and Harry helped Jez prepare the rooms for their "guests," giving everything a cursory dusting. The third floor of the house held what had once been servants' quarters. Drake sent Eric and Harry up there to continue cleaning, but took Jez aside.

She was looking wan and pale, her eyes distant. Still trying to contact Gabriel, no doubt.

"Jez," he said, and she blinked, coming back to herself.

"What?"

"I think Eric and Harry and I should stay here while the delegation is in the house."

She scowled. "Sure, invite yourself to stay. You've invited everyone else."

He sighed. "You know I had no choice. If they want to move in, there's nothing any of us can do to stop them."

Her eyes narrowed even further. "You're the kind

of guy who thinks that a girl shouldn't fight a rapist when she knows he can overpower her, aren't you?"

"What?" he asked, totally flummoxed by the question.

"Sometimes, you should fight even when you know you can't win."

He gritted his teeth. "So you would have preferred it if I refused to let them stay here, made them force the issue, and perhaps let some or all of us get hurt in the process?"

"Yes!" Jez snapped. "They weren't going to kill anyone, not when they think they can use us. And at least that way we wouldn't be acting like doormats. I didn't argue with you down there because I know it's important to show a united front, but I swear if you roll over like that again, I won't just sit quietly by."

"Yes, you will!" he snapped right back, crowding into her space. He'd given her the benefit of the doubt so far because of her fear for Gabriel, but enough was enough. "Remember, Jez, I'm older and stronger than you. As long as I'm acting Master of Baltimore, you'll do as I say."

Jez glared at him fiercely, baring her fangs. "Don't try to bully me, Drake."

He laughed humorlessly. "I'm not *trying* to bully you. I *am* bullying you." If he were more like Eli, he probably could have found the perfect words to soothe her brittle nerves and get her to regard the situation with her brain instead of her heart. But he didn't have Eli's diplomatic skills, nor did he have the effective wise-old-man image. The only way he could assert himself was through pure power, whether he liked it or not. "I might have to 'roll over' for the *Seigneur,* but I don't have to do it for *you.*"

A very unfeminine growl rose from her throat, and to his shock, she took a swing at him.

When Jez had been in Philly, she'd had some basic martial arts training, but Drake had learned his own fighting skills in a much tougher environment and at a much younger age. Even when totally taken by surprise, his well-honed instincts kicked in. He dodged the blow, grabbing Jez's wrist as her fist swung past his head. Adrenaline fueled by anger flooded his system, and his fangs descended. Momentarily forgetting his usual chivalry, he used her own momentum to shove her face-first against the wall, then pinned her there with her wrist behind her back. She tried to stomp on his foot, but he dodged that, too, and pushed her wrist up until she cried out in pain.

That small cry dragged him back from the brink of mindless fury, but he didn't let up on the pressure. This was for her own good, after all. If she attacked one of the *Seigneur*'s vampires, she could end up dead.

"If you have a problem with my decision making," he snarled in her ear, "take it up with Gabriel when we get him back. But until then, you'll do as I tell you."

"He'll kill you for this," she hissed, her teeth still clenched in pain.

Drake eased up on the pressure a bit. "Not if I keep you safe, he won't." Gabriel's leadership style wasn't exactly of the warm and fuzzy variety, and he would understand why Drake had to take a hard line. All three of his Guardians were young and volatile, inexperienced at controlling the natural aggression that came with being a vampire. Stress would weaken their impulse control even more than usual, and Drake had to make a strong impression.

Absorbed in his battle with Jez, Drake didn't realize he had an audience until she finally capitulated and he let go.

Eric and Harry stood at the base of the stairs to the third floor, watching him with wide eyes. Something twisted inside his gut. He knew that wary, guarded look, the look of frightened followers. He cursed under his breath.

Once upon a time, long ago, he'd wielded his strength as a weapon. He'd struck terror into the hearts of his enemies, and even his allies had feared him. It was a past he'd given up when he'd teamed up with Eli, and he'd barely allowed himself to think about it for over a century. Now the past seemed to be sneaking up on him again. He touched the pocket where the crumpled piece of paper lay, the insidious invitation echoing through his head.

Call me, said his maker's voice, the voice of temptation. *All is forgiven,* it seemed to say.

He shook his head violently. It didn't matter *what* Padraig had to say. Even if the note really was from Drake's maker, and not some construct of Brigitte's schemes. Drake had left behind the man he had once been. And even a momentary burst of violence wouldn't bring Johnnie Drake back to life.

Jez went to stand with the two fledglings as soon as Drake let her go. She rubbed her wrist absently and refused to meet his gaze as the other two closed ranks around her. He felt like a bastard. So much for his wishful thinking that somehow he might "fit in" among Gabriel's Guardians.

"I'm sorry I have to be a hard-ass about this," he said. "I'm just trying to keep us all safe."

Eric laughed nervously. "Hey, after Gabriel, you're an old softie."

Harry gave a halfhearted bark of laughter, but Jez didn't seem amused. She might have been about to light into Eric, but just then, the doorbell rang.

Despite what that ring portended, Drake was thankful for it. "It seems our guests have arrived," he said. "Jez, can you at least pretend to forgive me while they're around?"

The look she shot him was not even remotely friendly, but she nodded anyway.

* * *

AFTER HER LITTLE "chat" with the *Seigneur,* Faith wasn't surprised that she got her own room in their hosts' house. She supposed Armand thought she'd have a better chance of seducing Drake and getting him to spill all his secrets during pillow talk if she didn't have a roommate. Armand, Charles, and Lily had all merited rooms on the second floor. Faith and the "lesser" vampires of the entourage were relegated to the third floor along with the mortals. The others grumbled about being housed in servants' quarters, and grumbled even more that Faith got a room to herself.

Feeling like a puppet dancing on the end of the *Seigneur*'s strings, Faith left her unpacking for later and slipped down the stairs to the first floor, looking for Drake. She found him in a comfortable-looking den, complete with wide-screen TV and plush, overstuffed chairs. A room from the twenty-first century, in sharp contrast to the absurdly garish receiving room.

Unfortunately, Drake was deep in conversation with the female Guardian, Jezebel, their heads bent together, their voices low, and anger flashing in both sets of eyes. Faith cleared her throat softly to let them know she was there, and they both instantly clammed up and moved apart. Jezebel gave her a contemptuous once-over, then flounced out of the room in a huff.

Feeling almost unbearably awkward, Faith looked at Drake and found her voice trapped somewhere in her throat. He raised one dark eyebrow in inquiry.

"Is there something I can do for you?" he asked.

She swallowed past a lump of fear in her throat and moved farther into the room. "Armand tells me Guardians drink only animal blood," she said, then cursed herself. Hardly a seductive conversation topic, but she'd never tried to seduce anyone before. Actually, for the last six years, she'd been trying with all her might *not* to attract any masculine attention. Clearly, she had no idea how to go about such a thing.

Drake's lips twitched into a tense smile. "That's true, for the most part."

"For the most part?"

He crossed some of the distance between them, and she had to fight an urge to retreat. There was a predatory expression in his eyes that reminded her of Armand. His nostrils flared, as if he'd caught a whiff of her sudden, irrational fear of him.

"*I* don't," he said, and his smile went from tense to wolfish. He took another step toward her, his fangs descending.

Dammit! Had Armand known that when he sent her on her mission? She gritted her teeth. No doubt he had. Such details rarely escaped his notice. It wasn't possible to see from a vampire's aura whether he was a Killer or not, but Armand would not have set foot in potentially hostile territory without advance research.

"Why do you ask?" Drake asked, circling her like a shark.

Faith sucked in a deep breath. Like any predator, he could sense fear, and he knew from her reactions that she was weak and vulnerable. Doomed to be prey to older, stronger, more ruthless vampires as long as she refused to kill.

She swallowed past her fear. Despite his aggressive display, Drake would not dare harm her when his house was swarming with vampires many times his age. He was no doubt angry about his lack of power and had latched onto making her squirm as a way to reassert himself.

"Because I haven't fed, and I'm hungry," she said, though in fact she had fed before leaving France and would not need to do so again for at least a couple more days. She was pretty sure she could choke another meal down for a good cause.

Drake stopped circling, his brows drawing together in puzzlement. "You're not asking my permission to hunt in Baltimore, are you? Because that's something I will never allow."

She shook her head, wondering if he really thought he had the power to "allow" the delegation to do anything. "I'm not a Killer. I was hoping you could provide me with . . . what I need."

He looked at her with infinite skepticism. "You must take me for a complete idiot."

She huffed out a sigh of frustration. Why had she expected him to believe her? She could count on one hand the number of vampires she'd met who had resisted the lure of the kill—and most of those she had met today, in Drake's receiving room. Why on earth would he believe a vampire in Armand's entourage would have refrained?

"You don't have to believe me," she said. "You could just humor me."

He raised one shoulder in a halfhearted shrug. "I suppose I could, Miss . . . ?"

"Just call me Faith. No need to be formal."

"All right, Faith. Come on." Without looking to see if she followed, he strode out a door on the opposite side of the room.

Faith hurried to catch up. He led her down a long corridor that opened into a barren kitchen. "Grab a glass," he ordered, pointing at a cabinet as he opened the refrigerator.

Faith bit her lip, wondering what on earth she was doing here. She wasn't a seductress, and Drake didn't exactly seem to be open to flirting. Not that she'd tried yet. Sighing, she reached into the cabinet and pulled out a glass.

Drake emerged from the fridge with a stoppered green glass bottle in his hand. She forced herself to approach as he uncorked the bottle.

"You're not French," he said, pouring her glass halfway full with thick, preserved blood.

"No," she responded. Her nose wrinkled at the medicinal smell of the stuff. She realized it was a mistake when he scowled at her.

"I suppose you prefer it hot from the vein," he said. "As I do."

She shook her head and raised the glass to her lips. "No." She gulped down a swallow and practically gagged at the taste. She couldn't help making a face, no doubt cementing his conviction that she was a Killer—and a liar. "Armand keeps livestock on his estate, so I've never had to drink preserved blood before." She forced down another slug and shuddered. "This is truly foul stuff."

"I wouldn't know." Another of his wolfish grins. "The others mix it with milk, which I'm told makes it even more revolting."

"Why would they do that?" she asked, startled.

"They feel that making the task of feeding unpleasant will reduce the chance that they'll be tempted to kill." He stepped toward the refrigerator. "Shall I add some milk to yours?" he asked.

"No, thanks," she said hastily, sure he hadn't expected her to say yes. Unwilling to admit she didn't really need to feed, Faith took another sip. She distracted herself from the nasty stuff by giving her reluctant host an assessing once-over. No doubt about it, he was easy on the eyes. She especially liked his night-black hair, textured by a hint of curl. The well-defined muscles of his chest were a pretty attractive feature, too.

Drake grinned at her too-obvious gaze, turning so she could take in the rear view. Supple black leather clung appealingly to a tight, rounded butt, and something fluttered low in her belly. The flutter faded as soon as she noticed, and she wondered—had it really come from her, or had that been a touch of his glamour?

He turned to face her once more, an expectant expression on his face. She looked at the glass of blood and decided she couldn't bear another swallow.

Drake folded his arms over his chest and leaned that scrumptious butt against the counter. "Well?" he prompted.

She blinked. "Well, what?"

"I gave you the deluxe tour," he said with a sweeping gesture that indicated his body. "Now it's your turn."

Heat flooded her cheeks, and she was tempted to toss her drink in his face. But no, she was supposed to be flirting. It was a good sign that he would make such a remark. So why did she feel so dreadfully awkward? She couldn't even force herself to answer his taunt one way or another.

"So," Drake said when it became apparent she wasn't going to answer, "where are you from? I already know it's not France."

"I'm originally from Virginia," she said, staring at the floor. "I took my sister on a vacation to Paris, and . . ." She let her voice trail off.

"Your sister," he mused. "That would be Lily?"

She nodded. Lily had been all of ten years old at the time, had witnessed the attack that had forever changed both their lives. All because Faith had allowed herself to think with her hormones.

"Armand killed the man who made me. And he took me and Lily in."

"And how is it that you're not a Killer?"

"My maker told me I could survive on animal blood, and I found it was true. For reasons of his own, Armand has allowed me to indulge what he considers my eccentricity."

"I see."

He didn't believe a word she said, but she could hardly blame him. She would have been equally skeptical in his shoes.

If Armand had wanted someone to seduce information out of Drake, he should have sent Marie, who no doubt would have achieved an invitation to his bed by now. Of course, Marie wasn't exactly subtle. Or smart. She might have gotten Drake to bed, but her chances of charming useful information out of him were slim.

"What do you really want?" Drake asked. "It wasn't the blood," he finished, indicating the mostly full glass with a jerk of his chin.

She shook her head. She was not a seductress, and even with the carrot of her own and Lily's freedom dangled before her nose, she wasn't about to become one. So she'd have to settle for being herself—frank to a fault.

She met his eyes. "Armand thinks you know where Gabriel is. He wants me to seduce you and see if I can convince you to talk."

Drake laughed, standing up straight and uncrossing his arms. "Wow. That wasn't the answer I was expecting." He reached for her glass and tossed the contents down the drain.

She found herself laughing as well. "No, I guess not." She did a quick psychic scan of the area to make sure there was no one listening in on them. She stepped closer to him and dropped her voice.

"No matter what he might say, Armand is under orders to bring *La Vieille* Gabriel's head."

Drake's eyes widened, and he fixed her with a penetrating gaze. "Why are you telling me this?"

Why indeed? Her mouth seemed to be working independently of her brain. She rubbed suddenly sweaty palms on her pants legs, but her brain finally caught up with her and she smiled faintly. "I guess

I'm trying to play both sides. If you and your master come out on top, I don't want you to see me as one of *them*." She pointed at the ceiling to indicate the delegation.

"Gabriel's not my master," Drake said with some asperity.

She gave him a knowing look, and Drake visibly bristled.

"He's my *boss*. There's a difference."

"Uh-huh," she agreed. Let him cling to that illusion if he liked. She'd wager as a member of Armand's entourage, she'd met more vampires than Drake had ever known, and there wasn't a hint of democratic spirit in any of them. They ruled by pure power and fear. An employee could choose to disobey a boss. A lesser vampire had no choice but to obey his master unless he wanted to die.

"So Armand is *your* master," Drake said, no doubt trying to get a rise out of her.

She winced—she couldn't help it. But the answer was inescapable. "Yes. He is. In every way." Her throat tightened on the words, and she remembered the feel of his mouth on her breast as she sighed in pleasure under the influence of his glamour.

There was a moment of leaden silence. Then Drake reached out and touched her arm briefly. His hand dropped back to his side as if her skin had burned him. "I'm sorry," he said, not looking at her. "I didn't mean to be cruel."

She swallowed past the lump in her throat. "Neither does he." *Oh yeah,* she thought. *This is the best seduction attempt ever. Tell the guy what you're up to, then suggest you're sleeping with someone else.*

She shook the thought off. It was time to cut her losses and regroup. "I should go now." She forced something between a smile and a grimace. "Thanks for dinner."

Drake's only response was a brusque nod before he turned back to the sink to rinse the bloody glass. Faith slunk away.

* * *

CHARLES CLOSED THE door to his room and wondered how much sound would travel through these walls. Armand had the room next door, but a quick psychic scan told him Marie had joined the *Seigneur*. Surely that meant he would be distracted for a while, wouldn't overhear anything he shouldn't.

Hating himself, Charles pulled his cell phone out of his pocket and dialed the private number *La Vieille du Nord* had given him. She answered on the fifth ring.

"You have an update for me, *monsieur*?"

"Yes, Your Excellency," he said, the honorific tasting sour on his tongue. Having never risen in the ranks, Charles had had very little occasion to speak with her, being completely beneath her notice. How he wished it had stayed that way!

"Well?"

"We've taken up lodging at the Master's house, though Gabriel has made himself scarce. Apparently, Brigitte warned them we were coming."

La Vieille made a low sound that made the hairs on the back of Charles's neck stand on end. "My girl is a clever one and will no doubt make as much trouble as she can manage. But she won't outsmart you or the *Seigneur,* will she?"

He swallowed hard. "No, Your Excellency."

Charles had abandoned his faith in God long ago, but tonight he would pray nonetheless. *Please God, let us succeed. Don't cast me in the role of Judas.*

Because if they failed—if Brigitte or Gabriel eluded them, or if Brigitte was killed—the only way Charles could save his own life was to turn the man who'd been his best friend for more than six hundred years over to *La Vieille du Nord.* Armand's would be a fate worse than death, but to ensure himself immunity from her terrifying wrath, Charles would do anything.

By showing him how low he would sink to protect his own hide, *La Vieille* had eaten away a piece of his soul. And even if he never had to betray his friend, he would hate her—and himself—for the rest of his immortal life.

5

DRAKE RETIRED TO his borrowed bedroom at the crack of dawn, though at his age the daytime sleep wouldn't take him for another couple of hours. He didn't want to run into another member of the European delegation, and the Guardians had all succumbed to sleep already. He sat on a comfortable chair in the corner of the darkened room, watching as dawn began to glow around the edges of the heavy blackout curtains.

Try as he might, Drake couldn't imagine the current situation ending well. Not if the delegation was under orders to kill Gabriel. Drake might not have any personal attachment to the Killer, but he knew for a fact that Gabriel's death would destroy his fledgling Guardians. Drake might be powerful enough to bully them into following him in the short term—that remained to be seen—but he wasn't arrogant enough to believe he could do so indefinitely.

Eli could control his Guardians with wisdom and reason; Gabriel could control them with his iron fist; Drake could manage neither.

He grimaced, wondering if he was lying to himself. Once upon a time, during his mortal days, striking terror into the hearts of men had been his sole reason for existence. He'd beaten men bloody, broken bones, even killed in his role as enforcer. There hadn't been a soul in Five Points who hadn't feared Johnnie Drake. But terrorizing fellow gangsters—cutthroats, hooligans, and murderers all—had barely tweaked his conscience. He couldn't imagine treating Eric, or Harry, or, God forbid, Jezebel like that. And without that ruthless authority, he would not control them for long.

He reached into his pocket and pulled out the enigmatic note that had purportedly come from his maker. Smoothing out the wrinkles in the crumpled piece of paper, he stared at it and tried to decide if it could really be Padraig's handwriting. His gaze drifted to the phone that sat on a nightstand beside the bed. To find out if it was really Padraig, all he had to do was call.

With a grunt of frustration, Drake crumpled the paper again. If Padraig was alive, and if he wanted to talk to Drake, then Drake didn't dare make contact. Violent, cruel, and severely lacking in conscience, Padraig nonetheless possessed boundless charm and charisma, and he could persuade a scientist that the moon was made of cheese if he thought there was some advantage to be had in it.

No, Drake didn't dare risk falling under his maker's sway once more. Already he felt the insidious influence of Padraig's charm. Hadn't he found himself thinking that the note somehow meant Padraig had forgiven him?

Drake let out a little bark of laughter. *Padraig* had forgiven *him*? It was *Padraig* who'd condoned the murder of a fifteen-year-old innocent. Drake had never asked for, nor wanted forgiveness for his insubordination when he'd tried to stop it.

Knowing he should throw the slip of paper in the trash and have done with it, he nevertheless left it sitting in a crumpled wad on the side table. Then he tried to force his mind to shut down as he undressed and slipped into bed.

* * *

HE WOKE TO the sound of a shrill, feminine scream.

Elsewhere in the house, doors slammed and footsteps pounded. The screams continued. Still half asleep, Drake leapt from the bed, shoving his legs into yesterday's pants and not bothering with a shirt. He yanked his door open and stepped out into the hallway. The screams were coming from downstairs, and Drake emerged just in time to see the *Seigneur* practically fly past, fully clothed and groomed as if he'd been up for hours, which maybe he had.

Drake followed as more vamps filled the hallway behind him, milling about and looking disoriented.

The screams stopped, suddenly muffled, and then

turned into wrenching sobs. Drake followed the sound and found Armand in the den, the mortal girl, Lily, clutched in his arms. Her face was pressed into the *Seigneur*'s chest, her hands fisted in the lapels of his jacket, and she sobbed hysterically. Armand cradled the girl's head, turning his body slightly to shield her from something. He met Drake's eyes and jerked his chin toward whatever was behind him.

Drake took a step forward and flinched at what he saw—not because of his own sensibilities, but because he couldn't help seeing it through the eyes of a sixteen-year-old girl.

One of Armand's vampires, a pretty red-headed woman, lay sprawled on the floor, dead eyes wide and staring at the ceiling. The handle of a knife protruded from her ribs, and blood, many hours old, pooled on the floor beside her. One outstretched arm had apparently lain in a band of sunlight since her death, for the skin was blackened and withered, and the room stank of burnt flesh. Under that stink, Drake thought he caught a whiff of sex, though he couldn't be sure.

The hallway outside the room was filling with vampires and mortals—mostly Armand's entourage, but Drake also caught sight of Harry, who as a six-foot-four black man was hard to miss, and Jez, who'd pushed her way to the front. No doubt Eric was in there somewhere, too.

"Lily!" a voice called from the crowd, and people started moving aside as Faith, her face white, forced her way through.

"Faith!" Lily shouted back, struggling free of Armand and throwing herself into her sister's arms.

"Oh, sweetie, are you okay?" Faith asked, holding her tightly, but Lily just cried.

Armand's face was closed and shuttered as he looked from the body, to Drake, then to Faith.

"Everyone out except Drake and Faith," he commanded.

Drake could well understand why the *Seigneur* wanted to speak to him in private, but he couldn't understand why Faith needed to be here. Especially when her sister was in such distress.

"Seigneur—" Faith started to say, but he cut her off.

"I said everyone out!" he snapped, and Faith looked stricken as her sister clung tighter.

Jezebel, whom Drake had half expected to object to Armand's barked orders, stepped into the room and reached a hand out for Lily.

"Why don't you come with me, honey?" she prompted gently. "You don't want to stay in here anyway."

"Faith," Lily whimpered.

Faith swallowed hard, her eyes full of pain. "Go with her, Lily. Just give me a couple of minutes to talk with Uncle Armand." Her voice was calm and soothing, despite the turmoil in her eyes.

The *Seigneur* on the other hand looked like he was about to explode as he glared at Faith for no reason that Drake could fathom.

The others had all fled the fury in the *Seigneur*'s

expression, only Jez remaining to gently take hold of Lily's arm. Lily finally allowed herself to be led away, transferring her clinging hold to Jezebel. The door slammed behind them, but it was Armand's power that slammed it, not a human or vampire hand.

"Did you do this?" Armand growled at Faith the moment the door was shut.

Drake blinked in surprise. How interesting that after her avowal last night that she wasn't a Killer, she was the first one the *Seigneur* suspected of murder.

Faith kept her eyes glued to the floor. "No, *Seigneur,*" she said in a whisper.

Armand strode across the room and grabbed her shoulders in a brutal grip. "Look at me when you speak!" he shouted, giving her a shake.

Her face even whiter, Faith obediently raised her gaze and looked into his eyes. "I didn't do it, *Seigneur.*"

He nodded sharply. Anger still radiated from him, but it no longer seemed directed at Faith. "Very well. Get out." He gave her a little shove toward the door, and she hurried out.

Armand then turned his attention to Drake.

"If you or one of your people did this, I will kill you all."

Drake shook his head and looked at the dead woman. He didn't even know her name—Armand hadn't felt it necessary to introduce most of his entourage. "I can guarantee you it wasn't one of us. What reason could any of us possibly have to kill her?"

Armand frowned down at her. "Marie had a unique

way of making enemies, particularly among other women."

Drake almost laughed, but managed to swallow it. "Jezebel's never killed anyone, and if she were going to start, it wouldn't be when her home is occupied by half a dozen foreign vampires who can overpower her without breaking a sweat."

Armand glared at him. "My vampires wouldn't *dare* harm someone under my protection."

Drake met that glare, undaunted, and refrained from pointing out that Armand had accused Faith of doing just that. "Well *my* vampires have no reason to." He looked at the dead woman once more, not at all sorry she was dead. Faith's claims to the contrary, all the vampires of Armand's entourage had to be Killers, and death was no doubt what they deserved.

"Well, *somebody* killed her," the *Seigneur* said.

If it wasn't the Guardians, and it wasn't someone else in the entourage . . . "Brigitte," Drake responded.

The *Seigneur* looked momentarily startled by the suggestion. Then the expression on his face hardened. "I suppose she could be responsible. She can walk by day, so she could have done this when the rest of us were asleep." He frowned at the body. "Marie was my fledgling. I should have felt her death." The frown deepened. "But I was tired and slept before sunrise. *Anyone* could have done this, and I would not have known. Besides, if Brigitte had done it, she would have killed us all."

"Perhaps it wouldn't be as much fun that way."

Armand grimaced, then rejected the idea. "No. It was someone in this house. Brigitte's crazy, but not a fool. Charles and I are both old enough to keep watch during the day as long as we are not in the direct sunlight. She knows that. She's not stupid enough to give us a warning like this first."

Drake could hardly say he knew Brigitte well, but based on what he did know, he couldn't agree with the *Seigneur*. No, she was not a fool. But her ego was enormous. As far as she was concerned, she could play to her heart's content, and no one could stop her.

The *Seigneur* stared at Drake coldly. "When I find out which of your people is responsible, you will not stand in the way of my vengeance."

Drake shook his head. "I guarantee it was not one of my people. And if you harm one of them, I can guarantee you that Gabriel will hunt you to the ends of the earth to get his own vengeance." He made sure his own stare was as cold as the *Seigneur*'s.

"I find it interesting," the *Seigneur* said, "that you would threaten us with your master's vengeance when you claim that Brigitte has him imprisoned."

"I don't expect him to remain her prisoner forever," Drake answered calmly.

"I really must insist that I speak to your master," the *Seigneur* said, as if he'd lost his last doubt that Gabriel was available.

"You can insist all you want. Somehow, I don't think Brigitte's going to allow it."

The *Seigneur* waved off the protest. "You'll find a

way to reach him. You don't want to know the consequences of failing me."

"I can't—"

"Now," Armand said, "my ward has suffered a terrible shock. I'm going to take her mind off things by spoiling her shamelessly. I suggest you dispose of the remains while we are away."

He didn't wait for Drake to agree, instead turning and striding out of the room. Shortly afterward, Drake heard the thump of the *Seigneur*'s shoes on the stairs. Then silence.

Barefoot and shirtless, Drake climbed the stairs at a more sedate pace. By the time he reached the hallway that led to his room, the *Seigneur* had emerged with Lily. She was still pale and shaky-looking, but she tried for a brave smile. The *Seigneur* looked at her with what seemed to be genuine affection. Faith hovered nearby, her face almost as pale as Lily's. Ignoring her, Armand paused only long enough to issue orders to his entourage before leading the girl out into the chilly autumn night. Charles and the remaining vampires except Faith accompanied the *Seigneur*. The mortals disappeared into their various rooms. Leaving only Faith, who stood in the hall, eyes glistening with tears as she stared at the stairway down which the *Seigneur* and her sister had disappeared.

* * *

THERE WAS A damp patch on Faith's shoulder, the fabric of her nightshirt soaked with Lily's tears. She stroked her fingers over the dampened cloth as she followed Armand and Lily with her psychic senses until they were out of her range. Then, some of the strength seemed to fade from her legs, and she had to lean back against the wall for support.

The knowledge that he was out there right now, buying Lily's innocent affection, ate at her heart. And her own helplessness to stop him made her stomach clench into a painful knot.

She was so sunk in misery she didn't notice Drake approaching until he was practically on top of her. When she snapped out of it enough to see him, she sucked in a quick, startled breath.

He had obviously been roused from his bed by Lily's cries. His wiry black hair was messy and tousled by sleep, but that wasn't what stole the moisture from her mouth. Somehow, in the heat of the moment downstairs, she had failed to notice Drake's state of undress, his feet and chest bare. In fact, she suspected he was wearing *nothing* except for those sexy leather pants. She allowed herself one quick glance at the muscular planes of his chest before her eyes slid away in embarrassment.

Just out of bed, Drake looked sexy as sin, but the heat rose in Faith's cheeks as she realized what a sight *she* must be. Her oversized, shapeless nightshirt hung almost to her knees. Once upon a time, it had been a deep shade of purple, but repeated washings had faded it to a soft lavender that made her look even paler than she was, and the hem was beginning to unravel. She was sure her eyes were red and puffy, and she didn't even want to *think* about what her hair must look like.

"Was she a friend of yours?" Drake asked. His tone of voice was bland, as if he hadn't heard the *Seigneur* accuse her of murder, but she knew he was fishing.

Swiping the remaining tears from her eyes, she pushed her hair from her face and met his suspicious gaze. "No." She swallowed the lump in her throat. "I'm not sorry she's dead, either. She always saw me as 'the competition,' and she's threatened to kill me more than once. But I didn't kill her."

He leaned against the wall opposite her, arms crossed over that distractingly bare chest, legs crossed at the ankles. "But the *Seigneur* has reason to believe you might have."

She growled in disgust. "Yes, he *would* think something like that. Six years I've served him, and he hasn't a clue who I am." Dammit! She sounded for all the world like she had hurt feelings, which was ridiculous. What did she care what Armand thought of her? He was a ruthless Killer, and a leader of scores of other ruthless Killers, and there was no reason in the world why he should understand that she was different.

She ran a hand through her snarled hair. "It doesn't matter what he thinks. I didn't kill Marie." *No matter how much I might have fantasized about doing it.* "And I know none of Armand's other people would dare."

"Yes, I've already had this conversation with him.

My people would have had no reason to kill her. I suspect Brigitte."

Faith supposed that made a kind of sense, though she couldn't say she understood *La Vieille*'s daughter or her motivations. They had never been formally introduced, though Faith had seen her at Armand's manor house more than once. Her and her creepy fledgling, Henri, whom Armand sometimes used as a threat against people who incurred his wrath—toe the line, or the next time Henri came calling, Armand would lend you out to him for the duration of his stay. He had never followed through on that threat, thank God, and Faith had the distinct impression Henri held that against him.

Tears suddenly blurred her vision. "How could Armand bring Lily into the middle of this?" He was out there even now, with Charles and his other two surviving fledglings at his side. Could all of them together defeat Brigitte and Henri if they decided to attack? She wished she felt more confident that the answer was yes.

The thought of Lily in Henri's clutches made her sway dizzily. Drake reached out a hand to steady her. She held onto him, needing the anchor, as she closed her eyes and tried to calm the frantic rush of her heart.

Drake moved in closer to her, and she could feel the heat of his body. "I don't know what Brigitte's game is," he said, "but I do know she has delusions that she'll eventually talk Gabriel into becoming her ally. And she also knows how terribly protective

Gabriel is of mortals in general and children in particular. She won't dare harm your sister for fear that he would never forgive her."

Faith opened her eyes and chewed her lip. "You really think so?" she asked, desperately needing to believe him.

"There are two people in this house who are safe—your sister, and Jezebel." His face took on a grim cast, despite the hint of a grin on his lips. "The rest of us, though, are fair game."

The thought inspired little fear in Faith's heart. She would sacrifice every vampire here—including herself—if only she could get Lily free of them all. Because Armand had carefully sheltered her from the harshest realities of vampire existence, today was the first time Lily had seen a dead body. And though she knew intellectually that Armand and all his people were Killers, she gave herself the illusion that they weren't really bad people.

Armand was out there with her now, buying her expensive gifts to salve her emotional wounds, seducing her in ways that no words of Faith's could undo. Even if Faith should miraculously come up with a viable escape plan, she couldn't guarantee Lily would go along with it. She might have to kidnap her own sister to escape Armand's influence.

But if that was what it would take, then that was exactly what she'd do.

6

Gabriel had what Drake considered an ingeniously simple method for disposing of his victims—via a pet crematorium. During Camille's reign as Master of Baltimore, she had seduced one of the mortals who worked there with a promise of power and eternal life, and he had given her full access to his establishment. The victims of vampire kills in Baltimore vanished without a trace, their ashes mixed ignominiously with dogs, cats, and the occasional gerbil.

Camille had long ago killed her mortal henchman, but Gabriel had learned through him how the deed was done and had all the necessary keys. Having already had to dispose of a couple of his own kills, Drake had his own set of keys, which was how he found himself in the dark and depressing building in the early hours of the evening, carrying a dead vampire whom the mortal authorities could never be allowed to find.

When he'd finished his distasteful errand and slipped out the building's back door, he almost ran straight into Henri. He jumped back, startled and irritated with himself for not having performed a basic psychic scan of the area before stepping out into the darkness. Brigitte could mask her presence, but as far as Drake knew, Henri did not possess the same skill.

Drake belatedly performed the scan, but wasn't surprised that he couldn't pick up Brigitte's footprint. He had no doubt she was close by, however. He got the impression she kept her fledgling on a short leash.

"She was a lousy lay," Henri said, his thick accent making the colloquial words sound odd coming from his mouth. He wrinkled his nose. "I can't imagine why the *Seigneur* was so reluctant to share her."

Drake could only assume he was talking about the dead vampire. "So, *you* killed her?" Drake inquired, wondering what Henri was up to.

Brigitte's fledgling grinned. It was an unsettling expression, perhaps because of the unpleasant glow in his eyes.

Drake took that as a yes and frowned. "You killed her because she was a lousy lay?"

Henri laughed. "No, no. I would have killed her even were she the best lay in existence. A reminder of what happens when the *Seigneur* refuses to share his toys."

"What do you want?"

"I want the other toys the *Seigneur* has refused to share."

A muscle in the side of Drake's jaw ticked. He had the sinking feeling he knew just who Henri meant. But why would Henri tell him his plans?

"Here is the game," Henri said. "You tell the *Seigneur* exactly what my mistress and I plan to do. He can try to stop us. And he will find out just how helpless he is, even with his great entourage at his side. In France, my mistress bowed to him because he had the weight of *La Vieille* behind him. Here, he has nothing." He laughed again. "Except you."

"If she wanted to kill them all, she could have done it during the day while you were . . . visiting."

"That is not how my mistress wishes to do it. She prefers finesse to slaughter. They will slip through the *Seigneur*'s fingers one by one. And we will not enter the house again, so don't bother setting a trap." He got that nasty, eerie glow in his eyes again. "We will leave the girls for last. My mistress has promised I can have them both while the *Seigneur* watches." He reached down to stroke himself.

Drake's lip curled with distaste. "Brigitte would never promise you the mortal girl. Not if she ever hopes to win Gabriel's cooperation."

There was no mistaking the flash of jealousy in Henri's eyes, though he quickly suppressed it. "I can be most persuasive," was all he said, and his eyes narrowed with pleasure at his own touch.

"Why are you telling *me* this, anyway? Surely it's the *Seigneur* you want to talk to."

Henri was really enjoying whatever sickening image flickered through his mind. He unzipped his pants and reached inside. Drake met his eyes and refused to let his gaze drift.

"If we told the *Seigneur,*" Henri said, getting a little breathless as he continued to work himself, "then he'd know for certain it was us. This way, he'll never be completely sure whether it's us, or you Guardians, or even Gabriel himself. After all, we all have reason to want him and his entourage dead. You'll be under enough suspicion that you'll have neither the time nor the freedom to look for your master."

Brigitte's irritating giggle floated on the night air, and Henri's hand stilled, though he didn't let go of his equipment.

"I think you're embarrassing Jonathan," she said, coming into view from Drake's right.

"My apologies," Henri said, starting up again, the thought that he might be making Drake uncomfortable obviously exciting him even more.

Drake tried to ignore him. It wasn't the public masturbation that disturbed him—it was the thought of Henri getting hold of young Lily. And, Drake had to admit to himself, despite all his skepticism about her story, of Faith.

Brigitte watched her fledgling jerk off with rapt attention while she spoke to Drake. "I am not a good person to make an enemy of," she said. "Armand Durant has been one of my keepers for decades now, and I plan to pay him back for all his troubles. And if I can have some extra fun, make some extra mischief along the way, then I plan to thoroughly indulge myself."

Henri was still frantically wanking away, his breath coming in gasps, an occasional sound almost like a whimper rising from his throat.

"And, of course," Brigitte continued, "I plan to thoroughly indulge Henri, as well." He moaned, but still didn't come. Brigitte smiled at him, an expression far too sweet and innocent looking under the circumstances. "It's time for you to stop now, dearest," she said.

With a strained groan, Henri obeyed. He even zipped his pants, though Drake figured he had to have a major case of blue balls at the moment. Drake must have made some kind of face, for she laughed at him.

"We're saving him for the *pièce de résistance*," she explained. "He will be wonderfully primed by the time we get our hands on the *Seigneur*'s concubine. It will be soooo exciting to watch." She slipped her arm around her fledgling's waist and rubbed herself against him. Henri visibly gritted his teeth.

"You didn't feel the need to save him for the woman last night?"

Brigitte smiled, and for once allowed her innate malice to show in her eyes. "It would have been a waste. Armand cared nothing for her. I'll let the little one go in the name of friendship." She gave Henri a pat on the shoulder. "But only because I know how very much it will hurt Armand to see Henri with the other one. I doubt he realizes how much he cares about her. And by the time he finds out," her smile broadened, "it will be too late."

Drake kept his voice bland, though her gloating

sickened him. "Revenge quests rarely end as well as their perpetrators hope."

Brigitte's eyes widened. "But, my dear Jonathan, this has nothing to do with revenge."

Drake snorted. "Of course it does. You said yourself—"

"I said I would like to pay him back. And I would. But if he did not chase me, then I would let him and all his people alone. It is his choice whether to dance with me or not."

"But you know it isn't his choice. He can't afford to disobey your mother's orders."

She shrugged. "That is not my problem. If he will hunt me, then I will punish him for it." Her face went grim. "In the choice of the lesser of two evils, I'm afraid he would be wise to choose me. I can't compete with *La Vieille* for cruelty. But I won't grant a merciful end, either."

Brigitte shook off the grimness, putting on an impish expression. "Have you spoken to your maker yet? He was quite looking forward to hearing from you."

Drake scowled. "He can keep looking forward to it as long as he likes." He narrowed his eyes at her. "Why would you want me to call him?"

She sniffed daintily. "I don't care one way or another. I merely granted a favor to a friend and delivered his message."

"How did you—"

"Come, Henri," she said, turning her back before Drake got his question out. "We've taken enough of Jonathan's time."

Henri extended his elbow, and Brigitte slipped her hand through. Drake swallowed his curiosity about how Brigitte and Padraig had met. If indeed they had and this wasn't all an elaborate game.

If he wanted to find out, he knew exactly whom he should ask. And he knew that he would never do it.

* * *

ARMAND AND CHARLES sat side by side on an uncomfortable sofa outside the dressing room into which Lily had disappeared with a preposterously large bundle of clothing. He had set his other fledglings outside the store as guards. They might be powerless against Brigitte—if, indeed, Brigitte was hunting them—but Armand kept them firmly in his psychic radar. If anything happened to them, he would know, and he and Charles would be prepared.

Lily emerged from the dressing room, wearing a pair of hip-hugging, skin-tight jeans with a cropped, faded T-shirt. Why today's youth liked to buy clothes pre-aged, he'd never understand. She turned for him, displaying her considerable charms. Out of the corner of his eye, he saw Charles drop his gaze, a hint of pink in his cheeks.

Armand frowned when he took in the rear view. She'd tried to tuck the top of her thong down into the seat of her pants to hide just how low they rode, but when she turned, the panties slid back into place. She must have felt them pop free, because she hastily turned around to the front and clasped her hands behind her back, trying to look innocent. Charles crossed his legs and folded his hands in his lap, but his ruse was not any more effective than Lily's.

"No," Armand said simply.

Lily stuck out her lower lip in a pout while she made doe eyes at him. "Please? Everyone wears them at school."

"I don't care what anyone else wears," he said more firmly. "You're not wearing that, and that's final."

She rolled her eyes hugely. "I'm not *twelve,* Uncle Armand."

His temper stirred, and he narrowed his eyes. "I said no. One more protest, and the shopping trip ends now." She swallowed her next argument, though she was still giving him the doe eyes. "If you have anything decent in that dressing room, put it on and show it to me. If not, put everything back and start over."

Faith might worry he had designs on little Lily, but though she was a pretty young thing and would no doubt be a great beauty in just a few years, he found it difficult to feel lust for a girl he'd known as a ten-year-old. Unfortunately, it appeared Charles was another story. Lily hunched her shoulders and retreated to the dressing room. Without raising his voice or turning his head, Armand spoke to his fledgling.

"I can't blame you for finding her attractive," he said. "But if you so much as touch her, I will destroy you. Are we quite clear?"

The pink flush left his cheeks, and Charles looked both pale and hurt. "You know me better than that, surely. I would never molest a child."

Yes, Armand knew that. However, that wasn't the issue. He turned to meet his friend's eyes. "How old was your wife?"

When they'd marched off to war together, Charles had been married only three months, though already his wife was expecting his heir. He dropped Armand's gaze and squirmed.

"Those were different times," he murmured.

"How old?"

"You know how old she was!" Charles snapped, then heaved a sigh. "Forgive me, *Seigneur*. I would never dream of touching the girl, and I find the implication that I would . . . painful."

There was no doubt in Armand's mind that he had genuinely hurt his friend's feelings. But Charles was his fledgling first, and his friend second. "I will forgive you the outburst this once because there was no one but me to hear it. Speak to me like that again, whether anyone else can hear or not, and I will remind you of the definition of pain."

Charles accepted the rebuke with a nod. "I understand, *Seigneur*. But I must ask *you* to understand that I would not risk our friendship—or, for that matter, your wrath—by making advances on your ward. Even were she thirty years old."

Armand's lips twitched into a hint of a smile, which he quickly suppressed.

Lily emerged from the dressing room once more. The jeans she wore this time were considerably more demure, though they still hugged her hips suggestively. And the tank top did nothing to hide her bra straps. She grinned impishly at Armand, and he had to swallow twice to keep his temper under control. She was purposely playing with him, and it was his own fault for having so assiduously shielded her from the reality of who and what he was. If she had heard the threat he'd just issued to his closest friend, would she still tease him like this?

He rose to his feet. "Go put your clothes on. We're leaving."

Her mouth dropped open. "Uncle Armand—"

"Now!"

"But—"

"This is not a game we are going to play. You'll spend the remainder of the evening in your room."

She gave another one of those exaggerated teenager sighs. "I was just kidding around!"

"I don't care. Now go change."

Rebellion sparked in her eyes, but she lifted her chin and stormed back into the dressing room.

Charles laughed softly. "One might suppose she is over the shock of finding Marie."

Armand snorted. "Yes, one might." Though perhaps when they returned to the house and she had to spend the night locked in her room she might not be quite so sanguine about it. Still, it couldn't be helped. Typical teenage rebellion was not something Armand—or Lily—could afford.

Lily took her time changing back into the clothes she'd worn into the store, but Armand humored her sulking fit. At least, he humored it for a few minutes. When five minutes stretched to ten and she still hadn't emerged, he rose and moved to the dressing room doorway.

"Lily," he said in his firmest, most paternal voice. "We're leaving. Now."

When she didn't answer, his temper stirred once again and he strode through the doorway.

"I said *now*!" he growled, heading toward the only closed dressing room. He didn't care if she was stark naked. Sulking was one thing, refusing to answer him was another.

Armand pushed open the door, but as it swung inward, he noticed a bend in the hallway—and another curtain leading out of the dressing area into a different section of the store.

The dressing room was empty.

* * *

FAITH'S CELL PHONE rang as she was sitting on the bed in her room wondering whether Marie's death meant she would now be joining the *Seigneur* in bed for the remainder of their stay. On the one hand, it seemed a terribly selfish thought so soon after a brutal murder. On the other hand, it was hard for Faith to get too upset that Marie was dead.

She checked the number and saw that it was Lily. No doubt calling to tell her about whatever extravagant gifts Armand was in the process of buying her. She would endeavor to sound pleased, even while she ground her teeth.

"Hi, Lily," she said. "What's up?"

"First, you've got to promise you're not going to wig out."

Uh-oh. That was not a promising beginning to the conversation. What the hell had Armand bought her? Faith's imagination conjured up jewelry or furs, or something else entirely inappropriate for a sixteen-year-old.

"I'll do my best," Faith said, "but I can't promise until you tell me what I might wig out about."

The phone in the house rang, and next door Faith could hear one of the mortals' cell phones. She tried to suppress the shiver of unease.

Lily sighed dramatically. "Okay. I guess you'd probably wig out even if you promised not to."

Faith's pulse drummed in her throat. "Why? What's going on?"

"I gave Uncle Armand the slip."

The blood drained from Faith's face. "You *what*?" she yelled, leaping to her feet.

"I *knew* you'd wig!"

"Jesus Christ, Lily!"

"Oh, chill out already," Lily said, her voice dripping with disgust. "I'm not going barhopping or anything. It's just that Uncle Armand wouldn't let me try on anything that didn't make me look like a little girl, and it was no fun."

Faith's knees wobbled, and she sank back down onto the bed. Lily had no idea what she'd just done. Had no idea that Faith wasn't "wigging out" because she was worried about what Lily would do while unsupervised.

Heart throbbing in her throat, she tried to keep her voice quiet and steady. "Lily, listen to me very carefully. Park yourself in the most crowded place you can find, then call Armand and tell him where you are. Right now." If she was somewhere public enough that Armand was forced to control his reaction, there was an off chance he would calm down a little by the time he got Lily to privacy.

"He was going to lock me in my room for the rest of the night!" Lily protested. "I promise I won't get into any trouble. I'm just going to browse the stores for a little while and then I'll take a cab back to the house."

"You don't understand—"

"Will you stop worrying about me already! Plenty of girls my age go shopping without a squadron of adults with them."

"That's not—"

"What did you say?" Lily asked, then made a fake static noise in the back of her throat. "Sorry, guess the connection's bad."

"Lily!"

But the phone went dead, and when Faith frantically called back, her call went straight to voice mail.

For the second time that night, there was the sound of shouting and hurried footsteps in the house beyond her room. Armand was mobilizing a search, no doubt. Lily wouldn't be on her own for very long.

Faith's cell phone rang again as she hurried out her door, wondering what the chances were that she could find Lily before Armand or his vampires could.

Her heart leapt with hope, but the number was Armand's, not Lily's. Hands trembling, she answered the phone just as Drake appeared at the base of the stairs.

"Have you heard from Lily?" Armand snapped without preamble.

She could hear the unadulterated fury in his voice, and she quailed. "Yes, *Seigneur,*" she whispered. "But she wouldn't tell me where she was."

"We were at the mall when she eluded us." Every word was clipped with anger. Armand's was always a controlled rage, but it was rage nonetheless. "She can't have gone far," he said. "If you hear from her again, you call me immediately."

"Yes, *Seigneur*. But please—" He hung up on her. She sniffled, then touched her cheek and was surprised to find it damp with tears.

Drake started climbing the stairs as she descended, meeting her halfway. "Don't cry," he said soothingly. "I'm sure we'll find her in no time. And as I told you, Brigitte and Henri won't dare harm her."

Faith shoved the phone in her jeans pocket and dashed the tears away, continuing down the stairs. "That's not why I'm crying," she said as Drake followed. Fear for Lily gave her feet wings, and she was out the door and onto the darkened city streets before she'd formulated even the most halfhearted plan.

"Slow down!" Drake said, grabbing her arm. "Do you have any idea where you're going?"

She shook her head, panic thrumming through her chest. "I have to find her!" she cried, her breath coming in gasps. "He's going to hurt her if I can't find her first." For six long years, she'd managed to keep Lily safe from Armand's wrath. She'd tried to warn her sister about his ferocity while at the same time shielding her from it, making sure she never saw firsthand what Armand was capable of. And because of that, Lily had no idea what this childish prank would cost her.

Drake had hold of both her arms now and gave her a little shake. "Calm down!" he said. "You're not going to help her by panicking."

She snarled and bared her fangs at him, every instinct in her body calling her to action, insisting she had to run, fight, do *something* other than stand here and talk. Then she made the mistake of meeting his eyes, and his glamour seized her and held her still.

"Take a deep breath," he urged. He was still holding her arms, his fingers providing an almost comforting warmth.

Panic surged like wildfire through her veins, but she did as he commanded, sucking in one long, slow breath, then another. Either the deep breaths were working, or his glamour was having a calming effect, but her rational mind seemed to click back into gear.

Running out into the streets like a wild thing wasn't going to help Lily. If only she knew something that would! Armand couldn't—or wouldn't—forgive Lily for this. If he caught her, he was going to punish her, and Faith thought something inside herself would break if he did.

"This is all my fault," she murmured, not realizing

she'd said it out loud until Drake enveloped her in a hug.

She stiffened for a moment, but she felt as if her knees might buckle if she didn't hold on to something, so she put her arms around him and clung.

"She's a teenager," Drake said soothingly. "It's not your fault she's acting like one."

She shuddered. If it hadn't been for Faith, Lily would never have met Armand, much less fallen under his power. Guilt swept over her, gnawed at her heart. Six years they'd been with Armand, and still Faith hadn't figured out how to get Lily to safety. There might be nothing she could do to protect Lily from Armand's wrath right now, but Faith swore to herself that whatever she needed to do, Lily would *not* be going back to France with the *Seigneur*.

She pushed away from Drake, wiping the last of the tears from her eyes and sniffling. One thing was clear in her mind—she wasn't going to be able to free Lily without help. None of Armand's people would help.

That left Drake and his Guardians.

One way or another, she was going to win them over and use them to spirit Lily away, no matter what it cost her. Now, if only she could figure out how to manage that . . .

* * *

CHARLES WASN'T VERY good at thinking like a sixteen-year-old girl, nor did he spend much time in malls. However, after viewing Lily's performance at the department store, he had an idea what kind of clothes she was shopping for. He bypassed the shoe stores and the more sophisticated clothing shops, instead peering in stores that catered to a more flamboyant crowd.

Lily was not stupid. She had to know everyone would be immediately looking for her, which meant she would spend as little time as possible browsing the racks, and as much time as possible in the dressing rooms, where she wouldn't be seen.

Having reached the opposite end of the mall without finding her, Charles ducked in the first clothing store he passed on his way back, using his glamour to turn away mortal eyes while he marched directly to the dressing rooms and started pushing aside curtains. He saw several semi-naked women, one or two of whom were actually tolerable to look at, but none of them was Lily.

When he tried this same maneuver at the third store he passed, he met with some unexpected good luck. Behind the first door he opened, he found his quarry. His glamour held her motionless and sightless, and he slipped into the room and closed the door.

He'd caught her in the middle of pulling on another pair of jeans, no doubt as scandalous as the ones she'd modeled for Armand. She'd gotten the jeans up as far as her knees and was bent slightly at the waist, nothing but the minuscule thong covering her firm young bottom.

Charles swallowed hard and willed himself not to succumb to the sudden arousal the sight inspired. Tried to force away the image of peeling those barely there panties away and—

He closed his eyes and leaned his back against the dressing room door, taking deep breaths. She was only sixteen. A child, by modern-day standards. But Armand was right—having been married to a girl a year younger than Lily, it was hard for him to see her as a child.

He'd better damn well learn to do it, though! He had no illusions that Armand's friendship would keep him from carrying out his threat. He prided himself on being even-handed, on applying his rules—and his punishments—to *all* his people. Charles had tasted his wrath before. And no woman, no matter how tempting, was worth that risk.

Hoping logic and his instinct for self-preservation would help him quell his growing infatuation, Charles slipped out of the dressing room, closing the door behind him. Then he released Lily from his glamour. She would never know that he had invaded her privacy, had seen her in such a state of undress.

He knocked on the door. "The game's over, Lily," he said, and heard her groan. "Put your street clothes back on and come out of there. If you don't, I'll come in after you."

Clothing rustled, and he sincerely hoped that was the sound of her obeying his command. If he had to go in after her without clouding her mind with glamour, she might see the effect she had on him. If she told Armand . . . Concentrating on just what Armand would do to him if he didn't control himself, Charles managed to push the lingering arousal away.

Minutes later, Lily opened the door, her face a mask of teenage sullenness. Charles shook his head at her, then flipped open his phone to call Armand. He ended the call before it went through.

To say the *Seigneur* was furious right now was an understatement. Lily had never tasted his temper before, had always been protected from it, but every instinct told Charles this time would be different. The poor child was in for a rude awakening. Perhaps a delay of twenty minutes or so would give the *Seigneur* time to calm the worst of his temper—and perhaps redirect some of it to Charles. Charles might not be allowed to lust after Lily, but he could still care for her. So instead of calling Armand, he called a cab, and, taking Lily firmly by the hand, led her out to meet it.

7

DRAKE HAD COAXED Faith back into the house, and they were sitting in the den together, neither one speaking, when her cell phone rang. She answered instantly, muscles taut and aching with tension.

"I've found her," Charles said. "And she's fine."

Emotions chased each other around her mind. Relief that Lily was all right. And terror that she wouldn't be for long. There was no longer even the slightest hope that she could save her sister from Armand's wrath. Of all the vampires in the *Seigneur*'s entourage, Charles was probably the most likely to *want* to help, and the least likely to actually do so.

"I'm bringing her back to the house," Charles continued. "I waited until our cab pulled away to tell the *Seigneur,* but he won't be far behind us. It was the best I could do."

Her eyes prickled with tears. "Thank you, Charles,"

she said, keeping her voice low so he wouldn't hear the quaver. Then she hung up the phone.

"She's been found?" Drake asked.

She nodded. "Charles is bringing her back to the house, and Armand will be back soon, too."

Drake reached out and gave her shoulder a squeeze, his eyes filled with concern. "Do you really believe he'll hurt her?"

Clenching her teeth against the tears, she nodded. "He's been very . . . indulgent with her." And he'd kept her at boarding school for as many months of the year as possible. "But he won't forgive this."

His hand slid down her arm until his fingers twined with hers. "Perhaps we'll be able to reason with him," Drake said gently. "She's just a mortal, and a child at that."

It had been so long since anyone had shown her genuine kindness. She clung to his hand, squeezing hard as she fought for calm. "He doesn't see reason when his authority has been questioned." She knew that despite his ferocity, Armand would not do Lily any permanent harm. But that was cold comfort at best.

Drake's thumb caressed her knuckles. "Is there anything I can do?"

She had to blink away tears as she smiled at him. "Can you kill Armand before he has a chance to lay a hand on Lily?"

He sighed. "I would if I could."

And she believed him. His eyes looked so troubled,

his brow furrowed with concern. She drew in a deep breath and found a core of calm deep inside her.

Perhaps she was wrong in her assertion that there was nothing she could do to stop Armand from hurting Lily. An idea—a terrible, terrifying idea—tickled the edge of her mind. She would do *anything* to protect Lily. Swallowing a lump of fear in her throat, she hardened her resolve.

"Whatever happens," she said, "don't interfere. Armand would not take that well at all."

Drake nodded, but if he'd had anything to say about the matter, he was cut off by the sound of the front door opening. A quick psychic scan told her there was one vampire and one mortal in the foyer. She leapt to her feet and ran.

When she saw Lily and Charles, she gave a wordless cry and hurried to gather her sister into her arms.

* * *

DRAKE WATCHED FROM the doorway to the den as Faith hugged her sister fiercely. Her distress was like a physical force, creating a knot of guilt in Drake's stomach. Even if everything she'd claimed about herself was a lie, *this* was real, he'd stake his life on it. He wished he could spare her and Lily the ordeal, but what could he possibly do?

The Guardians had apparently heard the commotion, and they gathered at the base of the stairs. Drake's stomach clenched as he realized what was going to happen. They were young and impetuous, all of them. Drake knew better than to get into the middle of this mess, but he doubted the Guardians would be able to control their instinctual knee-jerk reactions.

He had to get them out of here before the *Seigneur* arrived.

Lily finally managed to extricate herself from Faith's embrace, her cheeks pink with embarrassment. "What is the *matter* with you?" she asked, exasperation clear in every nuance of her voice and posture.

Faith shook her head. "I tried to warn you," she began, her voice scratchy with tears, but at that moment the door flew open and everyone fell silent.

Drake cursed under his breath, knowing there was no way he could get the Guardians out of harm's way now. To keep them safe, he was going to have to act the bully again, and they might never forgive him for it.

The *Seigneur* stood in the open doorway, his two "lesser" fledglings at his back. From the buildup, Drake had expected a whirlwind of rage. Instead, the *Seigneur*'s expression was strangely blank, his eyes devoid of expression. However, the temperature noticeably dropped—a sure sign that there was an angry, powerful vampire in the room.

His eyes fixed on Lily, who didn't recognize the danger everyone else in the room felt. She jutted her chin out and crossed her arms, radiating a total lack of repentance.

Armand took a single step forward. Faith grabbed

her sister's shoulder and jerked her backward until Faith stood between the *Seigneur* and his quarry.

"Please, *Seigneur,*" she begged.

"Get out of my way, Faith," he said. There was no inflection in his voice, and still there were no external signs of anger except for the chill in the room. However, something about him, or about Faith's desperation, finally got through to Lily. She'd lost the sullen look and was instead biting her lip, a look of uncertainty in her eyes.

The *Seigneur* took another step forward. Keeping Lily behind her, Faith backed up.

"Please," she repeated. "She's only a child. She didn't know what she was doing."

He bared his fangs and took another step forward.

A little gasp escaped Lily's lips. "Uncle Armand?" she asked, her voice low and most definitely worried.

Armand's eyes slid away from Faith and locked with Lily's. The girl's face paled at what she saw there. Jez moved to stand next to Drake.

"Do something!" she urged.

Drake ground his teeth. "If you have a suggestion, I'd love to hear it."

"Punish *me, Seigneur,*" Faith pleaded, eyes impossibly wide. "You want to teach her a lesson. You don't have to hurt her to do that."

No one in the room could miss how much her own suggestion terrified her, but Faith took a step closer to Armand, head held high. Lily stood frozen in place, blinking in confusion.

"Uncle Armand?" the girl asked again, her voice even more uncertain this time. "What's going on?"

"You've indicated you would like me to treat you like an adult," he said coldly. "I plan to honor your request."

Faith took another step forward, putting herself within his reach. "Punish me, and she'll get the point."

Her eyes said she was still afraid, but she didn't back down. Drake couldn't help but admire her courage. And while he didn't want to see her get hurt, better her than Lily. Faith's vampire body could take the abuse without breaking. The same could not be said of Lily.

Armand said nothing, but his fist suddenly flew out of nowhere and sent Faith sprawling to the floor. Lily screamed and started to run forward, but Charles quickly grabbed her, lifting her off her feet when she struggled to break free.

Eric and Harry ran to Faith when she fell, their chivalric instincts getting in the way of their common sense. Armand's fledglings moved forward, then came to a stop at a signal from their master. Armand looked over his shoulder at Drake.

"Call off your vampires. This is none of their business. Or yours."

Jez made a growling sound, and Drake hastily used his glamour to freeze her. Harry had helped Faith raise herself into a sitting position, and Eric had stepped between her and the *Seigneur*.

"Back down, Eric," Drake ordered, hating that he had to do this. Harry's jaw dropped open, and he looked at Drake with horror.

Eric didn't move, didn't even glance in Drake's direction. "I can't just stand by and watch this!"

"Then go upstairs and don't watch," Drake said, his voice as cold as he could make it, all his own turmoil buried beneath the dictates of necessity.

Rebellion sparked in Eric's eyes, and his fangs descended. Drake wasn't entirely surprised. Gabriel had managed to intimidate Eric into submission, but it clearly wasn't a natural state for him, and up until now he'd had no reason to be afraid of Drake.

"Don't be stupid, puppy," Drake growled at the fledgling. "There's nothing we can do to help here. All we can do is make it worse." Not that Drake truly thought he could get through to Eric with logic when his primal instincts were in play.

Eric didn't withdraw his fangs, instead looking even more mutinous, his posture radiating hostility. Hostility aimed at Drake, but even so the room grew cold again, Armand's temper fraying around the edges once more.

Dammit! If Drake didn't get Eric under control, Armand was liable to kill him out of annoyance. At least Harry wasn't wading in, though the conflict on his face said he was thinking about it. Drake's glamour was easily strong enough to control the two of them, but he wasn't so sure he could control them with glamour *and* retain his hold on Jez. So he did the only thing he could.

Drake crossed the room, grabbed Eric by the collar of his shirt, then picked him up off his feet and hurled him into the next room. Even that tiny moment of distraction made his hold on Jez slip, and he just barely managed to get her back under before she said or did something to get them all killed.

That simple display of power was enough to get Harry to back off, and he raised his hands in surrender. But his eyes shone with a kind of sick sense of betrayal.

"Go upstairs," Drake commanded. "And don't come back down until I've given you permission."

Harry looked over his shoulder, where his maker was struggling to his feet.

"He may be your maker, but *I* give the orders," Drake said. "Go upstairs."

Harry hesitated only a moment longer before he obeyed. Drake heaved a mental sigh of relief. One Guardian safe, one under something resembling control—only one wildcard left. He kept his fangs lowered and glared at Eric as the fledgling finally got his feet under him.

"It's your choice, puppy," he said. "You can either go upstairs now, or go upstairs after I beat the shit out of you."

Eric's shoulders heaved, and his lip curled. Drake prayed Eric would come to his senses. It wasn't so much that Drake minded the idea of beating him up—it was more that he feared he wouldn't be able to do it and keep control of Jezebel at the same time. If *she* challenged him, he was in deep trouble, because if he hurt her—or was unable to stop the *Seigneur* from hurting her—Gabriel would kill him.

A long staring contest ensued, but Eric must have seen that Drake was dead serious. He gave Drake a look of pure disgust, then stormed out of the room and up the stairs.

In the foyer, Faith was on her feet once more. Blood from a split lip trickled down her chin, but the small cut was already healing, and her expression now was almost serene. Lily was still crying and struggling in Charles's grasp, though her struggles were weakening.

Armand glanced at Jezebel, then back at Drake. "Perhaps it would be better for all involved if you took *her* upstairs, too."

Drake couldn't help but agree. The effort of holding her was costing him, and the strain would no doubt get worse as time went on. He looked at Faith.

"I'm sorry I can't help," he said softly.

She nodded, but didn't speak. Pouring every ounce of his concentration into the effort, Drake forced Jez to walk with him as he mounted the stairs. Neither one of them looked back when they heard the sound of a fist hitting flesh.

* * *

DRAKE ESCORTED JEZEBEL to her room. He closed the door behind him, shutting out the sounds from downstairs. Then, he parked himself in front of that door and released her from his glamour.

He expected an explosion, was braced for it. Instead, Jez didn't say a word to him, crossing the room and sitting down in a chair with her back to him.

Anger, he could have dealt with, could have fought. Silent contempt hurt like physical pain. He shook his head.

"What could I possibly have done?" he asked. Not surprisingly, his only answer was more stony silence. "The Guardians have to be my first priority," he tried again. "I couldn't have risked any of you to save one of the *Seigneur*'s vampires."

Jez turned her head to look at him. "What about the mortal girl? Would you have risked anything to help her, or would you have just let him do whatever he wanted?"

Drake looked away. He would have hated it, and it would have eaten at his conscience for years to come, but no, he wouldn't have taken the risk. If there'd been even the slightest hope that he could have helped, that would have been one thing. But the *Seigneur* was six hundred years old.

No, he reassured himself. Nothing he could have done would have helped the situation. Most likely there was some small, human corner of Jezebel's brain that understood that. But Drake made a convenient scapegoat for her frustrated vampire instincts, so she would never acknowledge the truth.

It was a good thing *he* was the one in charge.

His thoughts brought him no comfort. Not wanting to see the condemnation in her eyes anymore, he slipped out of the room. Even so, he stood guard outside to make sure she didn't interfere until the sounds of violence had faded from below.

* * *

FAITH LAY ON the floor and concentrated on breathing. Her entire body ached and throbbed with the abuse, and her head swam from some of the more vicious blows. Unfortunately, she didn't pass out. Lily's heartbroken tears hurt almost as much as the punches, and Faith wished she'd been able to spare her sister the emotional pain as well as the physical.

Eventually, Armand stopped beating her. Her head felt thick enough that his voice seemed to come from a great distance as he coldly ordered Charles to take Lily to her room and make sure she stayed there.

When his fledgling had obeyed, and Armand and Faith were the only ones left in the foyer, he bent down on one knee beside her. His hand came to rest gently on her hair.

"For what it's worth," he said in a low whisper, "I'm sorry I had to do this. It was a mistake for me to hide my nature from her for so long."

Faith opened her eyes, though only her right eye would open all the way. The expression on Armand's face showed genuine regret, though he certainly hadn't allowed that regret to temper his punishment.

He brushed a finger over one of the bruises he'd given her and flashed her a sad half-smile. "You were very brave, *ma petite*, and I appreciate your sacrifice. I never had any intention of hurting Lily. As soon as

I realized what she'd done, I decided you would bear the brunt of my punishment. But we'll keep that between ourselves."

He bent to plant a kiss on her forehead, and Faith had to fight an urge to go for his throat. If he'd planned this all along, then at least he could have told her so and spared her the terror she'd experienced at imagining his ferocity unleashed on Lily. She stifled any number of retorts and remained lying on the cold marble floor as Armand slipped out the front door for destinations unknown.

Shortly after Armand left, she heard another set of footsteps coming from the stairs above her. Already her body was beginning to heal the damage, but she hadn't the strength or the will to raise her head to see who approached. She didn't even open her eyes, but her nose picked up the mingled scents of leather and sandalwood soap. Having not consciously noticed the scent before, she was surprised to realize she recognized it as Drake's.

With a little sigh, she opened her eyes to see him kneeling beside her, exactly where Armand had been moments before. She shuddered, remembering the sight of Drake's bared fangs, remembering him throwing the Guardian across the room. For some reason, even though she'd known almost since the beginning that he was a Killer, she'd allowed herself the romantic impression that he was somehow different from all the rest. She should have known better.

"Are you all right?" Drake asked, then laughed mirthlessly and shook his head. "Never mind. Foolish question. May I give you a hand up? I'm sure we can find somewhere more comfortable for you to recuperate."

"I'm fine," she lied. She pushed herself into a sitting position, gasping at the stabbing pain in her chest. Armand must have cracked one of her ribs.

Before she'd had time to recover from the pain, Drake had scooped her up in his arms. Instinctively, she put her arms around his neck to hold on.

Drake carried her up the stairs, then down the hall of the second floor, where she could see Charles standing guard outside Lily's room as ordered. Faith could hear muffled tears through the closed door, and her heart twisted in her chest. Charles shrugged and mouthed an apology as Drake passed by and started up the stairs to the third floor.

Faith noted with interest that he knew which room was hers, though it had been Jezebel who had handed out the room assignments. He carried her to the bed and laid her down gently. Every faint movement jarred something that hurt, and Faith bit her lip to keep from crying out.

Drake disappeared without another word, but he was back shortly with a handful of ice packs, a washcloth, and a bowl of steaming water. He put the ice packs on the worst, deepest bruises, then used the washcloth to dab away the blood from her split lip and bloody nose. All without saying a word.

She closed her eyes and let him minister to her, surprised at how good his touch felt. The ice began to numb some of the pain, and the minor cuts and bruises were well on their way to healing. The rib hurt worse than anything, and, naturally, would take the longest to heal.

"At home," she said to distract herself from the pain, "no one would dare help someone the *Seigneur* had just punished. They'd have left me on the floor, walking around me if I was in the way, until I was well enough to pick myself up and dust myself off."

"I don't work for Armand Durant," Drake said, his voice tight with anger, "and I'm not about to leave someone lying on the floor."

Her eyes blinked open once again, and she met his troubled, angry gaze. "What if your fledgling had refused to back down and you'd had to carry out your threat? Would you have let *him* lie on the floor while he healed?"

He averted his gaze as he dunked the washcloth in the bowl of water, rinsing off the blood. "First of all," he said, squeezing out the water before turning back to her, "Eric isn't my fledgling. I don't have any fledglings—never have, and never will. And no, I wouldn't have left him there."

She flashed him a faint smile. "Armand would have seen that as weakness."

"Armand can kiss my ass."

The unexpected rejoinder made Faith laugh, until her rib reminded her that laughing was a very bad idea just now. Drake had concentrated on the wounds he could see, so there was no ice on the aching rib.

"Could you put one of those ice packs here?" she asked, pointing at the source of the pain.

He lifted a pack from the side of her head, nodded in approval at what he saw, then laid it down very gently over her rib. The ice pack tried to slide off to the side with her first breath, so Drake held it in place. As she waited for the numbing effect, she couldn't help noticing that his hand was perilously close to her breast.

The thought of that hand sliding upward to touch her aroused a sudden tug of desire in her center. She swallowed hard, closing her eyes and telling herself that tug was just her imagination. She couldn't possibly be attracted to this man. Good-looking though he might be, kind as he might seem, he was a Killer and a bully, just like Armand.

"I wish I could have done something to help you," Drake said.

Once more, she opened her eyes. She could hardly blame him for staying out of it. There had been no sensible alternative.

"Armand and Charles are both six hundred years old. We both know what would have happened if you'd interfered."

"Doesn't stop me from wishing."

A lump formed in her throat. Even the knowledge that he'd wanted to help was somehow comforting. For six years, she'd had no sympathetic shoulder to cry on, no one who genuinely cared for her, except Lily, who spent most of the year at boarding school and who until now hadn't understood what Faith faced. She hadn't realized how much she'd missed companionship, hadn't realized how lonely she'd been.

"How did you and Lily end up in the *Seigneur*'s entourage, if you don't mind me asking?"

Not her favorite topic in the world. But at least if they had something to talk about, he would stay to listen. For reasons she didn't want to think about too closely, she didn't want him to leave.

"Lily and I went on a vacation in France. Our parents had died in a car crash a couple years before, and I'd become Lily's guardian. She was having a hard time adjusting." Faith gave a self-deprecating smile. "*I* wasn't having such an easy time, either. Try becoming mother to an eight-year-old when you're barely twenty-one yourself. We both badly needed some time away from the stresses of our everyday life, and our mom had been a huge Francophile. She'd taken us both to Paris when Lily was only a baby, and when I started talking about taking a vacation, Lily said she wanted to go back there now that she was old enough to enjoy it.

"So anyway, we went, and on the first night, I went down to the hotel bar after Lily went to bed." That had been the first of her many mistakes. "I met a man there, and I let him buy me a drink." She smiled faintly at the memory, despite everything that had happened afterward. "It made me feel so worldly and adult, sitting at the bar sipping a martini with a handsome Frenchman. I didn't notice that he never actually took a sip of his own drink. Either the jet-lag had killed my powers of perception, or he used glamour to make sure I didn't notice.

"We had a nice time, and he was a perfect gentleman. I went back to the room afterward and thought that would be the end of it. But the next night, after an exhausting day of touring, I went back to the bar, and there he was. We talked some more, and I was really starting to like him.

"He claimed he was in Paris on a business trip and that his work kept him busy all day. But we got together every night. He even took me and Lily around the city, showing us his favorite spots. We'd always go back to the hotel and put Lily to bed afterward. Then we'd have some private time once she was asleep.

"By the end of the first week, I had a major crush on him, and I was pretty sure he felt the same way about me. François and I talked about our future, but only vaguely. Until the end of the second week, when it was time for Lily and me to fly home."

The memory of that dreadful night seared through her, and for a long moment, her voice stuck in her throat. Drake didn't prod her, instead waiting patiently until she found the strength and will to continue.

"After Lily went to bed, François and I took a moonlit walk by the Seine, and he told me he didn't want me to go home. He told me he loved me, and that he was rich enough to support both me and Lily so I didn't have to worry about money." She smiled again, and she suspected her expression held an odd combination of wistfulness and bitterness. "I was so tempted. I really believed I was in love with him, and he with me, and the notion of staying with him in

Paris was so romantic—a young girl's dream come true.

"But I also knew that I couldn't do it. Lily was already showing signs of getting homesick, and after all that she'd been through, I couldn't imagine uprooting her like that, taking her away from all her friends and family and familiar surroundings. I told François that maybe one day in the future, I'd take him up on his offer, but I couldn't do it right then.

"At first when I refused, it was almost like he didn't hear me. Then, when he realized what I was saying, he tried to persuade me that staying was the right thing to do. When I kept saying I had to go home, he got mad and started yelling at me. He was so angry I was actually kind of scared of him suddenly. I walked away, and we were in the middle of a public place so he didn't dare try to stop me."

Faith heaved a sigh, noticing absently that she managed it without pain. Either the ice was helping, or her rib had healed.

"He came to the hotel later that night, once I'd gone to sleep. He said we were meant to be together, and he wasn't going to let me leave him. So he bit me. Lily woke up in the middle of it and started screaming, but François used his glamour to make her be quiet."

She would never forget the sound of Lily's screams. Nor could she ever forget that she had invited François into her life and into Lily's. If it hadn't been for her girlish infatuation, none of this would have happened. She and Lily both would have gone home to live as normal a life as they could with both their parents dead.

"And how did you get from being made a vampire to being in Armand's entourage?" Drake prompted.

"François was barely more than a fledgling himself. Only the *Maître de Paris* was authorized to create new fledglings. François had some crazy idea that he could hide me, I suppose. I think in his own twisted way, he really did love me. He spirited me and Lily out of Paris into the countryside and nursed me back to health as I went through the transition. And, thank God, he didn't turn Lily or kill her.

"He tried to explain how he'd made me with the best of intentions, how we were meant to be together. And he told me that just because I was a vampire didn't mean I had to kill anyone or drink from humans.

"Anyway, I was still too weak and dazed to do anything about the situation. And Lily had been seriously traumatized and wouldn't let François near her unless he used his glamour. He tried to keep moving us around to stay hidden, but we just weren't up to it.

"Armand found us and dragged us all back to his manor house in Rouen. He was actually very kind to Lily and managed to win her over despite all the trauma. And he wasn't unkind to me, either. He just asked me what happened, and I saw no reason not to tell him the truth.

"He executed François. He offered to let me watch, but I had no interest in seeing anyone die. He didn't tell me so at the time, but I know now that he didn't kill François quickly—he made an example of him." She shuddered. "I don't know exactly what he did, and I don't want to. But he can be very creative in his cruelty.

"So that's how I came to be with him. He somehow managed to get legal custody of Lily by claiming to be her uncle. I'm sure there was a lot of glamour involved. Ever since then, he's managed to keep me with him because he has Lily as a permanent hostage. If it weren't for her, I'd have run away from him long ago."

Drake raised an eyebrow at that. "Or died trying?"

She winced. "Yeah. Probably. It's not that Armand is that bad, at least not compared to other *Seigneurs*. It could have turned out a lot worse."

Drake nodded. "But you deserve better."

She smiled at that, not entirely sure that was true. She had let her own selfish infatuation with François blind her to his every fault, until it was too late and he'd turned her life—and Lily's—upside down. Yes, Faith had been young at the time, but she didn't think she would ever forgive herself for bringing that Killer into their lives.

The rib was definitely feeling better, so she pushed herself up into a sitting position. Drake moved the ice pack away from her rib, then reached out to help her sit up, and once again the touch of his hand stirred something inside her. Her body still felt sore and stiff, but the worst of the pain was gone, and in a half hour at most, she'd be as good as new.

"Thanks for taking care of me," she said, and her

cheeks heated with the hint of a blush. Was it only because Armand had sent her to seduce him that she was suddenly finding Drake so attractive? Surely that had to be the case. She had vowed to herself that never again would she allow a Killer into her heart, not even as a friend. Because the cold, hard truth of the matter was that Killers were always going to look out for number one first. They proved that with every kill they made, choosing to end another person's life to preserve their own.

Faith forced a smile, deciding not to risk falling victim to blind infatuation once more. Having Drake in her bedroom was dangerous. "I'm feeling much better now," she said. "You don't have to stay."

Drake blinked at her, then frowned. "Are you still trying to seduce me? Because if so you're not doing a very good job of it."

She couldn't help laughing, and he laughed with her, the sound warm and strangely intimate. She got the feeling he didn't laugh very often, at least not with any genuine humor.

"It's hard to feel terribly seductive when you've just been beaten to a pulp," she said wryly.

He sobered, meeting her eyes and capturing her gaze. "I'm not going to suddenly lead you to Gabriel, but if you wanted to seduce me anyway, I wouldn't object." His eyes darkened, and though he kept his lips closed, she suspected his fangs had descended.

Faith broke the stare quickly. Her heart pattered in her chest, and she'd have been lying to herself if she said she wasn't tempted. But it was pointless to start anything with him. When this was all over, she'd be either on the run, back in France, or dead. If she gave in to temptation, she'd probably let herself get too attached, and then she'd be miserable when she had to leave.

She smiled at him, no doubt a bit wistfully, and said nothing.

Drake rose with a shrug. "If you change your mind, I'm downstairs, second door on the left." He grinned at her, showing that his fangs had indeed descended.

Faith's gums tingled, and she knew if she didn't stop the flirting this instant, hers were going to descend also. Letting Drake see the evidence of her attraction was a bad idea.

"Second door on the left," she repeated, nodding. "Got it."

With a wink, he took her hand and kissed her knuckles. Then he walked out, hesitating only a moment at the door in case she should change her mind and ask him to stay. She clamped her jaws shut on the request and let him leave.

8

LEAVING FAITH TO her recovery, Drake retired to his borrowed room in Gabriel and Jez's house, glad to reach his destination without encountering either the entourage or any of the Guardians. Just as well Faith had turned him down when he'd flirted with her. While it might have been nice to drown his sorrows in the pleasures of the flesh, he knew the wise option was to stay as far away from her as possible. Never in his whole long life had he knowingly shared a woman with another man, and he was not about to start now.

Faith hadn't come right out and said so, but she'd made every implication that she was Armand's mistress, if a reluctant one. Drake had enough problems without getting himself entangled with the *Seigneur*'s mistress. Even if her delicate beauty tempted him. Even if her nobility and self-sacrifice moved him.

With a grunt of irritation, Drake shoved the lovely

Faith from his mind. He couldn't afford to have his head fogged with lust. His nerves felt brittle, his temper wavering on the edges of control.

If he let down his emotional guard, Drake kept flashing back to the look of hurt betrayal in young Harry's eyes when Drake had threatened Eric. Eli's Guardians would have been unruffled by Drake's show of aggression—they'd seen it all before, had sometimes knowingly provoked him—but Eli had always been there to calm things before Drake hurt anyone.

But Eli wasn't here now. If the youngsters mutinied, there was only Drake to control them. Perhaps all the years he had worked for Eli he'd been fooling himself, thinking that working for a benevolent leader had made him a better person. Maybe even a good person.

Drake practically slammed his bedroom door closed behind him. He was becoming maudlin, wallowing in self-pity. But recognizing that didn't seem to change the direction of his thoughts.

With a start and a shiver of unease, Drake finally realized what the increasing intensity of his emotions signaled—he was experiencing the beginnings of hunger.

His breath left him in a whoosh, and he had to sit down. In all the flurry of activity, he hadn't paid attention to his feeding schedule, but now that he actually thought about it, he realized it had been more than a week since his last kill. Under normal circumstances, he could go ten days without feeding, but stress made the hunger worse.

Dammit! No wonder his brain was in such a muddle. And his temper so short.

If he didn't feed soon, things were going to get a whole lot worse. He pinched the bridge of his nose, his head aching suddenly. One of the advantages of coming to Baltimore had been hunting with Gabriel, who could assure Drake that his chosen victims were indeed as corrupt as Drake thought. If he hunted without Gabriel, what was to say he wouldn't kill another undercover cop?

Drake banged his fist on the arm of the chair. The wood groaned in protest but didn't break. For all Drake knew, Fletcher had been making that whole story up. Logic said that there were far more criminals and predators in the neighborhoods he'd hunted than there were undercover cops. Chances were good he'd never accidentally killed an innocent. But the doubt that Fletch had awakened refused to go to sleep.

The phone rang. Drake practically leapt across the room to get to it, eager for anything to distract him from his self-doubt. And his hunger.

Hoping the call was from Gabriel, that he'd managed to free himself, Drake picked up the phone and uttered a greeting.

"Johnnie-boy!" said an all-too-familiar voice, sounding delighted.

Drake groaned and sagged onto the bed, the throbbing in his head getting worse. He should just hang up the phone, he knew. But somehow that's not what he found himself doing.

"So it really is you," Drake said. "I thought Brigitte was playing some kind of trick on me and you'd been dead for decades."

"Sorry to disappoint you, lad," Padraig said, a laugh in his voice. He'd lost most of the Irish brogue that had once colored his every word, but the flavor was still there, like an aftertaste. "I take it you got my note."

"Yeah."

"But you didn't call."

"I have nothing to say to you. And you have nothing to say to me that I want to hear." Once again, Drake urged himself to hang up. Padraig was a master manipulator, and Drake's defenses were compromised. He shouldn't take the risk of allowing Padraig to mess with his head. Unfortunately, he didn't follow his own sage advice.

"Are you sure of that, Johnnie?"

Drake gritted his teeth. "I haven't gone by that name for over a century. And yes, I'm sure."

Padraig chuckled. "Yes, I've heard you've taken to using your da's name. Nice irony, my lad. And if you're so sure I have nothing to say you want to hear, you can hang up at any time."

Drake got the receiver within about an inch of the cradle, then found he couldn't lower it the rest of the way. Padraig was a gang lord, a murderer, a Killer without conscience or mercy. In short, he was a classic master vampire. He was also a charismatic leader of men, with keen intelligence, unparalleled street smarts, and not a hint of sentimentality. If he was reaching out to Drake, it wasn't just for the pleasure of hearing his fledgling's voice.

Drake lifted the phone back to his ear. "What do you want?" he finally asked.

"Eh, that's more like it," his maker said, putting a touch more Irish in his voice, dragging Drake back to the past he'd thought he'd escaped.

"I was pleasantly surprised to find you still alive and well," Padraig continued. "I must admit, I didn't have high hopes for you when you left New York."

"When you banished me, you mean," Drake said, then wished he'd kept the bitter words to himself.

Drake could almost hear his maker shrug. "I could have killed you."

Drake swallowed the bitterness. In truth, the banishment had been as close to an act of mercy as he'd ever seen from Padraig. By all rights, Padraig *should* have killed him for his insubordination.

"Why didn't you?" At the time, he'd been too furious, too guilt-ridden to ask, or even wonder.

"Perhaps because I would have done the same thing in your shoes."

Drake had to laugh. "You've never stuck your neck out for anyone but yourself!" And the thought of Padraig making an effort to save a doomed life was patently ridiculous.

"You are an uncommonly judgmental man, Johnnie-boy. Like you, I learned the hard way to pick my battles carefully. I'm a hundred years older than you. How can you say whether I've ever 'stuck my neck out,' as you put it?"

Drake shook his head. He was allowing Padraig to draw him into a conversation that was irrelevant. "If this is what you called to talk about, then the conversation is over."

Padraig sighed dramatically. "Judgmental *and* impatient. Still the same old Johnnie Drake."

Drake swallowed a number of vile curses. He was *not* the same old Johnnie Drake! Johnnie Drake had been as vicious and unfeeling as his maker. If he hadn't been, he never would have survived to adulthood in Five Points, where he'd been unceremoniously dumped at the age of ten by his socialite mother whose new husband had refused to raise the son of a "murderous, thieving potato-eater." When she'd foisted him off on his Irish immigrant father, Drake had been educated and well spoken, with the manners and bearing that befitted his privileged upbringing. To survive the scorn of his father, his half-brothers, and all the other predators who lived in that dreadful neighborhood, he'd had to remake himself.

"Johnnie Drake was never real," Drake said, his voice rough as sandpaper. "He was a part I played for self-preservation. But he was never *me*."

"Judgmental, impatient, and delusional," Padraig muttered, but continued before Drake had a chance to object. "How are you enjoying being Master of Baltimore?"

Drake's jaw dropped. "How do you know about that?" It hardly seemed like Brigitte would broadcast her activities to any vampire she happened to run across.

"Should I add naïve to the list? Do you have any idea what our fine lady is up to, lad?"

As far as Drake had known, her only plan had been to win Gabriel over and to keep the delegation from dragging her back home to Mommy. But then, he couldn't help wondering what she'd been up to during the six months that Gabriel hadn't heard from her. And he should have known she hadn't been touring the countryside for pleasure.

"No," Drake said. "Care to enlighten me?"

"Oh, I think I'll let her do the enlightening."

"If you're not going to tell me anything, then why the hell did you call?"

There was a moment of silence before Padraig answered. "When all is said and done, my lad, you may find yourself in need of a new position. I'm the only man who remembers Johnnie Drake and knows that he was banished from New York. If you should find yourself out of work when this is over, I would be happy to repeal your banishment. My oldest surviving fledgling at the moment aside from you is only fifty, and New York is a big city. I could use a man of your power and skills."

Drake laughed, a mixture of genuine amusement and bitterness. "You think I would come back to work for you? And you call *me* delusional!"

"Everyone responsible for young Eamon's death is

dead. You know I had nothing to do with it myself. There is no reason for you not to return."

"You bloody bastard!" Drake snarled. "You might not have done the deed, but you're every bit as responsible as the ones who did."

"As are you," Padraig said softly.

And finally, Drake found the will to do what he should have done from the moment he'd first heard his maker's voice on the line—he hung up.

* * *

CHARLES WAS STILL standing guard outside Lily's door when Faith ventured out, her injuries all healed. She'd showered and changed out of her bloodied clothing, and it was almost as if the beating had never occurred.

"Am I allowed to see her?" she asked Charles.

He nodded, then moved a little farther down the hall. "I'm to keep watch," he said, "but I'll give you what privacy I can."

She smiled at him gratefully. Charles always seemed surprisingly decent, though she knew that was an illusion. He was a six-hundred-year-old Killer, slavishly loyal to Armand. Still, he seemed to have a spark of humanity to him.

Faith knocked softly on her sister's door, then entered even when Lily didn't answer.

Lily huddled on the bed, her arms clasped around her knees, her back pressed to the wall. Her cheeks were dry, but the puffy redness of her eyes said it hadn't been long since her last crying jag. When she caught sight of Faith, her lower lip quivered, but she held the tears inside.

Faith climbed onto the bed, sitting beside her sister and throwing an arm around her shoulders. Lily sniffled.

"I'm sorry," Lily said in a voice that was barely a whisper.

Faith's throat tightened. How many times had she wished Lily would see behind Armand's civilized mask to the beast that resided within? Now that she had her wish, she'd do anything to hide the *Seigneur* behind that mask once more.

"It's not your fault, sweetie," she said, giving Lily a firm squeeze. "You couldn't have known."

Lily sniffled again. "You've told me a thousand times that he wasn't as nice as he pretended. I should have believed you."

Faith sighed. "Armand and I both made sure you *didn't* believe. I might have told you what he was like, but I made sure you never saw it."

Lily snuggled close to her, forgetting her usual teenage standoffishness. "Are you all right?"

"I'm fine. There are some advantages to being a vampire."

Lily giggled nervously, and the giggle turned to tears. Faith couldn't think of anything to say, so she merely held on and made soothing sounds until the tears came to a stop. Then she put some distance between them so she could look into her sister's eyes.

"Do you understand that we *have* to get away from Armand?"

Wiping the last of the tears from her eyes, Lily nodded. Faith felt a guilty surge of relief. In the past, when she'd contemplated escape, she'd always had to plan for resistance on Lily's part, which made a difficult endeavor into an almost impossible one.

Faith swept her into another hug. "I got us into this mess," she said. "I promise I'll get us out of it, too."

Lily wriggled free and shook her head. "It's not your fault."

Faith snorted. "Of course it is." She smoothed a lock of hair away from Lily's face. "It was my job to protect you. Instead, I let François into our lives and—"

"I liked him, too, you know," Lily interrupted. "François, I mean." She smiled faintly. "I was actually kinda jealous of you. I thought he was a hottie."

That prompted an answering smile. "Well, he was nice to look at, I have to admit." The smile faded. "If only the inside had matched the packaging."

"It's not your fault you fell for him," Lily said again, chin lifting. "And if you say it is, then I'll say it's my fault I fell for Uncle . . . For Armand."

Faith ruffled her hair before Lily had a chance to duck away. Lily's laugh was a balm to Faith's soul. But of course, it was far too early to allow herself to relax. She reached out with her senses, making sure Charles was still down the hall, far enough away not to overhear.

"I haven't figured out how yet," she whispered,

"but somehow we have to make sure we don't go back to France with him. We'd never be able to escape him there."

The expression on Lily's face was far too grave for a sixteen-year-old. "And where would we go? If we go into another vamp's territory, they'll kill you."

"I'm still working on that problem. First, we have to figure out how to get away."

She did another brief psychic sweep to ensure privacy, and that's when she sensed another vampire coming down the hall. Instinct told her who it would be, and she pressed her finger to her lips. Lily's eyes widened, her face turning a shade paler.

There was a perfunctory knock on the door, but Armand didn't wait for an invitation to enter. The expression on his face was blandly neutral, though Faith thought she saw a hint of pain in his eyes when Lily flinched away as he approached. His sigh sounded heartfelt.

He sat on the edge of the bed. "I am sorry," he said to Lily. "You are too old to be indulged like a child, and I should have warned you of that long before tonight. I am a *Seigneur,* and I cannot allow defiance to go unpunished."

Lily crossed her arms over her chest and refused to meet his eyes. Faith tensed, but thankfully, Armand didn't take offense.

"I understand you're angry with me," he said. "But I think perhaps we understand each other better now, and nothing like this need ever happen again."

Lily met this statement with stony silence. The corners of Armand's mouth tightened with displeasure, but he let it go. He rose gracefully from the bed, holding his hand out to Faith.

"Come, Faith," he said. "I believe we need to . . . talk."

Lily looked alarmed, and Faith forced a reassuring smile while her insides curdled. She had a good idea just what kind of "talking" Armand had in mind.

"Don't worry, Lily," she said, the smile still plastered on her face. "Everything's fine now."

Lily's eyes said she didn't believe it, but she made no protest as Armand led Faith from the room.

Armand nodded briefly to Charles as they passed, but didn't relieve him from guard duty. With every step they took closer to his room, Faith's stomach clenched tighter. How could she bear to let him touch her now? And yet how could she stop him?

An idea leapt to mind, and relief swept over her.

"Seigneur?" she asked tentatively.

He looked at her and raised his eyebrows, and she presumed that meant she had permission to speak.

"Drake is expecting me to, er, visit with him tonight," she said, feeling the blood rush to her cheeks as she did. If the *Seigneur* were to find out she was lying, she was in for another beating, worse than the last. She hoped she looked more embarrassed than guilty.

The *Seigneur* stopped with his hand on the doorknob, then let his hand fall away. His eyes bored into her. "Is that so?" he murmured, and she noted a definite trace of skepticism in his voice. "You work fast."

The color in her cheeks deepened, but she didn't look away. "It wasn't my doing. *He* approached *me*." Which, she realized, wasn't far from the truth. He *had* let her know which room was his, and that had been a blatant invitation—just not an invitation either one of them expected her to accept.

"I see," the *Seigneur* replied, not sounding any more convinced. His gaze sharpened even more. "And given the choice between going to my bed and going to a complete stranger's, you would prefer his?"

Faith's jaw dropped at what she could swear sounded like jealousy. "This was your idea, *Seigneur*," she reminded him.

He pressed his lips together into a tight line. "So it was." He didn't sound happy about it. He reached out and brushed the back of his hand over her cheek. "I would like to make up for hurting you this evening."

Again, her stomach tightened with dread. How could he think forcing her to his bed would "make up" for anything? How could any man be so blind?

"Make it up to me by allowing me to try to win my freedom," she said. "Please."

He still didn't look happy about it, but he gave her something approximating a smile. "How can I refuse when you ask so nicely?"

There was a hint of bitterness in his voice, but Faith pretended she didn't hear it. "Thank you, *Seigneur*."

She felt his eyes on her back the whole time as she

made her way down the hall to the door to Drake's room and knocked.

* * *

DRAKE HEARD THE tentative rap on his door and felt absurdly grateful for it. Not so long ago, he'd retreated to his room to escape from company. Now he needed something to keep him from brooding about Padraig's parting shot. Even a crisis might be welcome.

When he opened the door to find Faith in the hallway, he had to admit she was a nice alternative to a crisis. She ventured a smile.

"May I come in?" she asked, and he couldn't fail to hear the hint of nervousness in her voice.

Drake opened his door wider, and Faith took about five steps into the room, then stood there looking awkward as Drake closed the door behind her. With a pulse of disappointment, he realized she hadn't come to continue her seduction attempts—or allow him to continue his. But of course he shouldn't be disappointed. She belonged to the *Seigneur,* whether she wanted to or not.

She rubbed her hands together and licked her lips. A light sheen of sweat covered her face, and her eyes were too wide. Drake took pity on her near-panic, guiding her to a pair of ornamental chairs nestled in the far corner of the room. He saw her gaze flick to the king size bed as they passed by.

When they were both seated, Faith sighed and flashed him a rueful smile. "Clearly I'm not meant to be a temptress."

He laughed, leaning back in his chair, feeling much more at ease than she looked. She'd changed into a plain white button-down shirt and dark blue jeans, but what would have looked nondescript on anyone else looked classically elegant on her. Her long dark hair was fastened by a barrette at the nape of her neck, but a few silky tendrils framed her face.

"Did you come here meaning to tempt me?" he asked, hearing the amused lilt in his own voice.

She leaned back in her chair but didn't manage to look any more relaxed. "No," she admitted. "But . . ." She blushed. "This is very awkward." She huffed out a breath and met his gaze with what looked like a concerted effort. "I told Armand you'd invited me, and I can't afford to be caught in a lie."

A few pieces clicked into place in Drakc's mind. "Ah. You were forced to pick the lesser of two evils, and I won the prize." The color in her cheeks deepened, and Drake felt like a jerk. "Sorry," he said quickly. "That came out sounding hostile, and I didn't mean it to."

"It's all right for you to feel hostile. This whole situation sucks, and I keep imposing on you." She smiled again, but the expression wasn't any more heartfelt than her last one. "Besides, you think I'm a Killer and a liar and I have no way to prove you wrong."

He winced. "I don't believe any such thing," he said, and realized it was true. It was possible that he was being a naïve, gullible fool, that Faith was playing him to perfection. But every instinct in his body told him she was telling the truth.

She regarded him carefully. "You've changed your mind since last night?"

"Let's just say you don't act like any other Killer I've known. If you're an actress, you're a very, very good one."

Her smile was wan. "An actress is one thing I'm not."

He nodded, believing her, though logic told him he should doubt her. "How's your sister?"

Faith shrugged. "About as you'd expect. Armand has always been so . . . civilized around her before. It was a rude awakening."

Words failed him as he read the misery in her eyes. What did the *Seigneur* have planned for young Lily? It seemed a natural assumption that he would make her a vampire when she grew up. He didn't strike Drake as the type to let her walk away to live a normal mortal life.

A lightbulb seemed to suddenly turn on over Drake's head, and he finally realized why Faith wanted to spend time with him—and it wasn't because she was trying to seduce him. He fought against a stab of disappointment, but he could hardly blame her for wanting to protect her sister.

"You're hoping I can help you get her away from him, aren't you?" he asked softly.

Faith didn't bother to deny it. "I can't let her go back to France with him. There would be no escape for her there." She bit her lip. "I'd take her and run, but as you can see, Armand makes certain we're never alone and unguarded together. And even if we got away, I don't know where we could go that I wouldn't attract unwanted attention, if you know what I mean."

He did indeed. And he also knew exactly where they could go—to Philadelphia. Eli would be happy to take Faith in, and he surely had the resources to take care of Lily until she reached adulthood. On top of that, even with his entire entourage, Armand wouldn't stand a chance against Eli and the Guardians.

He picked his words carefully. "If we can get Gabriel back so that we're not so helpless, then I might be able to help you," he said. "I have to protect the Guardians first, and I can't afford to cross the *Seigneur* without someone like Gabriel to back me up. But if you were to find a chance to escape with Lily, you should go to Philadelphia. That's where the original Guardians are, with Gabriel's father. They would take you in, and they'd offer you even more protection than Gabriel."

A smile brightened her face, and a hint of hope shone in her eyes. "Thank you. One problem solved, only a thousand more to go."

She yawned suddenly, and Drake realized it was nearing sunrise. He cast a sidelong glance at the bed. A hint of desire stirred his groin, but even if Faith truly wanted him, the daytime sleep would be on her soon.

"You should spend the day with me," he said, not

meeting her eyes as he spoke. "If you left now and ran into the *Seigneur,* he'd know nothing had happened between us." With a vampire's keen sense of smell, he'd be able to tell by scent alone that Faith hadn't had sex. No doubt she could come up with an explanation—such as dawn being too near—but then she might end up in the *Seigneur*'s bed. It was not a vision that sat easily in Drake's mind.

He risked a glance upward and saw that her face had colored again. She had such an easy blush for a woman who had been the *Seigneur*'s concubine for six years.

"It's a king-size bed," he continued. "We can share it without even touching." Though the thought of sharing the bed with her set his pulse to drumming.

"Thank you," she said, still blushing faintly. She yawned again.

Drake rose and moved to the chest of drawers across the room. The image of her climbing into his bed burned into his brain, and he fought against the arousal. No doubt this was another symptom of his growing hunger as all his more primal instincts rose to the surface.

He hadn't brought a huge supply of clothes with him, but he managed to find a T-shirt he could lend her to sleep in. He sent her into the adjoining bathroom to change as he continued to struggle against the tide of desire. When she stepped out of the bathroom, the T-shirt leaving her legs bare from midthigh down, he knew she couldn't help but see the effect she had on him.

Luckily for him, the pull of the daytime sleep quickly overpowered her.

* * *

IT WAS PERILOUSLY close to morning when Charles made his call to *La Vieille*. He was old enough that he could fight off the lure of the daytime sleep throughout the daylight hours as long as he remained out of the sunlight, but stress and guilt made the fatigue stronger than usual while at the same time making it harder to sleep.

Every muscle in his body went tense when he heard *La Vieille*'s voice on the line, but he had no choice but to speak to her. To report everything that had happened and hope that nothing he said contradicted Armand's report.

His nerves became almost overpowering when he recounted Lily's rebcllion. Would Armand have mentioned that to *La Vieille*? He suspected not, but he couldn't be sure. He had no choice but to tell the whole truth, for if she caught him in a lie or omission . . . He shuddered all the way down to his soul.

A sense of doom hovered over him. By spying for *La Vieille,* he'd already betrayed his friend, even if Armand never found out about it. It was a bitter truth to swallow. But more bitter still was the fear that wouldn't go away, the fear that this mission would fail. Brigitte and Gabriel had already shown they had the upper hand by killing Marie.

Charles could hardly bear the idea that he might

have to betray Armand to death by torture if the mission failed. But even worse was realizing that any surviving members of their delegation—save himself, of course—would be doomed to the same terrible fate. Including Lily.

La Vieille would have no mercy because of the girl's mortality or her tender age.

As his stomach churned at this realization, an idea came to him. An idea for how he might be able to keep Lily from *La Vieille*'s clutches even if they failed, without risking himself in the process.

So he told *La Vieille* about *everything* that had happened tonight. Including his lustful thoughts about Lily and Armand's chilling reaction to the idea of him touching his pretty little ward.

The seed was planted, and Charles could only hope it would grow in fertile ground. With her mortal frailty, there was only so much physical torture the girl could survive. Especially if *La Vieille* insisted Armand deliver it himself. Chances were high that the *Seigneur* would "accidentally" kill the girl.

But if Charles could subtly convince *La Vieille* that seeing young Lily as his betrayer's concubine would be a greater torture for the *Seigneur* . . . Yes, the idea had definite possibilities.

9

LIGHT STILL SHONE around the edges of the dark curtains when Armand awoke for the evening. He rose from his bed, fatigue dragging at his limbs though he knew he couldn't get back to sleep if he tried.

Before retiring for the day, he'd had another call from *La Vieille*. It hadn't been pretty, not when he hadn't been able to report any progress. Tonight he would launch a hunt of the city. Brigitte might be able to mask her psychic footprint and thus make herself to all intents and purposes invisible, but Henri did not have the same ability. If they could find Henri, they could find Brigitte.

Then all they'd have to do was find and kill Gabriel.

That thought, unfortunately, made him think of his ill-conceived plan to discover Gabriel's whereabouts. Reaching out with his psychic senses, he found Faith's footprint nearly on top of Drake's. His jaw tightened and his hands curled into fists.

When he'd suggested Faith attempt to seduce information from Gabriel's lieutenant, he hadn't for a moment guessed that the idea of her in another man's arms might . . . bother him.

Shaking his head, hoping to clear the cobwebs and irrational thoughts, he slipped into the bathroom and started the shower. But as he waited for the water to warm up, he remembered standing in the hall outside his door last night, intent on drowning his worries in Faith's body. And he remembered the tug of pain that had so shocked him when she'd confessed to her assignation with Drake.

Once upon a time, more than six centuries ago, when he'd been a mortal man, he'd been in love with a woman. As had been inevitable for a nobleman in that day, his marriage to Isabelle had been an arranged one, but they had fallen in love before their first month as husband and wife had passed.

Even now, thinking of her made his heart squeeze in his chest. She had just given birth to their fifth child when he'd marched off to his date with destiny on the field of Agincourt. He'd never seen her again, and for six hundred years whenever melancholy crept into his soul, he thought of her and wondered how she'd fared after his "death."

Armand looked at himself in the mirror over the sink. Outwardly, he looked like the same man he had been when Isabelle had kissed him goodbye for the last time. But inside, he knew he bore little resemblance to Armand Durant, the mortal. The mortal man could afford to love. The *Seigneur* could not.

And so this jealousy of his was nothing but foolishness, a side effect of the stressful mission, of his fear for himself and for all those who depended on him.

* * *

DRAKE WOKE TO a most unusual feeling—a woman's body snuggled up against his chest. He forced his gritty eyes open and confirmed that yes, Faith had somehow found her way across the bed and into his arms. And that he'd somehow managed to wrap those arms around her even in the grip of the coma-like daytime sleep.

Blinking in the darkened room, he realized that it was past sunset already. Usually he woke in the late afternoon, an hour or two before the sun set. Hard to believe he'd actually slept in when so many troubles besieged him!

Faith stirred in his arms, snuggling a little closer, and he couldn't help his instant reaction to the feel of her body against his. The T-shirt he'd given her to wear to bed had bunched up around her hips, leaving her legs bare against his. He usually slept in the nude, but he'd donned a T-shirt and boxers this morning. Still, that left plenty of bare skin, and before he was even fully awake, his fangs had descended and his cock hardened.

He hadn't woken up with a woman in his bed since his mortal days. For the last century, he had never been able to be so unguarded with a lover. With every mortal woman he'd bedded since then, he'd made sure their tryst took place at her home or at a hotel, leaving him the freedom to slip away in the middle of the night so she couldn't find out what he was.

Swallowing hard, he glanced down at Faith's face, still relaxed with the innocence of sleep, her lips slightly parted. If he kissed her, he wouldn't have to cloud her mind with glamour, as he'd had to with mortal women to keep them from noticing his fangs. He imagined giving himself up to that kiss, letting go of the reins, letting her kiss *him,* not some glamour-fogged facsimile.

He'd bent to within a millimeter of her mouth before he came to his senses and jerked away. Bad enough she might wake to find herself in an uncomfortably intimate embrace with a man she'd made clear she didn't want. What would she think of him if she woke to find him stealing a kiss?

He must have moved too suddenly, for Faith's body stiffened and her eyes popped open. His arm lay draped around her waist, and though he knew he should move away, he found himself staying right where he was, drinking in the sight of her tousled hair and startled eyes. When she licked her lips, it was all he could do to stop himself from stealing that kiss after all. His hand slid up her body until he touched the silky hair that lay across his pillow.

Faith didn't push him away, instead staring at him with those wide, still-startled eyes. He wondered if she was trying to decide how to extract herself from this uncomfortable position, until he took in a deep breath and caught the unmistakable scent of feminine arousal in the air.

His whole body clenched with need, and he forgot all his chivalrous instincts, as well as his rival for her affections. When his lips tasted hers, she gave a little moan and pressed herself more tightly into his arms. Her leg slid across the length of his, the friction sweet and sensual as her mouth opened for him. He didn't hesitate to take advantage of the invitation, sliding his tongue into the heat of her mouth as he speared his fingers through her hair and held her head at just the angle he liked.

His tongue brushed against one of her delicate fangs, and a shudder went through his body as he remembered once again that she was a vampire. That he didn't have to hide from her, didn't have to lie, didn't have to *think* every moment he made love to her, keeping himself in control so that his glamour wouldn't slip.

Her leg slid between his, her thigh coming to rest at the warm, hard center of him. His rational mind turned off completely then, leaving only his primal instincts to guide his actions. With a possessive growl, he rolled her over onto her back, making sure his aching erection came to rest at the juncture of her thighs. She made no protest, her arms sweeping around him, her nails digging into his back as she kissed him with wild abandon.

His hand was making its way down toward her panties when someone knocked on his door. His first instinct was to ignore the sound—he had more important things on his mind. But Faith tensed up beneath him, and the knock sounded again, louder.

"Drake?" Jez asked. "Are you awake in there?"

With a grunt of pure frustration, he rolled off of Faith and sat up. He'd bet anything Jez knew perfectly well he was awake—and what he'd been up to. It wasn't like the walls were soundproofed here, and vampire hearing was supernaturally keen.

"What is it?" he asked, and tried not to sound as snarly as he felt.

"His Majesty has called a meeting for this evening," she said with heavy sarcasm. "He respectfully requests your presence."

"Fine!" he snapped, accepting Jez's sour tone because he didn't think he had an alternative that didn't involve violence. "I'll be down in a few minutes."

"Bring Faith with you," she finished, and her footsteps retreated before he had a chance to respond.

Silence draped the room, and Drake risked a sidelong glance at Faith.

She'd sat up in the bed and pulled the hem of his T-shirt down as far as it would go. It was too dark for him to tell for sure, but he suspected her cheeks were pink with a blush. He cleared his throat, meaning to say something suave and self-assured, but no words came to mind.

With every passing moment, he was more awake and more aware of how close he'd come to completely losing control of himself. There were a thousand reasons why he shouldn't let himself get entangled with Faith, even if he did find himself reluctantly liking her, even if his body longed for her in ways he didn't understand.

The beast stirred within him, the hunger making it restless. Drake's fangs started to descend yet again, and it was embarrassingly hard to stop the descent. He cleared his throat again.

"I'm, uh, sorry if I took advantage," he said, no longer daring to look at her. The scent of her arousal had faded, and he wondered if she regretted returning his kiss as she had.

She laughed softly. "I'd say we both took advantage, so we're even."

He echoed her laugh and turned back to her. Her head was bent forward, her hair veiling her expression, and before he knew what he meant to do, he had reached out and brushed it away from her face.

"I would have liked to have met you under different circumstances," he said, and meant it.

"Me, too," she murmured, then leaned toward him and pressed a soft, chaste kiss against his lips.

Arousal surged through him once more, his fangs descending at lightning speed before he could even muster the will to stop them. Faith slid out of the bed, and it was all he could do to keep himself from grabbing her and hauling her back in.

"Do you mind if I use your shower?" she asked.

He was struggling too hard against the beast within him to speak, so he merely made a gesture of acquiescence.

When the bathroom door closed behind her, he closed his eyes and took a deep breath. The shower turned on, and he imagined her stripping out of that T-shirt.

Dammit! He opened his eyes and shook his head fiercely. He was only a day or so late in his feeding. He shouldn't be so . . . raw yet. And yet his body refused to stop responding to the images his mind continued to conjure of Faith's naked body standing under the spray of the shower.

He had to get out of here before he completely took leave of his senses and joined her.

Sliding out of the bed, he hastily dressed in his trademark black leather pants and a fresh T-shirt. He'd go see what the *Seigneur* wanted and take a shower later. A *cold* shower.

* * *

FAITH DUCKED HER head under the shower and let the steaming water sluice over her face and body.

She'd come to Drake's room last night meaning only to escape Armand's unwanted attentions. But from the moment she'd slipped between the sheets of his bed, she'd started to think that perhaps the charade needn't stay a charade forever. When her head had touched the pillow and she'd picked up his unique scent, she'd wanted to draw him into bed with her. But the pull of the daytime sleep had been too strong, and she'd fallen asleep in a haze of unfulfilled desire.

She picked up the bar of soap and noticed instantly the distinctive sandalwood scent that clung to Drake's skin. It was going to drive her crazy to smell that all night, but if she'd gone up to her room, she'd have had to wait her turn for one of the guest bathrooms.

Besides, she might have bumped into Armand, and she'd prefer to put off seeing him again for as long as possible. She remembered too well how Armand had looked at her as she'd left him at his doorway last night.

He might not particularly value her—at least, not as a person—but the idea of her sleeping with someone else hadn't sat as easily as he'd thought. That could potentially make things very uncomfortable around here.

Drake was gone when she emerged from the bathroom. She wasn't entirely surprised. She didn't think either one of them had expected the heat that had arisen between them when they'd awakened together like that.

She hurried down the hall and upstairs to her own room to change into fresh clothes.

She couldn't believe how good his kiss had felt. And while she was tempted to tell herself that she wouldn't have reacted like that if she hadn't still been on the edge of sleep, she wasn't so sure.

In her six years with Armand, she'd experienced a great deal of physical pleasure. He'd brought her to orgasm more times than she could count, but even when she was in the throes of ecstasy, there had always been a . . . taint. A knowledge deep inside her, somewhere that he couldn't reach, that the pleasure was false, nothing but a product of his glamour. And always there was the knowledge of how she'd feel afterward, when his glamour no longer clouded her mind.

As she dried her hair and pulled it into a ponytail at the nape of her neck, she wondered if there was any reason she should continue to resist Drake's charms. What would be the harm in sleeping with him? Yes, she'd have to leave him, and yes, it would hurt more if she let herself get more attached. But maybe it would be worth it.

Once upon a time, she'd had the illusion that she would never sleep with a man she didn't love. It had seemed like such a romantic idea, that her body would only go where her heart directed. But Armand had long ago shattered the illusion.

Maybe making love with Drake, feeling pleasure that wasn't tainted, would erase some of the scars the *Seigneur* had put on her soul.

She smiled ruefully at her reflection in the mirror. Or maybe she had no such lofty goals but just wanted to get laid. Either way, she would be a fool not to take advantage of the situation the *Seigneur* had put her in. No, a long-term love affair with Drake was not among her options. But there was no reason in the world she couldn't enjoy a hot, short-term fling.

All she had to do now was convince him he wanted the same thing. Considering how hungrily he'd stared at her this morning, she suspected that might not be much of a challenge.

* * *

WHEN DRAKE DESCENDED to the first floor, he discovered that the *Seigneur* and his entourage had taken over the receiving room. Armand had appropriated Gabriel's chair, with Charles sitting at his right hand, and his other two vampires occupying the seats Drake had set out for Eric and Harry. The mortals milled around, looking smug and arrogant. Jez and the Guardians stood clumped together in one corner, being ignored by the delegation. Jez had objected to Drake sitting in Gabriel's chair; she must be nearly out of her mind to see Armand in it.

Drake heaved a mental sigh. There was no doubt the *Seigneur* meant this as a challenge. Were he not so badly outmatched, Drake would have known exactly how to handle it. As it was, he feared anything he said or did would only make the situation worse. Still, his own Guardians might lose what respect they had for him if he didn't at least voice an objection.

Hating this role, he crossed his arms over his chest and stared at the *Seigneur,* who looked poised to pounce.

"I see you've made yourself at home," he said mildly.

The *Seigneur* smiled at him, and his look was coldly calculating. "The chair was unoccupied when I entered. I find it is quite comfortable."

Drake shook his head. "I'm not going to start a war over a chair," he said, and thought the *Seigneur* looked disappointed.

"A wise decision," Armand said, his smile even colder. The look in his eyes suggested Gabriel might not be the only Baltimore vampire he hoped to kill before returning to France.

There was no question in Drake's mind that the *Seigneur* was seething with jealousy. If the situation weren't so grave, Drake would have laughed at the absurdity of it. After all, it was the *Seigneur* himself who'd pushed Faith into his bed.

Drake returned the *Seigneur*'s sharklike smile. "Faith should be down shortly. She was in the shower when I left her."

Armand showed no sign of the barb hitting home besides a slight tightening at the corners of his eyes. But it was enough, and the *Seigneur* knew it. All conversation in the room halted, and everyone seemed to hold their breath.

Drake's nerves buzzed, his senses sharpening as he became aware of the scent that surrounded him, the scent of mortal men. Men he was certain were not innocents.

His conscious mind pulled back on the reins, trying to control the beast. Getting into a pissing contest with the *Seigneur* when the hunger clawed at the edges of his control wasn't the wisest idea he'd ever had. Too late now, however.

"You look . . . tense, *monsieur*," the *Seigneur* said. "Is something wrong?" His tone was one of polite inquiry, but the expression in his eyes was far from polite. In fact, Drake suspected he knew exactly what was wrong and hoped to goad Drake into losing his precious control.

Drake breathed deeply. He wasn't going to give Armand the satisfaction of winning a battle of wills. He would keep control of himself if it killed him.

His eyes flicked to the cluster of mortals who served the *Seigneur,* four men who all had the look of hired muscle. Not that the *Seigneur* needed muscle. They had to be used to the presence of vampires, but they must have sensed the tension in the air. All four looked uneasy, and the scent of fear hovered about them.

"It's past my dinnertime," Drake said, still looking at the mortals. "I was wondering if you'd be willing to share your livestock."

The scent of fear sharpened, though one of the mortals went red in the face with outrage.

Drake turned his most charming smile on the *Seigneur*. "I assume you brought them so you wouldn't have to insult the Master of Baltimore by hunting in his territory."

The fear was almost overpowering now, and Drake made no attempt to stop his fangs from descending. He sincerely doubted the *Seigneur* had brought the mortals as food, but he'd certainly planted that doubt in their minds.

The tension eased when Faith entered the room. Her nostrils flared briefly, and she gave the mortals a puzzled look. Then the *Seigneur* held out his hand to her.

Very pointedly not looking at Drake, she crossed the room to the *Seigneur* and allowed him to pull her down onto his lap. Her face had turned into an impassive mask, and if she minded sitting on his lap like a child, she didn't show it.

This little demonstration of his power over Faith

seemed to restore the *Seigneur*'s good humor, and his smile lost some of its frost. "My mortals are under my protection as much as my vampires," he said. "I'm afraid you'll have to find your meal elsewhere."

Drake doubted the mortals were much relieved, but Armand seemed disinclined to reassure them more than he already had.

"After two nights in your fair city," the *Seigneur* said, "I already find myself longing for my own home. And I suspect you are equally anxious to see me gone."

That was certainly the truth.

"We have so far allowed ourselves to be distracted from our purpose," the *Seigneur* continued. "All of us wish to see Brigitte returned to the loving arms of her mother. I propose that we put aside our differences and work together to make that happen."

Since their major differences were that Drake suspected the delegation planned to kill Gabriel, and Armand suspected Gabriel had teamed up with Brigitte against him, Drake wasn't sure how exactly they could manage to put them aside. However, he could hardly say he objected to the idea of getting Brigitte out of the city, as far away from him and the Guardians as possible.

"I'm happy to help," he said, "though as we all know, Brigitte has other plans."

He told Armand about his encounter with Brigitte and Henri yesterday, but wasn't surprised to be met with skepticism.

"That makes a very nice cover story," Armand

said. "Plausible, even. However, I have only your word that any of this happened. The murderer could just as easily be your supposedly absent master."

Drake nodded. "Yes, that's exactly what she and Henri predicted you'd say. I'm sure she'll be most gratified to be proven right." The *Seigneur*'s eyes flashed with anger, but Drake continued before tensions could escalate. "Do you have a proposal for how we can capture Brigitte?"

For a moment, the *Seigneur* looked as if he was tempted to pick a fight. Then the fire in his eyes faded.

"Charles and I are both old enough to distinguish between vampire auras. We know Henri is about two hundred and fifty years old, and we sincerely doubt there is another vampire of his age anywhere near your master's territory."

Drake nodded, though he supposed it depended on one's definition of "anywhere near." The Master of Washington was of approximately that age and was far closer than either Gabriel or Drake preferred. Unfortunately, the Master of Washington also had an impressive flock of fledglings and was too dangerous a foe for Gabriel and his Guardians to take on.

"We will divide into two search parties," the *Seigneur* continued. "I will head one, Charles the other. We will search for Henri's psychic signature. If we can find Henri, we will find Brigitte."

Drake would have liked to find fault with the plan, but with nothing else to go on, it seemed a reasonable one. Henri had said he and his mistress planned to take out one member of the entourage each night. They had to be nearby to hope to manage it.

What would happen after they found Brigitte was another thing entirely. Could they actually capture her, even if they found her? Would she hold the Guardians personally responsible and betray Gabriel's location to the delegation for spite? Or would she say nothing whatsoever, leaving Gabriel to die slowly of starvation?

Drake shook off the questions. There were no answers for them, not now. And so he would put off worrying about them until Brigitte was captured.

10

CHARLES DIDN'T FEEL at all himself as he hunted Henri through the streets of Baltimore, a ragtag team of lesser vampires in his wake. The *Seigneur* had assigned Jacques, his second-oldest fledgling, to Charles, along with Drake and Eric, taking Faith, Harry, and his youngest fledgling, Louis, with him. The mortals and Jezebel had remained at the house. Charles had questioned the wisdom of leaving Lily without better protection—despite Drake's claim that Brigitte would not harm her—but Armand had silenced him with one cold look.

In a custom holster under his jacket, Charles carried the tranquilizer gun he was to use on Brigitte if he found her. He had his master's permission to kill Henri outright, which he would be glad to do. But he couldn't help wondering whether splitting up was a good decision. Brigitte was powerful, and far from stupid. It seemed the chances of the hunters becoming the hunted were distressingly good.

He tried to shake off the disloyal thought, concentrating instead on reaching out with his psychic senses. But there were no vampires nearby except those in his party. At least, not that he could sense. Brigitte could be practically on top of them and he'd never know.

A cloud of depression hovered around him. This mission was doomed. Brigitte had had the upper hand from the beginning, and Charles saw no reason to think that would change. And even if the mission succeeded . . .

They would go home to France as soon as possible. Armand would immediately send Lily back to the boarding school where she spent most of the year. And considering the threat the *Seigneur* had issued last night, Charles would be best off trying to forget the girl existed. She belonged to the *Seigneur* as surely as Faith did. And while Armand might never take the girl to bed himself, he wasn't about to let Charles do so, either. After having served Armand loyally for more than six hundred years, didn't Charles deserve better than to be treated like some kind of dirty old man?

He didn't want to, but he couldn't help calling to mind the image of Lily in that dressing room, her skin so smooth and white and tempting. He swallowed hard and tried to calm the sudden surge in his pulse.

If she was tempting now, he told himself, she would be equally or more so when she turned eighteen, or even twenty-one. And maybe by then Charles would be able to soften his friend's stance.

But mortals were so fragile. Armand might keep the girl as safe as he possibly could, but accidents happened. Cars crashed, innocent bystanders were killed in acts of senseless violence. Wouldn't it be better for everyone if she became a vampire sooner rather than later? For her own protection, of course.

"Any sign of Henri yet?" Drake asked, shaking Charles out of his meandering thoughts.

"Nothing yet," he said, feeling like he was dragging himself back from a thousand miles away. Thinking about his future was pointless. Either he would be forced to betray Armand, or he would be forced to give up on Lily—and there was nothing he could do to control the outcome.

Drake grunted and gave him something of an odd look. Perhaps Charles had looked as distracted as he'd felt. If only they could find Brigitte and Henri! Or if only Brigitte and Henri would find *them*. At least then the torturous wait would be over. The uncertainty of it all was worse than anything. No reality would be as dreadful as the possibilities he imagined for himself.

He reached out with his senses, hoping against hope to feel Henri, but there was nothing. Brigitte and Henri would prolong this game for their own amusement. Listening to Drake recount Brigitte's plans to kill them all, one at a time, drawing out the game, had chilled him to the marrow. Yes, it was possible Armand was right and Drake had been making the whole thing up. But Charles couldn't convince himself that was the case, couldn't shake his sense of doom. How he wished they could just go home!

And then an idea emerged from the depths of his psyche. An idea of how he could take control of his own fate and make their hellish exile end sooner. He tried his best to bury the idea back in the depths of his mind, but now that it had sprung to life, it refused to die.

* * *

DRAKE HAD A sneaking suspicion they were on a fool's errand. He believed Charles was capable of sensing Henri. And he even believed the tranquilizer could take down Henri or even Brigitte. What he *didn't* believe was that Brigitte or her fledgling would allow it to happen. If her psychic radar was anywhere near as good as Gabriel's, she'd "see" them coming long before they reached her, and that would be the end of that. It would be far more effective to set a trap, but the *Seigneur* had not been open to suggestion.

Charles came to a halt so suddenly Drake almost bumped into him.

"What is it?" he asked as Jacques and Eric stared warily into the shadows.

Charles's eyes lost focus for a second, then brightened. "I've got him!" he said, pulling the gun from its holster inside his jacket. "Up ahead. Come on!" He gestured for them to follow, then started running down the street.

"Hold on a moment!" Drake protested, but Charles ignored him. Jacques followed obediently behind, but Eric looked at Drake first.

"Damn fool," Drake muttered, shaking his head, then hurrying in pursuit with Eric at his heels.

"This is a bad idea," Eric agreed, but kept pace with Drake.

This was the most they'd spoken to each other since the incident the night before. Drake didn't for a moment imagine the puppy had forgiven him, but at least he wasn't being actively hostile.

Up ahead, Charles and Jacques turned a corner. Drake quickened his pace from a jog to an all-out run. He careened around the corner with Eric right on his tail . . .

. . . and the next thing he knew, he was sitting on the front steps of a house with Eric seated beside him.

His head swam in confusion, and he blinked rapidly.

"What the hell just happened?" Eric asked, voicing Drake's own question.

Drake rose to his feet, his head feeling thick and muddy with the aftereffects of glamour. "Whatever it was," he said grimly, "it wasn't good." He rubbed his eyes, but his wits were returning to him rapidly.

He and Eric caught sight of Charles at the same time. The older vampire was sitting on the sidewalk between a pair of stoops, his back resting against the brick wall behind him. And lying beside him, with his head on Charles's lap, was Jacques, his neck twisted at an angle that was all wrong.

"Shit," Eric muttered, and walked over to squat beside Armand's dead fledgling.

Charles looked pale and shell-shocked, barely seeming to notice when Drake and Eric approached.

"What happened?" Drake asked, though he had a good idea he knew.

Charles swallowed hard and shook his head. "I don't know. Jacques and I ran around the corner, and then . . ." He shook his head again. "Then everything just went blank. When I came to . . ." He looked down at Jacques's body.

"Jesus!" Eric said. "I've never felt anything like that before. And if she can do that to *you,*" he continued, pointing at Charles, "then how the hell are we supposed to capture her?"

Charles seemed to be in a state of shock and didn't answer. Eric's eyes were too wide, and Drake realized how little experience the fledgling actually had with vampires. At least hostile ones. No doubt this was the first time he'd experienced glamour of this magnitude.

"She's powerful and dangerous," Drake said, again trying for the soothing croon that Eli did so well, "but she's not invincible."

Something sparked in Eric's eyes as he glared at Drake. "Oh yeah? What the hell could we have done if she'd decided to kill us all just now?"

Once again, the beast within Drake stirred, the hunger making his temper more brittle than usual. He managed to stifle the sharp responses that came to mind, though.

"She has no interest in killing *us,*" he reminded Eric. "It's the delegation she's after."

"Yeah, for now," Eric said. "But the bitch is crazy. Who knows what she'll do next?"

Drake gave him a marrow-freezing glare. "Don't have a panic attack on me. We can't afford it."

The command had the expected effect, and the fear drained from Eric's eyes, replaced by outrage. He opened his mouth as if to respond, but when Drake continued to glare, he thought better of it.

Charles's cell phone rang, and he turned a shade paler. Sweat beaded his brow and upper lip, and Drake could smell his fear in the air. His Adam's apple bobbed as he swallowed hard, but he answered the phone. He listened for a moment, then said, "*Oui, Seigneur,*" and closed the phone. He stood up, lifting the dead fledgling easily and slinging him over his shoulder in a fireman's carry. "The *Seigneur* wishes us to return to the house."

Drake felt momentarily sorry for the Killer, who would bear the brunt of the *Seigneur*'s wrath. There was sure to be an ugly scene when they all returned to the house. Then Drake reminded himself who and what he was feeling sorry for, and the feeling passed.

* * *

BECAUSE ARMAND SEEMED to expect it, Faith walked at his side as they hunted the streets. Louis and the Guardian followed behind them. For the first fifteen minutes or so, no one spoke. But when Faith tried to drop back and let Armand take the lead by himself, he put a hand on her elbow to stop her. It took all her willpower not to jerk her arm out of his grip.

Unfortunately, the *Seigneur* read her first reaction. His eyes narrowed and his lips thinned.

"You may have spent the night in Drake's arms," he said quietly, "but you are still mine. Are we clear on that?"

His tone was chilling, but she met his gaze anyway. "Unless I can get him to reveal Gabriel's whereabouts. Right?" Her heart pattered as his expression darkened even more.

"I keep my promises," he said through gritted teeth.

As far as she knew, that was true. But the way he was looking at her, his expression so proprietary, suggested he might be tempted to break this one.

Which didn't matter, she reminded herself. Even if she thought Drake would tell her where Gabriel was, she wouldn't ask him. She wouldn't give up her last scrap of honor.

Even if it was the only way to get Lily away from Armand?

She realized the *Seigneur* was awaiting an answer. "I know, *Seigneur*," she said, and he nodded curtly.

"I take it you met with no success last night?"

She shook her head, hoping he couldn't read the lie in her face. "I thought it might be too obvious if I started asking questions right away."

"Most practical of you." The words were bland enough, but from long exposure Faith could still hear the strain in his voice. "I hope you did not find your duties distasteful."

She couldn't help the bark of laughter that escaped her. "Are you asking me to rate his performance?" she asked, then instantly regretted it. Armand Durant was not the kind of man a woman could get away with teasing, especially not when he was in high temper already.

For a moment, the fire leapt into his eyes, and she wouldn't have been surprised if he'd hit her for her impertinence. Then the fire drained, replaced with a rueful smile.

"Touché," he said. "I would be a liar if I said I did not feel any trace of jealousy."

Her eyes widened. It wasn't like the *Seigneur* to admit any human frailties.

"I'm only doing what you ordered me to do," she said.

"I did not *order* you to seduce him. It was merely a suggestion."

"A suggestion you're regretting?"

Another rueful smile. "As a matter of fact, yes. I find myself thinking that he doesn't deserve you."

Faith swallowed a laugh of disbelief. The *Seigneur* was hardly in a position to make such a declaration. She bit her tongue to keep from saying anything, and hoped her expression was appropriately neutral. She felt his eyes on her but kept looking straight ahead.

"Don't forget, *ma petite*, for all his supposed virtues, the man is a Killer. If you find yourself feeling sentimental toward him, remind yourself how many people have died to feed him over his long life."

This time, Faith couldn't suppress her snort. "You've killed far more than he, *Seigneur,*" she said, knowing how stupid it was to talk back but unable to stop herself.

"Only because I'm so much older," he replied, his voice still surprisingly mild. "Perhaps I cannot persuade you not to think of me as all things evil, but I *can* remind you that Drake is not exactly all things good."

She had no good retort this time, so she didn't answer at all. Nothing Armand said mattered anyway. Even if she were following his orders and trying in earnest to seduce Drake, that was an act of the body, not of the heart. It didn't matter whether Drake was a saint or the devil himself.

"Are you trying to tell me you've changed your mind about your offer?" she asked, praying that wasn't what he meant, because if it was, there would be no escaping his bed.

The *Seigneur* sighed. "No. No, I might not like picturing you in his bed. But I much prefer that to picturing you in *La Vieille*'s dungeons, and if you have to go to his bed to avoid such a fate, then so be it."

She shivered at the reminder. She kept thinking that only freedom for herself and Lily was at stake. But while she had never met *La Vieille* personally, she knew enough about her to know just how dreadful the consequences of failure would be.

"I don't wish to alarm you," Armand continued,

"but she has made clear that *all* of us will suffer if we fail. Even young Lily."

Fear clutched at Faith's heart. Armand slipped an arm around her, pulling her close to him, and she was unnerved enough not to object.

"I will do everything in my power to see that that doesn't happen," Armand said, his hand giving her shoulder a reassuring squeeze. "But if we fail, I'm not sure if anything I do can prevent it. So you see how vitally important it is—to *all* of us—that we succeed."

The thought of Lily being subjected to *La Vieille*'s vengeance was more than Faith could bear. It was a fate she wouldn't wish on anyone, even Armand. She would not weep for him if he was killed, but she would not want to see him tortured.

The *Seigneur* came to a sudden stop. One hand flew to his forehead, and he winced as if in pain, swaying dizzily.

"*Seigneur?*" Faith asked, reaching for him before she thought better of it. "What's wrong?"

Armand's hand dropped back to his side. His jaw set in a grim line, and unadulterated fury gleamed in his eyes.

"Jacques just died," he said, his voice a heavy growl.

* * *

THE MOMENT DRAKE pushed open the front door and stepped inside, he knew something was dreadfully wrong. There was a faint, yet distinct, scent of blood in the air.

At first, the others didn't seem to notice as they piled in behind him, Charles still carrying the dead fledgling. Then they either noticed the scent, or noticed the look on Drake's face.

Charles let the fledgling's body slide to the floor, then reached for his tranquilizer gun. A quick psychic check told Drake that other than themselves, only a single human and a single vampire were in the house. A least, those were the only ones alive.

"Lily!" Charles cried in dismay, then leapt toward the stairs.

This time, Drake was ready and reached out to grab the older vampire's arm.

"Slow down!" he barked, earning himself a growl. "Remember what happened the last time you went charging out like the Lone Ranger?"

Charles's eyes glittered dangerously. "You and that baby," he said with a jerk of his chin in Eric's direction, "arc of no possible use against a foe like Brigitte. Now let go of my arm before you lose that hand."

Drake held on. "We might not be of much use, but neither are you. So let's all go up together, okay?" He let go of Charles's arm and was relieved when the older vampire didn't charge up the stairs. Instead, the three of them climbed the stairs together.

No doubt Brigitte was long gone, Drake told himself as he kept straining with his psychic senses. Neither the vampire nor the mortal he'd sensed had moved since they'd entered the house. He wasn't sure what that meant.

The smell of blood grew stronger when they reached the head of the stairs. The scent teased Drake's nostrils, and the hunger flared to life. His fangs descended almost without warning, and his skin felt thin and stretched over his body.

"Maybe we should wait until the *Seigneur* gets here," Eric suggested in a voice not much louder than a whisper.

There was a certain wisdom in the idea of waiting for reinforcements, but if Brigitte was in the house and wanted to kill them, she'd be sure to do it before the *Seigneur* showed up.

Communicating with hand signals, Charles motioned for Drake to open the first closed door they came to in the dark and suddenly ominous hall. The smell of blood was stronger still, but Drake did his best to ignore it.

He sensed no sign of life behind the door—though of course he wouldn't be able to sense Brigitte if she didn't want him to. Making sure Eric was out of the line of fire, he shoved the door open.

Charles stood in the hallway, his finger on the trigger of the gun, but there was no sign of movement. Drake reached in and flicked the light on.

One of the *Seigneur*'s mortals lay sprawled on the floor, his throat torn open. Blood still trickled from the wound, but nowhere near as much as there should have been. Whatever vampire had attacked this mortal had drunk his or her fill.

They continued down the hall. The next room was the source of the vampire presence Drake sensed.

"Someone very young," Charles said. "Certainly not Henri."

"Jezebel," Drake guessed, then pushed the door open without ceremony.

Jez was tied to a chair, almost mummified by the quantity of rope around her, with a gag cutting into the edges of her mouth and a blindfold over her eyes. Drake quickly crossed to her, ripping off the blindfold and gag. The ropes that bound her were going to take considerably longer to get rid of.

"What happened?" he asked as he knelt by the chair and started prying at one of the knots.

"I have to look for Lily," Charles said impatiently, then was gone before Drake could object. Not that he felt inclined to at the moment. Whatever Brigitte's game, he sincerely doubted it included the death of the Guardians. At least, not yet.

"I don't know what happened," Jez said. Drake finally managed to tear through the first knot and started working on the next. "I was sitting in the den minding my own business. Then the next thing I knew, I was tied to this chair and the only other presence in the house was a single mortal." Another knot released, and Drake began to unravel the bindings.

"You didn't see or hear anything?"

"No," Jez responded.

"Sounds familiar," Eric said, and Drake had to agree. But powerful as Brigitte was, she couldn't be in two places at once. She and Henri could have split up, but Drake seriously doubted Henri had the kind of power necessary to cast that strong a glamour on his own.

Downstairs, the front door opened and then closed with an earth-shattering slam. The *Seigneur* had returned.

"Charles!" he bellowed, no doubt puzzled to find Jacques's body abandoned on the floor.

Jezebel was finally able to work her way out of the ropes. Drake and Eric helped her step away without getting tangled up. The *Seigneur* shouted again. Charles responded, but the sound was muffled by distance.

Drake stepped out into the hallway just in time to almost collide with the *Seigneur*. The air temperature dropped sharply as the *Seigneur*'s eyes blazed.

It must have suddenly dawned on him that something more than Jacques's death was wrong, for he came to an abrupt halt and his jaw dropped open.

"My mortals . . ."

"Lily!" Drake hadn't even seen Faith climb the stairs until he heard her cry of distress.

Luckily, at that moment Charles emerged from Lily's room, leading the frightened-looking girl by the hand. She pulled away from Charles and ran toward her sister. When Faith met her halfway and Lily threw her arms around her neck, Drake noticed the rope burns on the poor child's wrists.

Armand must have noticed at the same moment, for the temperature in the room dropped still more.

"What has happened?" he asked, and you'd never

know from the tone of his voice that he was practically livid with rage.

Charles approached warily, not eager to be the bearer of bad tidings. Drake couldn't blame him.

"The mortals are all dead," Charles reported. "And all drained."

"What?" Armand cried. "There were *four* of them. Brigitte and Henri couldn't have drained them *all*!"

Charles raised his hands in a helpless gesture. "I know, *Seigneur*. But they are drained, just the same."

The *Seigneur* glared at his lieutenant. "So you're telling me that Brigitte and Henri managed to entrance your entire search party, kill Jacques, and drain my mortals dry. All at the same time."

Charles stared at the floor in front of his feet. "I don't know what to tell you, *Seigneur*. Except that Brigitte and Henri can't be in this alone."

The *Seigneur* whirled on Drake. "Do you still claim Brigitte has your master captive?"

With the scent of blood making his nerves vibrate, it was all Drake could do not to lunge at the *Seigneur*'s throat. There was no chance in hell he could get the fangs to retract.

"Yes, I still *claim* that," he snarled. "And even if I were lying, three vampires couldn't drain four people."

The *Seigneur*'s fangs had descended as well, and he took a menacing step forward. "Don't bare your fangs at me."

Drake struggled against his visceral urge to attack. Dammit, he had to feed soon, or he'd never keep control of himself.

"I can't help the fangs," he admitted, fighting back his temper. "I haven't fed recently, and the smell of blood . . ."

The *Seigneur* didn't look in the least bit appeased. "Yes, the scent is tempting, isn't it?" He tongued one of his fangs, then licked his lips. "It's making me quite hungry, in fact."

Both Drake's fists clenched at his sides, and something twisted in his gut at a premonition of where the *Seigneur* was going with this.

"In fact," the *Seigneur* continued, "I think Charles and Louis and I should go for a hunt. It wouldn't do for us to let our hunger cloud our judgment."

"If you hunt in our city, Gabriel will see you dead before this is all over."

The *Seigneur* laughed. "He's either a prisoner or he isn't. Make up your mind which."

"We've had this discussion before. He's a prisoner *now,*" Drake said, "but I don't expcct him to remain one forever."

"Let's test the theory, shall we? I shall lead my vampires on a hunt. If your master objects to us hunting his city, then let him come stop us. If he's not in a position to do so, then his threat carries no weight."

Drake wished like hell there was something he could do to stop them. "You're signing your own death warrant," he warned, but wasn't under the illusion that the warning would matter.

The *Seigneur* shouldered him aside, Charles and Louis trailing behind him. Eric hurried to block their path. Drake groaned. The fool was going to get himself killed.

The *Seigneur* bared his fangs, but Drake stepped between them and stared into Eric's eyes.

"Stand down," he ordered. "There's nothing we can do to stop them."

Eric's lips pulled back to reveal his fangs, and his eyes narrowed. Once again the temperature in the room dropped. Eric wasn't anywhere near powerful enough to have that effect, which meant the *Seigneur* was once again getting pissed off. And if he was pissed off enough to ignore protocol and hunt without Gabriel's permission, he was pissed off enough to kill Eric.

"I don't give a shit," Eric growled. "I'm not letting them hunt our city without a fight."

The beast within Drake stretched and flexed its muscles. He tried to hold his temper in check, but with his hunger, the smell of blood, and the younger vampire's blatant challenge pounding at his self-control, he just couldn't do it.

His first punch connected with Eric's jaw and sent the youngster flying. Jez gave a little cry of distress and took a step toward him, but one look from Drake was enough to back her off.

Moronically, instead of giving up, Eric sprang from the floor and charged Drake, an incoherent battle cry rising from his throat.

Something snapped within him, and Drake suddenly felt like he was watching his own actions from a distance as he met Eric's charge and jammed a fist into his stomach. The fledgling doubled over in pain, but Drake hit him again anyway.

Distantly, he was aware of his anger and of his paradoxical concern for Eric's safety. He still felt the blood pounding in his brain, the quickening of his breath, the stirring of his hunger. But he was more strongly aware of the overpowering sense of déjà vu as he grabbed Eric by the shirt and hauled him onto his feet.

The fledgling's eyes were filled with pain, his scent tinged with fear as he realized how thoroughly helpless he was. Drake slammed him into the wall, and Eric cried out.

Johnnie Drake was at work again, delivering a beating that would leave his victim bedridden and in pain for days on end, if he were mortal. The anger disappeared from his consciousness, replaced by something cold and numb. Johnnie didn't feel anything when he delivered a beating. He beat whomever his master told him to, whether that master was his father or, later, Padraig. He didn't ask why. He didn't ask whether the victim deserved it. He just did his job, neither liking nor disliking the experience.

A backhanded slap sent Eric to the floor again. Absently, Drake noticed that the *Seigneur,* Charles, and Louis were halfway down the stairs. Jez and Harry were both reaching out to him, begging him to stop, though neither was stupid enough to actually touch him.

Eric lay on the floor, in too much pain to make

even the slightest effort to protect himself. Johnnie casually pulled back his leg to deliver a kick, but then his eyes fastened on Faith, standing in the hallway and watching. Lily's head was buried against her sister's shoulder, and Faith held her there as if to block her view. Faith's face was white with shock, her eyes wide and betrayed.

And suddenly, Drake came to himself once more. His momentum was too great for him to stop the kick, but he managed to take most of the force out of it.

Eric lay still, and Drake sucked in deep, frantic breaths of air as he struggled to lay Johnnie to rest once more. The lingering scent of blood didn't help matters. But dammit, Johnnie Drake didn't exist. He was a character Drake had once played, never a part of the real him. And he wouldn't play that part ever again.

With a shake of his head, he banished the last of his rage and knelt by Eric's side. The fledgling's eyes were open, but the bones of his jaw stood out in sharp relief as he gritted his teeth.

"I'm sorry," Drake said, wincing at how lame that sounded under the circumstances. Eric struggled to sit up, and Drake helped him.

"The hunger makes my temper very brittle," Drake continued. "I lost control of myself."

Eric made a grunting noise, but didn't say anything. Jezebel came to kneel on the other side of Eric, draping his arm over her shoulder. She glared at Drake.

"I think you've done enough for tonight," she said, then helped Eric to his feet.

Drake had nothing to say in his own defense. Jez guided Eric toward his room, Harry tagging along beside them. Faith and Lily had already disappeared.

Alone in the hallway, Drake was haunted by a past he'd give everything he owned to deny.

11

Lily looked older than she'd looked when they'd first stepped off the plane, Faith realized as they sat together on the bed in Lily's room. Lily had stopped crying shortly after they'd entered the room, and now looked deep in thought as she idly rubbed one of the rope burns on her wrist.

Faith reached out to still her sister's hand. "You'll just make it worse."

Lily frowned at her wrist, but stopped rubbing at it. "Have you figured out how we're going to get away yet?"

Faith stifled a sigh of frustration. "I'm working on it, sweetie."

Lily gave her a narrow-eyed glance. "Do you still think Drake's going to help us?"

"There's no one else," Faith answered, though right now she desperately wished there were. Drake had shown his true colors tonight, proven once and for all that he was just as much a bully as Armand. Which suggested that like Armand, he would always put self-interest first. Try though she might, Faith couldn't imagine how she could make it worth his while to help her.

"Maybe we don't need any help," Lily suggested. "If the vamps are all out hunting, and the mortals are all dead, what's to stop us from running away right this minute?"

Hope and terror battled in Faith's chest. Drake had told her that she would find a safe haven in Philadelphia. That wasn't too terribly far away, and even a vampire as young as she could manage enough glamour to relieve mortals of their cash, so money wouldn't be an issue. But if Armand should catch them . . .

Holding on to Lily's shoulders, Faith peered into her eyes. "We can do this," she said. "We can make a run for it, and thanks to Drake I know where we can go. But I want you to understand it's a terrible risk. If the *Seigneur* catches us, there will be hell to pay. He'll hold me responsible. You have to promise me that if the worst happens, you won't interfere."

Lily shook her head. "He could *kill* you!"

"I doubt he would. And even so, there'd be nothing you could do to stop him, and you'd get yourself hurt in the process."

Lily blinked rapidly, her eyes shining with tears she seemed determined not to shed. "I don't want to put you in that kind of danger."

Faith forced a smile. "You're not putting me in danger, sweetie. I'm doing that all by myself."

"But if it weren't for me, you wouldn't be trying to run."

Actually, if it weren't for Lily, she'd have run long ago and probably died in the process. But that wasn't something she could say.

"I have to get away from him," she said. "It's not all about you. If I don't get away now, I'll be stuck with him for who knows how many centuries." She shuddered. "Trust me—I'd be running for it even without you. Okay?"

Lily bit her lip, but nodded.

"And you promise you won't make a fuss if we get caught?"

Lily's chin jutted out stubbornly, but when Faith refused to back down from her demand, she gave another halfhearted nod.

"All right," Faith said, trying to project utter calm. "Let's go."

"Now?" Lily cried, then lowered her voice. "Don't we have to pack some stuff?"

Faith shook her head. "There's no time for that. Who knows how long they'll be gone? Let's just get out of here while we can. We'll worry about supplies later."

She took Lily by the hand, and Lily didn't object. Faith did a quick psychic scan, but there were no vampires lurking about in the hallway. Moving quickly and as quietly as possible, she and Lily descended the stairs. Faith groaned at the sound the front door made when she swung it open, but no one came charging down the stairs after them.

"Here goes nothing," Faith muttered under her breath.

And then she and Lily were jogging down the street, trying to put as much distance as possible between themselves and the house. Faith used what glamour she had to turn away the attentions of curious pedestrians. A few people gave the fleeing pair a speculative look when Faith's concentration broke, but no one tried to stop them.

At least, not until they'd gotten about a block and a half from the house.

Then Charles stepped out of the shadows and blocked their way. Faith came to a stop with a muffled shriek, and Lily gasped. Charles crossed his arms over his chest, but he didn't look like he was angry or about to attack them.

"The *Seigneur* decided that leaving the two of you unsupervised might not be a good idea," he said with a hint of a smile. "I see he was right."

Faith swallowed hard around the lump of fear in her throat. "Please, Charles. You've always been kind to us. You're a decent man. Please let us go."

But Charles shook his head. "I'm truly sorry, but I can't do that. The *Seigneur* is angry enough with me already. I can't afford to anger him again."

Faith wanted to beg some more, but what was the point? As she'd always known, Killers were self-interest incarnate. Never would Charles risk his neck for anyone. Her shoulders sagged, and she tried not to drown in the tide of fear that swept over her.

Lily stepped out from behind Faith's back and

looked at Charles with imploring eyes. "Please! Uncle Armand is going to . . ." A fat teardrop rolled down her cheek, and she grabbed Charles's arm. "You know what he'll do to her!"

Charles smiled benignly and wiped away the tear. "I won't let you run away, but that doesn't mean I have to tell the *Seigneur* you tried."

Relief weakened Faith's knees, even if she couldn't help noticing the odd way Charles was looking at her sister. Like Armand, he'd always played the role of the kindly uncle with Lily. He wasn't looking terribly avuncular at the moment, however. His thumb stroked over Lily's cheek once more, ostensibly to wipe away another tear, but Faith wasn't so sure.

"We'd better get back to the house," she said, casually drawing her sister away. "If Armand finds us outside, it won't matter what you say."

"Very true," Charles agreed.

And with Charles hovering nearby to crush all hopes of escape, Faith and Lily returned to the house.

* * *

DRAKE FIGURED THAT a truly wise man would stay away, but he couldn't stop himself from stopping by Eric's room to check on the fledgling's condition. Eric was stretched out on his bed, his back propped against the headboard by a stack of pillows. Both Harry and Jez had pulled up chairs to sit beside him, and when Drake stepped into the room he had the distinct impression that Eric was growing impatient with their coddling.

Jez had been in the middle of saying something, but she cut herself off when Drake entered. The look she gave him was cold and angry, and there wasn't a thing he could say to make that look go away. Harry looked uncomfortable, his gaze fixed on the floor. Eric's expression was conspicuously neutral, except for his eyes, which couldn't conceal his antipathy.

Drake had felt more welcome in Eli's meeting hall on the day Fletcher had dropped his bombshell.

"I'm sorry for what I did," he said. "I lost control, and there's no excuse for that. But Eric, if I hadn't stepped in, there's a very good chance you'd be dead right now." He met the fledgling's mutinous gaze. "Neither Gabriel nor I would kill you for being a pain in the ass. The *Seigneur* would. Maybe you think getting up in his face is brave, but you're wrong. It's just stupid."

"You've made your position on that very clear," Jez said, not in the least appeased.

Drake set his jaw. "I'm going to do everything in my power to keep all of you alive while Gabriel is gone. Hate me for it if you have to. I'm used to it." His gut twisted with the truth of his own words, but he hid his pain under a stony façade.

"No one hates you," Harry said, startling everyone because he was usually so quiet. "We just hate feeling helpless."

"Believe me, I hate it, too." And he hated being *responsible*. He hated that he had to make all the hard decisions, with no one here to back him up. How he wished he could hand this whole mess over to Gabriel or Eli. Hell, even Padraig!

"Unless we all want to keep playing doormat," Jez said acidly, "we've got to get Gabriel back. And we haven't made the slightest effort to do it."

Drake shook his head. "You have no idea how much I want him back right this moment. But if we find him, we'll lead the delegation right to him. Don't forget, they're under orders to bring his head to *La Vieille*."

"Their delegation is down to only four vamps!" she protested. "The four of us together could take Faith and Louis, and you know Gabriel can take Charles and Armand."

"Are you sure of that?" Drake asked, and her hesitation was all the answer he needed. "What would happen if his glamour gave out on him at the crucial moment?"

Jez's shoulders slumped, and Drake knew she saw the truth, even if she didn't want to admit it.

"Look," he said, "this situation sucks. We all know it. But we have to play it smart. We won't do anyone any good if we get ourselves killed."

No one answered him, but at least they didn't argue, either. A leaden silence descended, and Drake could think of no way to break it. He looked at the three Guardians sitting there together, providing a united front, and he felt more keenly than ever his role as the outsider looking in.

When his mother had abandoned him in Five

Points to the tender mercies of his father, he had turned himself into Johnnie Drake and earned himself an insider's position. But it seemed that while he had managed to create a convincing gangster persona, he'd never be able to turn himself into the kind of man the Guardians would accept. All these years, he'd told himself the only rift that divided him from the Guardians was his status as a Killer. But perhaps the differences ran far deeper than he'd realized.

Shaking his head, Drake slipped from the room without another word. He started down the hall, but the door behind him opened and Jezebel stepped out. She closed the door behind her, moving to stand within a foot of him and lowering her voice. The censure in her eyes was almost more than he could bear.

"For the time being," she said, "I have no choice but to accept you, since I'm not powerful enough to kick you out. But when Gabriel gets back, I want you gone."

The pronouncement should have sparked his temper. Instead, it just hurt, though he tried to keep the pain from showing on his face.

"Ask yourself this, Jez. What would Gabriel have done in my shoes?" He knew the answer to that perfectly well, as he was sure she did. Gabriel had spent five hundred years wallowing in violence, and Drake doubted he'd be suffering any remorse right now.

"He might have attacked," Jez conceded. "But I could have stopped him. He wouldn't have . . . brutalized Eric like that."

Drake suspected her perspective was a little off

where Gabriel was concerned. Gabriel had never raised a hand to her, but Drake had personal experience with just how brutal he was capable of being. Of course, that experience predated Gabriel's relationship with Jez, so perhaps he really had changed since then.

"If it weren't for the hunger, *I* wouldn't have done that, either," Drake said, hoping it was true. "I just . . ." He sighed heavily. "I don't want to feed without Gabriel. I don't want to take that chance."

He thought there might be a slight softening of her expression, but her stance remained unchanged. "When he gets back," she repeated, "I want you gone."

This time, the pain those words inspired roused his temper. He clenched his fists and sucked in a deep breath, holding himself together for all he was worth. Then, knowing he risked another explosion by staying, he turned on his heel and retreated to his bedroom.

* * *

AFTER THE ABORTED escape attempt, Faith was more convinced than ever that her only hope for getting Lily away from Armand was Drake. Despite what she'd seen him do tonight.

She left Lily ensconced in her room, IMing with her friends from school, and set out in search of Drake. A quick psychic scan told her he was in his bedroom. Unbidden, the memory came to her of waking up to find herself pressed against his body, his arm draped around her. The memory made her whole body flush with warmth, but she dispelled it by thinking about the very different side of him she'd seen tonight. She had to remember he was a Killer, had to remember that despite moments of kindness, he was no knight in shining armor.

However, knight or not, he was all she had. And tonight's escape attempt had revealed an unpalatable truth—with Armand on his guard, there was little to no chance that she and Lily could escape together. If only one of them was going to escape, it would have to be Lily. The idea of leaving a sixteen-year-old girl in the hands of a Killer she barely knew was enough to turn her insides to water. But the idea of leaving her in the hands of a Killer she knew all too well was even worse.

She rapped lightly on the door, but Drake didn't respond. She still had no idea how she could persuade him to help Lily escape. There was nothing in it for him. Quite the contrary, if Armand were to find out Drake helped Lily get away, he'd be a dead man. Biting her lip indecisively, she waited what must have been a full minute before knocking again. She might not know what she could offer him in return, but whatever his price, she would pay it.

She was debating whether to knock a third time or just slink away in embarrassment when his door finally swung open. He looked tired and haggard, and for a moment she felt a surge of pity.

"May I come in?"

"I'm not good company right now."

Faith fought her natural instinct to retreat. "Better than Armand, surely." He hadn't returned from his hunt yet, but Faith could only imagine what sort of a mood he'd be in when he did.

Drake shook his head, but swung the door open for her anyway. "Come in then."

"Are you all right?" she asked, then almost laughed at her own question. *He'd* been the aggressor tonight. Eric hadn't landed a single blow, and even if he had, any damage would be healed by now.

Drake sank down into one of the chairs across the room, leaning his head back and closing his eyes. "Not really," he admitted.

Uncertain what to make of that statement, she came and sat across from him, peering at his face. "What's wrong?"

He laughed but didn't open his eyes. "Other than the fact that there are three Killers hunting innocent mortals on my watch and I can do nothing to stop them?"

Instinct told her there was more to it. "Yes, other than that."

He laughed again, this time raising his head and opening his eyes. "Other than that, my hunger has put my temper on a razor's edge, I've acted like a brute and a bully because of it, and Jezebel has told me I'm to leave the city as soon as Gabriel returns." He scrubbed a hand through his hair. "Oh, and if I'm forced to leave the city, I have nowhere to go except back to my maker, who would separate me from what remains of my humanity in no time at all."

Pity stabbed at her again, though why she should feel sorry for him at the moment was a mystery. "Couldn't you go to Philadelphia?" she asked. "That's where you told me I could go if I somehow got free."

But Drake shook his head. "I've already been kicked out of Philadelphia." The pain that shadowed his eyes was impossible to miss. "No, if I'm forced to leave here, my only choice will be to return to my maker. And I think everyone, including me, would be better off if I died instead."

Faith raised her eyebrows. "Surely it can't be *that* bad." She definitely felt a pang in her gut at the thought of Drake dying. Killer or no, bully or no, he still seemed like he was at heart a decent person. But then perhaps she was romanticizing him, just as she had François. "Your maker can't change who you are."

"Maybe not," Drake admitted, looking no less haunted. "But the question then becomes just who am I?" His eyes were distant and unseeing. "For more than a century, I've convinced myself I'm one of the good guys. That the people I've killed to keep myself alive were all people the world was better off without. I can't help wondering if that was all a lie. Maybe I'm no better than your *Seigneur*."

Even though she'd had that very thought herself, Faith found herself leaping to his defense. "You're nothing like Armand!" she insisted. "I know you hurt Eric, but Armand hurt me far worse, and for a far less noble cause. If you hadn't stepped in, Armand might well have killed him. Hell, if you'd just stopped him without hurting him, Armand might *still* have killed him, thinking you were too nice to punish him." Her voice rose as she gained momentum. "And at least you have the excuse of hunger fraying your temper. Armand might have been angry when he hurt me, but he was hardly out of control." She shook her head. "No, there's no comparison between the two of you."

Drake smiled at her, but it was a bitter expression. "I appreciate the sentiment, but I'm afraid it's misplaced. Yes, this time I must admit to being spurred by the hunger, but in my youth I delivered beatings as dispassionately as the *Seigneur*. I thought I'd exorcized that part of myself, but I'm not so sure anymore. And if I find myself in Padraig's orbit again, I have no doubt I'll fall back into old habits."

Faith couldn't stand the haunted look on his face. How could she have told herself he was just like Armand? Had Armand ever shown a single sign of remorse for the pain he'd caused?

Not knowing what she could do to ease his spirit, she still found she longed to do so. She rose from her chair and moved to stand behind him, laying her hands on his shoulders and giving the tightened muscles there a firm squeeze. She meant to say something clever and comforting, but the moment she touched him, words fled.

His body felt warm under her hands, and the tight-fitting T-shirt let her feel the ripple of his muscles. She gave another exploratory squeeze, looking down at his face from above, and saw his eyes drift shut as he sucked in a hissing breath. She didn't think he meant it as a protest.

Her hands slid up from his shoulders to his neck, finding more tightened muscles and, more importantly, bare skin. She shivered at the feel of him under her fingers, then forgot her original intention to soothe him and instead bent over to smooth her hands down the planes of his chest.

The movement brought her face closer to his, and she inhaled his scent as her cheek brushed against his hair.

"Be careful," he whispered as her hands drifted lower, reaching the bottom of his sternum. "You know how little self-control I have just now."

She inhaled again, drawing in his warm, spicy, arousing scent. A little voice inside her tried to remind her why she'd come here in the first place but was drowned out by the tide of desire. Instead of answering him, she nuzzled his ear, her fangs descending as her hands curled in his T-shirt to untuck it from his trousers. When her hands found the warm skin of his abdomen underneath, they both groaned.

"Last warning," he breathed in a hot whisper. His hands clutched the arms of his chair hard enough to turn the knuckles white, and as Faith continued to caress him, she couldn't help noticing the bulge that strained against the zipper of his pants.

She really should stop, she thought as she hesitated for a moment. She'd come here to propose a plan to free Lily from Armand, and sex would be nothing but an unnecessary distraction.

Her eyes fastened on the bulge that stretched the

black leather to its limits, and desire chased the last of her common sense away. Instead of stopping, she teased his earlobe with a flick of her tongue.

Before she'd had a chance to register the taste of his skin on her tongue, he'd tilted his head back and captured her mouth with his. The hands that had clutched the chair arms now fastened onto her, holding her in place while his tongue stabbed into her mouth. A moan escaped her, despite the awkwardness of the position.

Drake released her mouth but grabbed her arm and pulled her around to the front of the chair. She leaned eagerly into another kiss, then decided she wanted even more contact. There was just enough room on the seat for her to climb on and straddle his lap. His hands skimmed down her back then fastened on her bottom, holding her securely in place while his mouth ravaged hers.

Faith felt like she was drowning in pleasure. His touches were rougher, needier than Armand's, and yet there was no denying how perfectly they stoked her desire. Desire that came from within, not as an artificial construct of someone else's will.

Beneath her, Drake's erection continued to swell, a hardened core of heat that pressed into her and showed her just how thoroughly her desire was returned.

Suddenly, his hands clamped down harder on her bottom and he surged to his feet. Instinctively, she wrapped her arms and legs around him. Not breaking the kiss for an instant, he carried her to his bed and laid her down, his body coming to rest on top of hers.

Faith kept her legs wrapped around him, unwilling to let go, as her hands raked up and down his back. She tugged on his T-shirt, wishing there was some way to get it off him without his mouth leaving hers.

With a low growl, Drake pulled away from the kiss. Before she had a chance to protest, he'd practically torn the T-shirt off his body in his haste. His chest was as mouthwatering as she remembered, and she gave in to her desire to taste it. Sitting up just enough, she flicked her tongue over one hardened nipple. His hiss of pleasure emboldened her, and she did it again.

Drake's eyes were closed as he savored her licks and caresses, but his hands unerringly found the buttons on her blouse. His fingers were clumsy as he tried to slip the buttons free.

"Tear it," she murmured with a wanton laugh, amazed at her own boldness and lack of inhibition.

He didn't need to be told twice. Buttons flew every which way, and then his hands were on her bare skin and it was all she could do to string together two coherent thoughts in a row. She forgot to continue her sensual assault on his chest and merely lay back and *felt*.

His hands were warm and sure, his touch surprisingly gentle in light of his rampant need. His fingers traced the lacy edges of her bra, causing her back to arch and her breath to catch in her throat. She wanted a firmer touch, but Drake didn't give it to her, continuing to tease as she writhed. When she reached for his hand to guide it to where she wanted it, he grabbed her wrist with his free hand and pinned it to the bed beside her. She opened her eyes in surprise. His feral grin, showing lots of fang, made her shiver deep inside.

"There will be no rushing things," he scolded.

She made a moue of discontent. Laughing, Drake leaned over and kissed the expression away, making her forget her complaints. His fingers resumed their teasing dance.

After what seemed like forever, Drake finally relented and slid the lace of her bra away from her nipple. The light caress of his thumb set fire to her senses. She instantly wanted more.

This time, he gave her what she wanted. His kisses trailed down her throat, tasting and nipping all the way down until his lips brushed the top of one breast. He'd let go of her pinned wrist, so she reached up to spear her fingers through his hair and urge him on. But by now, he needed no urging.

When his mouth closed over her nipple and he gave a gentle draw, Faith thought her heart was about to explode. The pleasure was overwhelming, and yet somehow . . . pure. Her mind was clear, her thoughts her own, and all she could think of was pressing closer to his heat.

Trailing her hands down his ribs as he continued to torment her, she finally met the waistband of his pants. She slipped her hands between their bodies and pried at his belt buckle. He raised up enough to give her room to maneuver, but didn't otherwise help. Just as she felt like screaming from impatience, the buckle finally loosened and she went to work on the button and then the zipper. She nearly swallowed her tongue when she managed to coax the zipper down and found he wasn't wearing anything beneath those pants.

Drake gave a heartfelt moan when her fingers grasped him. She reveled in the velvety smoothness of his taut skin, stroking him from tip to base. His mouth left her breast, and she was enjoying the feel of him in her hands enough not to protest.

Eyes night-dark with desire, he unfastened her pants in record time, then started tugging them down. She hated to let go of him, but if she didn't, he wouldn't be able to get her pants off, and that was unacceptable. His wicked grin suggested he read her thoughts.

With a sigh, she released him, and he dragged her pants and panties down her legs. She took the opportunity to shuck the remains of her shirt and her bra. Then she was naked, her whole body flushed with heat and yearning as Drake sat back on his heels, his erection jutting out of his pants as his eyes took a leisurely tour of her body. She felt his gaze like a physical touch, but she wanted—no, *needed*—more. She arched her back temptingly, and that was all it took to make him see things her way.

Moving considerably faster now, Drake peeled

away his pants, then climbed up her body like a predatory cat, skin rubbing against skin the whole way. She spread her legs eagerly and slid her arms around his neck as soon as he was within reach.

His muscles quivered under her hands, his skin dewed with sweat. She felt his strain as his erection nudged her entrance and he tried to ease his way in. But whether because his desire was too strong or because his hunger overwhelmed his control, he soon abandoned the effort and plunged into her with a single hard thrust.

An incoherent cry rose in Faith's throat. For half a second, Drake looked indecisive, like he thought he might have hurt her. But one look at her eyes must have told him just what that cry meant. His mouth came down on hers, his tongue tasting her as his hips began to thrust.

Fingers digging into his shoulders as she tried to absorb everything he gave her, Faith wrapped her legs around him and gave in to the pleasure. She sucked eagerly on his tongue, ran her hands over his sweat-dewed skin, inhaled the mingled scents of sex and Drake. Within seconds, she was on the brink of orgasm, but she held on desperately, not wanting it to be over yet.

His hips pumped ever more frantically, his breath wheezing in and out of his lungs. Faith knew it wasn't from exertion, but from the same effort she was making to hold off climax, to make it last.

Hard though she fought, the pleasure was too intense, rising steadily from inside her until she couldn't contain it anymore. And once she cried out in release, she burst through the last of Drake's self-restraint. His whole body stiffened, and his moan was pleasure, and release, and relief, all rolled into one.

12

Usually, a good hunt would restore Armand's mood as much as good brandy used to in his mortal days. But tonight's hunt had failed to erase even the tiniest bit of the stress and strain. He had brought the tranquilizer gun in hopes that Gabriel would make an appearance and try to stop the hunt. If Armand could just make *some* progress . . .

Instead, he returned to the house empty-handed. Two of his vampires were dead. Four of his mortals were dead. And he had no leads on the whereabouts of either Gabriel or Brigitte. His heart quailed at the idea of telling all this to *La Vieille,* but he had no choice but to make his report.

The phone call was as hellish as he'd expected. *La Vieille* had ranted at him, her fury prickling his skin like needles as he tried to pretend he still felt hopeful of success.

Afterward, he lay on his bed and stared at the ceiling, feeling strangely numb. Perhaps this had been a lost cause from the very beginning.

Armand grunted in exasperation. This was not the kind of battle one could give up on. Had he given up on the field of Agincourt? The forces of the French army had been overwhelming; the English had been exhausted, bedraggled, and vastly outnumbered. But when victory had turned first to defeat, then to bloody rout, Armand had never once considered the possibility of fleeing. When he saw Charles fall from his horse, Armand had cut a swath through the enemy to save his friend's life, then held off three men while giving Charles the chance to run.

He'd never blamed Charles for running, even though Armand had taken a killing blow himself trying to defend his escape. Charles had been wounded, his horse and sword lost. There would have been nothing he could have done except die at his friend's side, making Armand's gesture futile.

Armand had been willing to stand his ground in that blood-soaked, muddy field, and he would stand his ground now. And, dammit, he was going to win.

Desperate for some relief from his own thoughts, Armand was out of bed and halfway down the hall before a sweep with his psychic senses told him Faith wasn't in her room tonight. Grinding his teeth, he turned to look behind him, eyes focused on the room at the other end of the hall. The room where Faith lay in the arms of a Killer.

While Armand had pushed her into Drake's arms for his own purposes, he was not a total fool. He knew she went willingly to Drake's bed when she would only come to his under the influence of glamour.

Jealousy, sharp and bitter, flooded his senses. Why should she prefer Drake? As Armand had reminded her earlier, the man was a Killer, and when he was as old as Armand, he would most likely have killed the same number of people. So why did she somehow judge him the lesser of two evils? Why didn't she see how much Armand had done for her, and for Lily, in the years she had served him? He'd protected them both—she had to know that—when he had no selfish reason to do so. He'd never forced her to kill, never forced her to embrace her true nature and make herself a useful part of his entourage. Was it so unreasonable of him to expect her to be grateful?

Knowing he was acting like a besotted fool, he nonetheless crept down the hall, closer and closer to that closed door. His nostrils flared as he picked up the ever-so-faint scent of sex. Unexpected pain stabbed through his chest, and he gritted his teeth against the urge to burst through the door and kill the man who dared to touch her.

Still fighting against those primitive urges, he stood before the door and seethed. Until he heard the faint murmur of voices within. Then he leaned forward and closed his eyes, listening to what he most definitely did not want to hear.

* * *

THOUGH DAYLIGHT WAS still hours away, Drake found himself dozing, his body deliciously sated, his chest against Faith's back, his arms around her as he drank in her warmth. He was far more relaxed than he'd been ever since the *Seigneur* had arrived on the doorstep—perhaps since much longer ago than that—and he wished he could bask in the afterglow forever. He didn't want to think anymore, didn't want to worry or plan. He inhaled Faith's womanly scent, spiced with the musk of their lovemaking, and felt his lips curve in a contented smile.

He was starting to drift off to sleep again when Faith stirred against him, the delicious friction of skin against skin waking his body and his mind.

"May I ask you a personal question?" she asked, sounding almost as sleepy as he felt.

He kissed a line from just below her ear all the way down to her shoulder, and she shuddered with pleasure.

"I take it that's a no?" she asked breathlessly.

He chuckled and planted another kiss on the curve of her neck. "Do I get a reward for answering?"

She spun in his arms until she faced him. Her cheeks were flushed with color, her eyes wide and dark, but her expression was grave despite her obvious arousal. "You don't have to answer if you don't want to."

He brushed the back of his hand over the softness of her cheek, her presence warming him from the inside out. "What do you want to know?"

She bit her lip anxiously. "How did you become a vampire?"

Drake stared at Faith's upturned face and for the first time in his life felt tempted to answer that question. Eli had only asked him about his transition once and had gracefully accepted Drake's unwillingness to answer. Drake couldn't count how many Guardians had asked him, and never had he been willing to tell them anything. It was almost as if by not talking about it, he could maintain the illusion in his mind that it had never happened.

"Is it really that terrible?" Faith asked, a frown puckering her brow.

He smoothed the frown away with his thumb. The temptation to talk didn't go away.

"It's not that it's so terrible. It's just that . . . I hate to talk about the man I once was." But he realized he was going to do it anyway.

"My mother was a socialite in New York. She and some of her friends visited Five Points, which was one of the most dangerous and reviled neighborhoods anywhere, on some kind of charitable mission, and she and my father struck up a flirtation. My father was a charming Irishman, and my mother was dreadfully naïve.

"I was the result of their dalliance, but of course she wasn't about to marry a man like my father. Not that I think he'd have married her, either—he was a hard-hearted gangster who wasn't exactly known for his honor.

"Her family tried to marry her off to avoid disgrace, but things just didn't work out. There was too much gossip, too many people who knew who the father of her baby was.

"When I was ten, my mother finally met a man who could overlook her past. He married her, and made a cursory effort to be a stepfather to me, but he was one of those people who believed that bluebloods were inherently better than everyone else. That I was some kind of lesser being because of who my father was. So when I got caught shoplifting a piece of candy on a dare from my friends, my stepfather felt sure that my true breeding was shining through. He threatened to leave my mother if she didn't get rid of me. So she handed me off to my father in Five Points, and I never saw her again."

Faith made a little cry of distress, and Drake could see the pity in her eyes. He couldn't blame her—he pitied his younger self, too.

"My father was married by then, and had three other sons. He thought I was soft and spoiled, and my half-brothers took their cues from him. It was mutual hatred from the first time we all met."

Still hating the memories, he told Faith how he'd molded himself to the culture of Five Points, how he'd toughened himself, hardened his heart, locked out everything his mother had taught him.

"To carve out my place, I didn't just have to be as mean and tough as everyone else. I had to be meaner and tougher." He grimaced. "And I was. By the time I was eighteen, it was almost as if my time with my mother had never existed. I'd erased it from my mind." Or at least locked it in a dark closet.

"My father was working himself up in the ranks of his gang, and when I was twenty-five, he finally scratched and clawed his way to the top. I was his enforcer, the guy he sent to beat the crap out of anyone who crossed him." He closed his eyes to avoid seeing Faith's face. "I even killed for him. These weren't innocents I was killing by any stretch of the imagination. But it really bothers me now to remember how little it bothered me then."

"If you'd let the killing bother you then," Faith said, "you'd have opened the floodgates to let everything else bother you, too."

He opened his eyes and was surprised to see no censure on her face. She must have seen his surprise, for she gave him a sympathetic smile.

"Do you think I don't know what it's like to shut yourself off from your feelings to protect your sanity? How do you think I managed to survive six years with Armand?"

"At least you have a noble purpose," he countered. "You're trying to protect your sister."

She reached up and stroked his face again. He loved the feel of her fingers on his skin. "Protecting yourself is a noble purpose, too. You didn't deserve what happened to you."

Her warm-hearted defense moved him so much his throat tightened and for a moment he couldn't speak. But there was still a lot left to this story, and she might not be so forgiving when she'd heard it all.

"My half-brothers still hated me, and they resented any attention my father paid to me. Once he'd trained me to be a true Five Points gangster, he started treating me like some kind of favorite. You can imagine how much my brothers appreciated that. The more my father seemed to like me, the worse my brothers treated me. Except for the youngest, Eamon, who was born shortly after I came to Five Points. He was different from the rest. By the time he was old enough to notice such things, my father had accepted me, and Eamon could never understand why the others didn't.

"It was no secret that except for Eamon, my brothers hated me. But because of what I did for my father, there were plenty of other people in Five Points who hated me at least as much. So one day, my brothers decided they'd had enough of me, and that there were enough people who hated me that they could pin my death on someone else.

"They cornered me and tried to beat me to death. Obviously, I wasn't quite dead when they left me, but they had every reason to believe I would be within minutes.

"And that's how Padraig, my maker, found me. He was the leader of a rival gang who called themselves Blood and Death, and we knew each other on a casual level. He certainly knew of my reputation. When he found me, he figured I'd make a good addition to his crew, so he made me."

Faith shuddered in his arms. "A gang of vampires? How could they have any rivals when everyone around them was human? Surely they should have been top of the heap."

Drake nodded. "I'm sure they could have been, had they wished to. But in the U.S., where we have a relatively low vampire population, secrecy is crucial. Padraig knew better than to set himself and his vampires up for the kind of violence and scrutiny that would go with being on top. It wasn't like he rolled over for anyone, but he never fully stretched his wings, either.

"When I came to and found out what had happened to me, there was a part of me that was just sick to death of the whole lifestyle. A part of me that remembered how . . . civilized my life had once been. You have to realize, there is no place in modern America that is as vile and lawless as Five Points was back then. It was a dreadful, soulless way to live, and my brush with death had made me question just what I'd become in my effort to survive.

"But there was another part of me that overflowed with hatred for my brothers. It's not like I hadn't known they hated me, and it's not like I felt any particular loyalty to them beyond what was absolutely necessary based on our belonging to the same gang—and the same father. But I'd honestly never thought they hated me enough to kill me.

"Even *that* I might have been able to . . . well, not forgive, but maybe let go. But they didn't just shoot me in the head and have done with it. They made sure my death was as slow as they could manage with fists and feet, and any time I passed out, they made sure to revive me until I was so close to death they couldn't anymore."

Drake had let his eyes slide closed, his mind spiraling back to the past, to the misery and pain of that encounter. He was jerked back into the present by a wet tickle on his chest.

He opened his eyes and saw tear tracks on Faith's cheeks. His heart squeezed at the sight, and he tried to brush the tears away with his fingers.

"Please don't cry," he begged. "This was all a very long time ago, you know."

She sniffled. "I know. I just can't imagine how I would have felt in your place."

No, he very much doubted that she could. Perhaps her experiences with the *Seigneur* had hardened her in some ways, but she couldn't possibly imagine the seething mass of hatred and resentment that was Johnnie Drake. No doubt somewhere deep inside him, he'd been emotionally traumatized by his brothers' betrayal. But that hurt was buried under layer upon layer of fury and hate.

"I told you before that Padraig was a very charismatic and influential man. He wanted me just the way I was, as an explosion waiting to happen, a bogeyman to frighten even the strongest of men. So he fed and nurtured my hatred while I recuperated. And he kept my identity hidden for months, letting my brothers believe I was dead—even though my body was never found, which I suspect worried them.

When I went out, it was always in the darkest part of the night, and the targets he sent me after never lived to tell the tale.

"Then finally, he gave me permission to take my revenge, and he sent three of his older fledglings with me for backup. It was overkill, but the idea was that I would personally kill each of my brothers, and the other fledglings would make sure no one escaped while I was busy.

"So one night, we managed to corner them in the perfect dark, deserted alley." Drake's soul cringed at the memory. At the time, he'd been so wrapped up in being Johnnie Drake, the soulless Killer, that he'd felt nothing but a surge of triumph.

Since he'd gone to Philadelphia and changed his ways, he'd never felt much in the way of remorse for the people he'd killed. His surety that they were evil had shielded his conscience. But there'd always been a tinge of sadness in him. A wish that he didn't have to kill, and a wish that there weren't so many reprehensible human beings in the world.

When he'd confronted his brothers, he hadn't felt a single scrap of such honorable emotion.

"I killed them all," he said, his voice flat and dull. "I showed them my fangs from the first moment we managed to surround them, then I killed them one at a time. I didn't use any glamour, and neither did my fellow fledglings. We used brute force to keep them contained, made sure that they were fully aware of what we were and how they would die."

Drake's mouth tasted sour, and the memory felt so

dirty he wanted to take a shower. When he'd done his father's bidding, Drake had felt next to nothing for his victims. He'd shut off every human emotion and just done his job. But when he'd taken his revenge against his brothers, he'd been overcome with every imaginable unclean emotion.

With distance, he knew that much of what he'd felt then was the triumph of the predatory instincts that were inherent in all vampires, even the Guardians. But he still hated to remember the gleeful killing machine he had been.

"When they were all dead," he continued, "I didn't feel a hint of anything that resembled remorse. My fellow fledglings congratulated me on a job well done, and it looked like I'd firmly cemented my place in the Blood and Death gang.

"Until we discovered young Eamon, who'd witnessed the whole thing.

"He was fifteen years old, a scrawny kid who didn't have the family gift for violence. He'd been following my other brothers around, hoping to find a way to sneak into their inner circle. He'd been hidden behind a pile of rubbish, and we'd all been too engrossed in our game to notice him until it was all over and he couldn't help sniffling.

"There really and truly was no such thing as an innocent in Five Points, but Eamon was about as close as you could get. He was the only one of my brothers I had any loyalty to, and he was basically a good kid. But not only had he seen me kill my other brothers, he'd seen how I'd done it, seen that I was a vampire. He had to have seen the fangs on my fellow fledglings.

"The moment we found him, I knew he was in big trouble. My . . . companions offered me the chance to kill him, but of course I refused, and I tried to convince them that Eamon would never tell anyone what he'd seen. Hell, even if he'd told, no one would have believed him.

"But Blood and Death believed in keeping the secret of our powers buried deep so no mortal would know what we were until it was too late.

"The other fledglings were all older and more powerful than I, and they also outranked me. I got between them and Eamon and told him to run. They ordered me to stand aside, and I didn't. But it was a useless effort.

"I tried my best to fight them, but all I managed to do was piss them off. One of them ran off to catch Eamon while the other two detained me. Eamon didn't get far, and the vamp who caught him dragged him back to the alley. They again gave me the opportunity to kill him myself, but I was determined I was going to save him.

"If I'd just used my head and accepted the inevitable, I could at least have given him a quick and painless death." Drake heard the hoarseness that had crept into his voice and shut up. In his mind's eye, he still saw Eamon's terrified face, still saw the way he'd pleaded with Drake with his eyes.

Even after what Eamon had seen him do to his other brothers, he'd believed in Drake, had trusted him to save him.

"I made it so much worse for him," he said, his voice little more than a whisper now. "I prolonged his misery because I just wouldn't accept that there was nothing I could do to help him. And because I was being so difficult, I made the others mad. Instead of taking it out directly on me, they took it out on Eamon. He didn't die quickly."

Drake's heart slammed against his breastbone, old pain gnawing at his belly as memory forced its way past his defenses. The aching lump in his throat wouldn't let another word out, and every muscle in his body was stretched taut by tension.

Faith wrapped her arms around him and pulled him closer, holding him tightly as he struggled for control. He inhaled the rich, womanly scent of her and tried with all his might to drag his mind back into the present.

"I'm so sorry," Faith said, and in her voice he heard the tears that he refused to shed.

They lay in silence, holding each other, giving each other warmth and comfort, for a long while. Eventually, Drake managed to pull back at least partway into the present. He cleared his throat to get rid of any remaining tightness.

"Afterward," he said, "the fledglings brought me back to Padraig and reported what I'd done, how I'd refused to follow their orders. I was barely coherent at the time, in as close to a state of shock as a vampire can be. Padraig ordered the others out and used that legendary charm of his to help bring me back to myself.

"He then offered me my choice of punishments. He could kill me, or he could exile me. I knew that for a fledgling as young as myself, exile was as good as death. I was bound to infringe on some older, more powerful vampire's turf, and that would be the end of me. But even knowing that, and even though a part of me felt I deserved to die, I couldn't resign myself to it. And so I chose exile."

"I'm so glad you did," Faith said, hugging him harder. "You're a good man, Drake. The world's a better place with you in it. No matter what mistakes you may have made in the past."

He appreciated her words and her sentiment. But that didn't mean he was convinced.

If Drake hadn't been so full of hatred, if he hadn't been so hell-bent on getting his revenge, Eamon would have lived to be an adult. Maybe he even would have escaped from Five Points and lived a good life.

No, Drake might have tried his best to live a virtuous life ever since that dreadful night. And he might even have succeeded for the most part. But he doubted anything would ever erase the lingering taint of guilt that had clung to him now for more than a century.

13

CHARLES COULDN'T SLEEP. The sun had risen hours ago. For a while, he'd tried lying down and closing his eyes, but the effort to keep still had only made him more agitated. And so he'd sprung from his bed and gotten dressed once more, pacing the confines of his room and wondering if he'd completely taken leave of his senses.

Last night, everything had suddenly become so clear to him. The mission was doomed. Armand was doomed. Nothing Charles could do would help him.

The only person he could even hope to help was Lily. If only Armand had listened to him and left Lily at home where she'd belonged! Charles had felt sure they could ensure her safety, but Armand had been adamant that she couldn't remain in France without his protection. The damn fool.

If Armand kept bumbling around as he'd been doing, with Brigitte and Henri picking them off one by one, how could Charles know Lily's wouldn't be the next dead body they found? He couldn't let that happen! And there was only one way he could think of to make sure she was safe—they had to get her back to France as soon as possible. Unfortunately, there was no chance in Hell they were going home until their mission either succeeded or failed.

It had been childishly easy for Charles to overcome the search party he'd been leading. He'd killed Jacques before the fledgling had any idea what was happening, and Drake and Eric were no match for the glamour of a six-hundred-year-old vampire. Clearly, it had been the only way. They needed to get home, and Brigitte would draw out the game as long as she could for the sheer pleasure of it. All he'd done was hurry things along a little.

Only after he'd retired to his bedroom had Charles begun to absorb the enormity of what he'd done.

When *La Vieille* had first approached him with his secret mission to spy on his best and oldest friend, he'd been sickened by the idea. Consumed with guilt. And he'd prayed that the betrayal she'd planned would never come to pass. Now, he was actively trying to bring about the very fate he'd sworn he'd give anything to avoid.

What kind of monster was he?

Worst of all was coming back to the house and discovering all the mortals slaughtered—and Lily left alive. Suggesting that Brigitte did indeed intend to spare the girl. He had killed Jacques for no reason. He hadn't had any particular fondness for the fledgling, but he hadn't disliked him. Hadn't really *wanted* him to die. But it was too late now.

Had he been lying to himself all along? The gnawing, knotted feeling in his gut suggested that he had.

The sun was high in the sky, and though the pull of the daytime sleep made every movement of his limbs sluggish, Charles knew he would not be able to succumb. He didn't have the energy to pace anymore, so he sat on the edge of his bed and tried to figure out where to go from here.

When his cell phone rang, he practically jumped out of his shoes, his heart leaping into his throat. The phone rang a second time, and he took a deep breath, trying to soothe his shattered nerves. Who could possibly be calling him at this hour? *La Vieille* would be awake, no doubt, but she wouldn't expect Charles to be.

Approaching the phone as he might a poisonous snake, he flipped it open and looked at the number. It wasn't familiar. He answered anyway.

"Hello?"

"I hope I didn't wake you," Brigitte said.

Once more, Charles's heart seemed to stutter in his chest. "What do you want?" he asked, his voice little more than a gasp.

She laughed. "I heard the so-sad news about Jacques's untimely demise last night. You can imagine how surprised I was to find out what Henri and I had been up to. Considering you and I both know we were nowhere near the scene of the crime."

Charles swallowed hard. If Brigitte were to make a

similar phone call to Armand—or worse, to *La Vieille* . . . ! Armand might take Charles's word over Brigitte's, but *La Vieille* would not. Dread suffused him until he could hardly breathe.

"One can only deduce that you yourself were the culprit in that particular murder," Brigitte continued, her tone light and playful despite her words. "One then begins to wonder what you're up to."

He could think of nothing to say, the terror that gripped him too overwhelming to allow a single sound from his throat. He'd thought himself safe from *La Vieille*'s wrath, had been willing to damn his soul to escape a fate worse than death. Had he just condemned himself to the very fate he'd been so desperate to avoid?

"Come now, Charles," Brigitte prompted. "Tell me *everything*. Perhaps if I like your story, you and I can come to some kind of . . . accord?"

Charles hesitated only a moment. Brigitte had him completely in her power now. He hadn't thought she cared about him enough to sink her claws into him, but if she did, he was doomed. All he could do was hope that she might find some advantage in keeping his secret.

And so he did exactly as she commanded. He told her everything, including his desire to keep Lily from *La Vieille*'s clutches.

"Why, how sweet of you, Charles," she said when he was finished. "I never knew you were such a sentimental creature." She giggled. "Who am I to stand in the way of true love?"

Charles swallowed hard. "Do you think it's possible we could come to an agreement?" If he was willing to betray Armand to *La Vieille,* surely it was no more evil an act to betray him to Brigitte and Henri.

"I must admit, I could find uses for a six-hundred-year-old ally, as long as he proved himself worthy of me."

"And what would I have to do to prove myself worthy?"

He could almost see her tapping her chin while cold calculation filled her eyes. "First of all, you could rid me of the other useless fledgling Armand has by his side."

Charles's conscience twinged at the thought of killing Lily's sister, but once again he reminded himself that death was a far preferable fate to the one that awaited her in France.

Then he frowned, belatedly realizing that Armand still had his own fledgling with him. "Do you mean Faith, or Louis?" he asked.

"Louis. I have something entirely different in mind for the lovely Faith. Henri is quite taken with her, you know, and I've promised him a reward for all his years of faithful service."

Charles fought a shudder. Handing Faith over to Henri would be another in the long list of black marks against his soul.

"And of course, if you were to prove yourself as faithful as Henri, I would be happy to reward you as well. The girl could be yours for all eternity. It's true that if you took her home to my mother, she might agree that giving her to you would hurt Armand dreadfully. But I still think Armand is sentimental enough that he'd prefer her to live as your love slave than die in my mother's dungeons. And my mother would know that. Your chances of winning her are much greater if you ally yourself with me rather than with my mother."

Charles hardened his heart, realizing that Brigitte was right. He could be useful to her. And it would make sense for her to keep him happy by giving him Lily. *La Vieille* might make him *Seigneur* in Armand's place, but Charles had never hungered for that kind of power. If he could have Lily, at least he would have saved one innocent life. Even if saving that life came at a terrible price.

"Very well," he said. "Louis will not live to see another sunset."

"I'm delighted to hear that. We'll talk again later, I'm sure. Have a lovely day."

The line went dead, and Charles gently lowered the phone. Trying his best not to think about what he was doing, or how far he'd fallen, he slipped out of his room and padded down the hall, then up the stairs to the third floor, where Louis slept.

* * *

IT WAS AFTER sunset when Armand woke and realized something was wrong. His limbs still felt heavy, his mind sluggish with the remains of the daylight sleep—even though he usually awoke hours before sunset—and it took a while for him to discern the cause of that feeling of wrongness.

He came fully awake and let out a stream of curses when he realized he no longer sensed Louis in his head. There was only one reason why he should be unable to sense his fledgling—Louis was dead.

An additional jolt of adrenaline rushed through him, and he reached out with his senses, holding his breath until he found Faith's psychic footprint. Relief washed over him, but it lasted only until he realized that she was not alone.

He gritted his teeth when he recognized Drake's psychic footprint beside her. Jealousy flooded his veins, and a white-hot anger filled his senses as he remembered standing outside that door last night, listening to Faith forgive Drake's every sin, listening to her make excuses for behavior she would have condemned in Armand. It had taken every scrap of his will not to burst through that door and tear her from the bastard's arms. The image of the two of them together had haunted him as he'd tried to sleep, and even when his mind had slipped into unconsciousness, he'd been plagued by dreams.

Since he'd begun his dalliance with Marie, he'd gone at least three months without taking Faith to bed and had never felt particularly deprived. But then, she had still been there, a fixture in his life—with no other man daring to sniff around her skirts.

Armand let out a sigh of frustration. Louis was dead, and here he was mooning over a woman whose heart would never be his. For years, he had mastered her body, but never her heart. He hadn't realized until now that the lack had bothered him.

About Louis's death, he felt next to nothing. Once upon a time, Louis had been one of his favorites, which was why Armand had brought him along in his foolish hope to protect him from *La Vieille*. But he had to admit that something inside him was shifting, changing. His sense of hope was dying, and a part of him had already started to let go.

Compared to the fate awaiting the rest of the delegation, Louis was lucky to be dead.

Furious, exhausted, filled with despair, Armand headed to the shower and hoped he could gather the shreds of his self-control before he had to face anyone. If he couldn't, he might not be able to stop himself from killing Drake tonight out of sheer spite. And though Faith might hate him for it even more than she already hated him now, he wasn't entirely sure it wouldn't be worth it.

The steam and hot water that should have been soothing served only to further narrow his focus and hone his fury. Even with Louis dead, Armand could think of nothing else except the image of Faith opening her legs, and maybe even her heart, for Drake. His hands curled into fists at his sides and he choked on a cry of rage.

And then, everything suddenly became clear in his mind. The difference between himself and Drake, at least in Faith's eyes. She'd seen Drake lose his temper last night, seen him driven to violence by his hunger. But she'd seen Armand do far worse. Hell, she'd *experienced* far worse from Armand. She knew Drake was a Killer, knew he wasn't the paragon of benevolence he pretended to be. But knowing something and seeing it were two very different things.

Armand knew Drake was hungry, though he didn't understand why the idiot didn't just go out and feed. If Drake wouldn't hunt, perhaps Armand could bring the food to him. His lips curled into a feral smile. He knew exactly what would happen when a hungry vampire came into contact with a helpless, wounded mortal. And if Faith were to witness the reality of Drake's nature, the clouds would be stripped from her eyes, and she would see him for the Killer he was.

* * *

FAITH WOKE TO the sound of the shower running. She stretched and yawned, a silly grin tugging at the corners of her mouth.

The room was almost pitch dark, the heavy black curtains blocking out all but the tiniest sliver of city lights. She rubbed her gritty eyes, then sniffed the air and found the scent of sex. The seductive smell sent a bolt of arousal straight to her center, and she rolled her eyes at herself. When had she become such a nympho?

The answer was easy: since she'd started having sex that touched something other than just her body.

But no. She couldn't allow herself to think that way. Privately, she could admit to herself that she felt an emotional connection to Drake, something that went beyond the physical. But she couldn't allow that emotion to rule her. Not when in all likelihood she would be forced to leave Baltimore in the near future.

More awake now, she remembered that she had come to Drake's room last night not with the intention of sleeping with him, but with the intention of begging him to help her spirit Lily away. Somehow, she'd never gotten around to asking him. She would have to remedy that soon. For all she knew, tonight could be her last chance. *La Vieille* was not famous for her patience, and everything had been going so dreadfully wrong since the moment they'd set foot in Baltimore. How long would they have before the witch ordered them to return to face an unimaginable punishment?

She heard Drake turn off the shower, and the thought of him naked and scrubbed clean, with beads of water trickling down his chest, derailed her train of thought completely. When moments later he emerged from the bathroom with a towel wrapped around his hips, her fangs instantly descended, and desire filled her mind.

Drake stood in the bathroom doorway, crossing his arms over his chest and grinning as he watched her watch him.

"You look like you have evil plans for me," he teased.

Unquestionably true. But she shook her head to try to dispel the fog of lust. As much as she might want him right now, sex couldn't be her first priority. Remembering Armand's threat about what would happen to Lily, to them all, if their mission failed, she managed to tame the raging of her blood.

Drake sensed her change of mood and came to sit on the edge of the bed. He was careful to keep the towel modestly wrapped around him, but it wasn't exactly lying flat. Faith's hormones acted up again, but she beat them back down.

His fingers twined with hers, and though there was no missing his continued arousal, he spoke mildly.

"What are you thinking that has you looking so serious?"

She took a deep breath. "I have an enormous favor to ask of you."

He kept his hold on her hand, but she could see walls springing up around his emotions as the expression in his eyes went blank. "I'm not telling you where Gabriel is. I don't know the answer, and even if I did, I wouldn't tell you. I'm sorry."

Faith jerked her hand out of his grip, anger flushing her cheeks. "You think I'm still trying to seduce information out of you? You think *that's* why I slept with you last night?" Hurt and anger warred in her chest, and if she weren't naked she might have made a sprint for the door.

Drake sighed and bowed his head. "I'm sorry," he said softly. "That was unfair of me."

Faith clamped her jaw shut and put a muzzle on her temper. What right did she have to bite his head off? She might not be planning to ask him for Gabriel's location, but she was still asking a favor after sleeping with him. It was a similar form of emotional blackmail, and once upon a time she'd never have imagined she'd sink so low.

"No," she murmured. "I'm the one being unfair. Asking you for favors on the morning after, so to speak, then snapping at you for questioning my motives."

Drake took her hand again, fingers twining with hers in a way that made her throat ache. She couldn't bear to look at him. When she'd come to his bed last night, she hadn't given a second thought to how her behavior would look the next day. Now she wondered how she could have been so naïve.

Drake's fingers tightened on hers, a reassuring squeeze that felt like an anchor when she was in danger of being swept away.

"Tell me what favor you wanted to ask," he said. "I can't promise anything, and my first responsibility has to be the Guardians, but if I can help you, I will. I hope you know that."

She forced a smile as she met his eyes. "I know." She swallowed hard around the painful lump in her throat. "Armand will never leave me and Lily unguarded. But he might leave Lily in the house when he goes hunting for Henri again. If there's any chance you or one of your Guardians could get her out . . ."

Drake frowned. "And do what with her? She's not a vampire, so it's not like she's a candidate to go to Philly and join the Guardians there." Faith opened her mouth to protest, but Drake cut her off. "Besides, the *Seigneur* would know we helped her, and I have a feeling he'd be able to persuade someone to tell him where we'd taken her. I don't have firsthand experience with how strong his glamour is, but I have every reason to suspect he'd be able to drag an answer out of anyone, even me, if he wanted to badly enough."

Faith knew that was true, but the image of Armand lying naked and asleep on the hotel bed suddenly flashed in her mind. She remembered thinking how helpless he'd been at that moment, how easy it would be to put a gun to his head and pull the trigger.

At the time, she'd still had the whole entourage to get through, even if she managed to kill Armand. Now, only Charles and Louis remained. The Guardians could take Louis, who was the youngest of Armand's fledglings now that Marie was dead, and she doubted Charles had the kind of ferocity necessary to interrogate anyone effectively.

"He couldn't drag an answer out of anyone if he was dead," she said, her voice calm even as she contemplated murder.

Drake regarded her steadily, his face giving nothing away. "What are you saying?" he asked.

She swallowed hard. "If you get me a gun, I can hide it in his room while he's out hunting tonight. Then when he comes back, I can . . . go to him. You can get Lily to safety while he's distracted. Then afterward, I can shoot him." While he lay helpless and sated and totally unaware of his danger.

"No!" Drake barked immediately.

"Why not?"

Drake calmed himself with a visible effort. "Let me count the ways. One, it's way too dangerous for you. Two, you'd still be leaving a child with no resources on her own in the streets. And three . . ." His voice died and he looked away. "Three," he started again more softly, "I really don't want you in his bed."

There was a warm glow in her chest at that admission. "I don't want to be there, either," she admitted. "But if that's the only way I can keep him away from Lily, then I'll do it. She deserves the chance to lead as normal a life as possible, given the circumstances. And she's resourceful. Worst case is she goes into foster care somewhere. That has to be better than life with Armand. Eventually, he's going to turn her and make her into his—" She couldn't say it, could hardly even bear to think it.

Drake's jaw visibly worked. "I understand. And I'll do whatever I can to help. But not this."

She clutched his arm, pleading with him with her eyes. "What if it's the only way?"

He cupped her cheek in his palm, and she closed her eyes to revel in the caress even as desperation continued to claw at her.

"Are you sure you could do it?" he asked softly. "Shoot him in cold blood?"

She nodded without opening her eyes. "I won't like it, but I'll do it. I want Lily safe, and she won't be until he's dead. If I have to be the one to send him to Hell, then so be it."

Taking in a deep, slow breath, she opened her eyes. If she thought too much about what she was proposing, she'd probably make herself sick. "Will you get me a gun?" she asked. "If it's the only way?"

He looked away, his hands clutching the edge of the bed so hard his knuckles turned white. It looked like a great battle raged behind his eyes, but he finally gave a short, curt nod.

"If I'm convinced it's the only way, then I'll get you a gun. But I'm not convinced yet. There's still hope."

Faith let out a deep sigh of relief. She, too, hoped there was another way. But she couldn't help fearing that her options were becoming more and more limited each day.

Tentatively, she reached out and touched Drake's shoulder, hating the tension that radiated from him, that showed in the tautness of his muscles and the stiffness of his posture. He didn't react to her touch at first, but when she trailed her fingers softly over his collarbone, a little of the tension eased away. Her own body reacted instantly to the feel of his bare skin under her fingers.

Her eyes roved the length of Drake's body. Their serious discussion had lowered the tent in the towel, but her scrutiny brought him up to full mast immediately.

"I don't want to talk about Armand anymore," she said, her voice suddenly husky.

"Good," he said, leaning in to her. "I don't, either."

His kiss started off deliciously soft, his lips roaming over hers as if he were discovering them for the first time. The tenderness of that kiss made her chest ache with longing. She wrapped her arms around him, feeling the lingering dampness of his skin, smelling the sandalwood soap that would forever be imprinted in her mind. His tongue dipped into her mouth, and she couldn't suppress a moan of pleasure. She felt his smile against her lips.

He pulled back just far enough to meet her gaze. "You haven't had your shower yet," he murmured.

She laughed without breaking eye contact. "Is that your way of telling me I smell bad?"

"No, that's my way of offering my services. I wouldn't want you to tire yourself out with the back-breaking labor of washing."

She laughed again, wondering how he could look so playful and so lustful at the same time. "You're right. That would be *exhausting*."

Brushing the covers aside, he scooped her up and carried her to the bathroom. Somehow the motion seemed to have dislodged his towel. Why did she think that wasn't an accident?

He had to put her down once they reached the bathroom, but at least she got another chance to devour him with her eyes as he turned the water on and adjusted the temperature. She couldn't resist the urge to reach out and pinch one firm cheek when he turned his back.

Drake jumped a little, then turned to face her with narrowed eyes. She might have thought he was genuinely angry with her, except there was an amused glint in those eyes.

"I'm going to make you pay for that," he warned.

"Oh yeah?" she taunted. "You and what army?"

Faith felt as if she'd transformed into a different

person entirely. Who was this playful creature who pinched her lover's butt and teased him when they were on their way to making love? She'd never thought of sex as anything even remotely playful before. But then, with Armand as her only lover for the past six years, was that any surprise?

Without warning, Drake pounced, crossing the short distance between them at lightning speed. Before she could even react, he'd grabbed her and turned her around, pressing her back firmly against his chest and pinning her arms to her sides with one strong arm. He bent his head so his breath tickled her ear when he spoke.

"No army. Just me."

Still keeping her arms pinned, he walked her forward until they were both inside the shower stall. He used his foot to slide the door closed, then positioned them both beneath the warm spray. His erection was a firm, hot presence in the small of her back.

"How exactly is this making me pay?" she asked, trying to wriggle to torment him a bit. Unfortunately, he was holding her too tightly.

"You'll see."

With his free hand, he grabbed the bar of soap. After wetting it, he touched the soap to her collarbone and began moving it in slow, sensuous circles, leaving a trail of lather across her skin.

Her eyes slid closed as the circles traveled across her body, slowly, slowly inching lower. When they reached the tops of her breasts, her breath hitched and she tried to arch her back to move his touch where she wanted it. Again, she found his grip too firm.

"Are you beginning to get the picture yet?" he whispered in her ear.

Oh yeah. She was getting the picture all right. Every nerve in her body seemed to have come to life and clamored for his touch. She knew his plan was to tease her unmercifully. And while she enjoyed being teased, now wasn't the time for it. Who knew when Armand would decide it was time to go hunting? It was in Faith's best interests to hurry things along a bit. Which would be a hell of a lot easier if she could move!

Drake set the soap back on its dish and began working the lather into her skin. The sandalwood scent surrounded her as steam billowed in the air. He rubbed the lather down the valley between her breasts, then along their undersides. Faith had to bite her tongue to keep from begging.

This was ridiculous. She was hardly powerless, even if he did have her practically immobilized. He was a hungry vampire. Which meant his self-control was questionable at best. His little torments had to be revving him up almost as much as they were her. All she had to do was try to push him past the breaking point. She might not be able to move, but that didn't mean she couldn't speak.

"If you let me move," she said in a breathless whisper, "I promise I'll make it worth your while."

His laugh was a breath of warmth against her neck.

His free hand caressed the lather onto the top of one breast, and once again she found herself trying to arch into the touch.

"I don't believe you," he said, then tasted the skin of her throat with a quick flick of his tongue.

Infuriating man! She squirmed some more with no success.

"You don't think I could make it worth your while?" she asked, trying to sound insulted.

"Oh, I'm sure you *could*. I'm just not sure I believe you *would*. I think you'd torture me just for spite. Women can be so vengeful."

"Yes," she agreed. "Maybe you should listen to your own words. If you let me move now, I'll give you time off for good behavior."

"I'll take my chances."

His hand slid between her breasts again, then drifted lower, soaping her ribcage and then starting on her abdomen. She bit her lip on a protest, imagining just how desperate he could make her by continuing the tease on her lower body. She couldn't bear it! So she decided to offer him a temptation she sincerely doubted he could refuse.

"I want to taste you," she said, her voice low and sultry.

Drake lost a little of his self-assurance, and his hand stilled for an instant. The hesitation brought a smile of feminine triumph to Faith's lips, even though he quickly recovered and reached for the soap.

"Nice try," he said. There was no mistaking the

desire that roughened his voice. He wet the bar of soap, then began to rub it up and down what he could reach of her thigh.

The touch almost made her forget her evil plan, but she recovered enough to whisper again.

"I want to feel you in my mouth." The pulsing heat at the small of her back told her how much he liked the idea. "I want to explore every inch of you with my lips and tongue." Another, more definite pulse, and the hand gripping the soap slowed its movements. "I want to suck you until—"

The bar of soap slipped from Drake's fingers and hit the shower floor. His grip on her loosened, and Faith took advantage, slipping out from under his arm and settling on the floor of the shower on all fours.

Water poured over her head and ran into her eyes, but her questing fingers found the soap. Even over the sound of the water pattering on the walls and floor, she could hear the shortness of Drake's breath, and she was surprised he hadn't fallen on top of her the moment she'd hit the floor in such a provocative position.

Wiping wet hair and rivulets of water from her face, she looked up at Drake from her knees and smiled.

"You dropped something," she said, holding up the bar of soap.

His eyes were dark with desire as he ran his tongue over his lips, flashing a whole lot of fang. He plucked the bar from her hand and shoved it back into the soap dish.

Faith suspected he was about to reach for her, but she was determined to keep her promise. She took a firm grip on the base of his erection, effectively freezing him in place. Then she touched her tongue to his tip, and he gasped.

This was something she'd never done when not under the influence of glamour. But there was no denying how much she wanted to, nor was there any denying that the desire came entirely from *her,* was not something being forced upon her by the will of another.

She opened her mouth wide and took in as much of him as she could manage. What she couldn't reach with her mouth, she stroked with her hand. Drake groaned, and from beneath her half-closed lashes she could see his hands fisted at his sides. He tasted rich and exotic, and her tongue glided over his flesh as she sucked gently, careful not to nick him with her fangs.

His hands opened and closed a couple of times as she continued to work him, loving the taste of him, loving the knowledge that while *she* was the one on her knees, *he* was the one who was helpless against her assault.

His fists turned white at the knuckles, and suddenly a low growl rose from Drake's throat. Before she knew what was happening, he'd torn himself from her mouth and hauled her to her feet. Then her back was against the wall, and his hands were under her bottom, lifting her off her feet. She did the only sensible thing, which was to wrap her legs around him.

His mouth crashed down on hers in a kiss that tasted of raging desire. One hand supported her bottom while the other slid between their bodies to adjust his position against her. Faith wriggled and helped as best she could.

When he finally slid inside her, they both paused the kiss to groan in bliss.

The pause didn't last long. Soon, he was pounding into her, his mouth once more melded with hers. She clung to his shoulders, digging her nails into his flesh. Drake didn't seem to mind.

Once again, his hand slipped between their bodies, and he began to stroke her as he thrust. There wasn't room for thought anymore. Only sensation. Only pleasure.

Faith felt herself teetering on the edge and tried desperately to hold on, waiting for Drake to reach the edge with her. He tore his mouth from hers and pressed his lips right up against her ear.

"Come for me," he commanded, and she couldn't help but obey.

The pleasure raced through her, starting at her center then radiating outward in rapid pulses until her fingers and toes curled with it. Over the pounding throb of her own heart, she heard Drake's half-strangled cry and knew that though he had pushed her over first, he'd followed right behind.

She clung to him with arms and legs, letting her

head come to rest against his shoulder as she drew in one burning breath after another. And though she knew that Lily had to be her first concern, she desperately wished that just this once, she could selfishly go after what she wanted for herself.

14

DRAKE WAS TUCKING his T-shirt into his pants, and Faith had just tied the belt on the robe he'd lent her, when the door to his room suddenly burst open. Faith jumped and whirled, but though Drake was as startled as she must have been, his first reaction wasn't fear, but . . . something else.

His fangs descended even before he had a hint of what was happening, and his heart rate skyrocketed as his nerves set up a clamor he could almost hear.

Standing in the doorway with an expression halfway between a smirk and a sneer, was the *Seigneur*. Faith was gaping at him, but at the moment he seemed to have eyes only for Drake. The smirk turned into a malicious smile as his nostrils flared.

"I see you've been the most accommodating of hosts," he said, and Drake's pulse picked up even more.

"Armand, what are you doing?" Faith asked, still looking at him like he'd lost his mind.

Armand kept his gaze on Drake even when he spoke to her. "Are you growing overfond of this man, Faith?"

"What?"

A low growl rose from Drake's throat, and he took a step forward. His rational mind reminded him that he was no match for a six-hundred-year-old Killer. But something had roused his most primitive instincts, instincts that didn't seem inclined to listen to his rational mind.

"I think you've been enjoying yourself in his bed," Armand continued as Drake fought to keep control of the beast inside him. "I think you've deluded yourself into believing he is a kinder, gentler Killer. I wouldn't want you to lose your heart to a lie."

"Armand, what are you talking about?" Faith asked, and she sounded genuinely confused.

Drake growled again, a feral sound that caused Faith to turn her puzzled look in his direction.

And that's when his mind finally caught up with his senses and he understood the clamor of his instincts. His nostrils flared as he recognized the scent of blood in the air, and the hunger roared in his ears.

"What have you done?" he asked the *Seigneur*, his voice barely his own. His muscles quivered with the strain of keeping his feet rooted in place.

The *Seigneur*'s malicious smile widened, and he stepped aside just enough to allow someone else into the room.

The girl was at most twenty years old, but it had been a hard twenty years. A passably pretty face was marred by far too much makeup, and the blond tresses that curled down over her shoulder had the coarse, brassy look of a cheap wig. She wore a midriff top that showed too many bony angles to be sexy, and her tight black miniskirt barely covered her sex. Clear plastic platform shoes made her look taller than she really was, and the mingled scents of alcohol, spearmint gum, and cum blended with the blood.

Drake swallowed hard, fighting desperately against the hunger that surged through his veins. The scent of blood came from a small cut along the fragile skin of her neck. She made no attempt to stanch the flow, her eyes glazed as she stared into some inner distance, her mind a slave to the *Seigneur*.

The *Seigneur* reached out and dipped a finger in the trail of blood, then stuck it in his mouth and made an appreciative sound.

"Why don't you have a taste, *mon ami*?" he taunted. "I assure you, the world will not miss one more whore."

"Armand, stop it!" Faith cried, stepping closer to him until he froze her with a glare.

"You forget your place, *ma petite*. Do not think to give me orders."

She bit her lip and her eyes widened in supplication. "Please don't do this."

He sniffed. "I'm doing nothing. Our friend here needs to feed or he risks losing control of himself. You wouldn't want such a thing to happen around young Lily, now, would you?"

"You bastard," she whispered, shaking her head.

Armand snarled at her. "Be careful what you say. I'm losing my patience with you."

The scent of blood filled Drake's head, and though he could see both Faith and the *Seigneur* in his peripheral vision, he couldn't drag his gaze away from the crimson trail down the prostitute's neck. She was just the kind of victim vampires like the *Seigneur* favored: the kind who could disappear from the face of the earth and cause nothing more than a raised eyebrow, if that, from the community. The kind even the mortal authorities saw as expendable.

"Come now, *mon ami*," the *Seigneur* said, his voice low and coaxing. "I know you are hungry. And here is a tempting morsel for you. You may be too far gone in your hunger to sustain your glamour, but I will hold her for you. She won't feel a thing."

Faith murmured something too low to hear. Drake tried with all his will to drag his gaze away from the blood, to look at Faith and remind himself of his humanity. But he couldn't do it. His breath came in short gasps, and his tongue tested the sharpness of his fangs. The vacant-eyed prostitute took a step closer to him.

"Look at him, Faith," Armand said. "Look at his eyes, how he stares at the blood. Why, he's practically drooling. He's a Killer. Not the saint you'd like him to be."

"He can't help it," Faith gasped.

"Neither can I," Armand countered. "I was a vampire for more than a century before I even heard rumor it was not necessary to kill. Far too late to break the addiction."

Faith sniffled, and the mortal woman continued to inch closer to Drake, the scent of her blood filling his senses so that everything else in the room seemed far away.

"Look at him and understand what he is. I will force myself to bear it if you share his bed, but I will not allow you to give him your heart."

Against his will, Drake reached out and touched the mortal's shoulders. His muscles quivered with the need to draw her to him, to sink his fangs into her neck and feed on her blood and her life.

"Please," Faith said, her voice faint and shaking. "Don't do this."

Drake didn't know if she was speaking to him or to the *Seigneur,* and at the moment, he hardly cared.

"You still think he's some kind of hero?" Armand asked, a hint of incredulity in his voice. "Ask yourself this—if I were to call Lily right this moment, would you trust him around her?"

Even in the haze of his bloodlust, Drake heard the oppressive silence that suddenly filled the room. Pain lanced through his heart.

"Answer the question, Faith. Would you trust a man like this around Lily? You've been with me six years. Have you ever for a moment feared for her life in my presence?"

"Please," Faith said again, her voice even softer than before.

"Answer the question. Shall I call Lily right now? Shall I take you and this bleeding creature out of the room and leave him alone with Lily? Answer me, dammit!"

"No." Faith's voice was barely a whisper, full of anguish.

"Say that again," the *Seigneur* demanded. "Would you trust Drake around your sister?"

"No," she repeated on a sob.

The pain in Drake's heart made him hunch his shoulders and wince. The prostitute was in his arms now, her body pressed against him, her bleeding throat within easy striking range. Drake peeled his lips away from his fangs. He closed his eyes for the strike, but something held him back despite the urgency of his need. He turned his head and opened his eyes, meeting Faith's horrified gaze.

There was only the barest scrap of humanity left in him, but he used it to shove the prostitute away from him. He had to get out. Now. But Armand stood between him and the door.

Without thinking, Drake ran for the window, ripping the curtain aside and flinging himself at the glass. He heard Faith's shrill scream as the glass shattered, the shards biting into his flesh to leave trails of pain. In the street below, someone else screamed as he fell from the second-story window to the pavement. He rolled with the impact, more shards of glass slicing his skin as he did.

The breath was knocked out of him for a moment, and he lay there dazed as the nearby pedestrians ran to him, shouting at each other to call 911. The hunger surged at the smell of his own blood in the air. Using every last ounce of his will, Drake pressed his lips together so no one would see the fangs, then forced himself to his feet and ran, ignoring the cries of the Good Samaritans behind him.

* * *

FAITH STARED AT the window through which Drake had jumped. Shards of glass clung to the frame like jagged teeth, some of them stained with Drake's blood. Not speaking to her, Armand crossed the room and looked out the window. The sacrificial mortal he had brought still stood frozen in the middle of the room, her eyes staring straight ahead, seeing nothing.

Someone pounded on the door, and Faith heard Armand utter some bland explanation for the disturbance, but all she could think about was the look on Drake's face when she'd said she wouldn't trust him with Lily. The misery in his eyes had stopped her breath in her lungs, and she hated herself for letting Armand manipulate her like this. Again.

She sensed him coming near her and stepped away, eyes averted. She couldn't stand even to look at him, and if Drake had gotten her the gun already she would have shot him dead.

"I'm sorry—" Armand started, and Faith actually snarled at him like a feral cat, her sense of self-preservation overwhelmed by her outrage.

"Don't even speak to me," she spat, so angry she wanted to gouge his eyes out with her nails.

To her surprise, he didn't snarl back. For long, agonizing minutes he stood there beside her, not speaking, not moving. Faith struggled to calm herself, to put the anger she usually kept so carefully contained back in the cage where it belonged. Every cell in her body revolted at the idea of submitting to him, of following his orders and treating him with the respect he demanded. But she had to think of Lily. If she gave in to the urge to tell him exactly what she thought of him, then very likely she wouldn't be around to protect Lily. And that was unacceptable.

When Armand spoke again, his voice was very soft and held none of the malice he'd exuded earlier.

"I meant to show you that Drake was as much a monster as I," he said. "It appears I've merely proven to you how monstrous I myself can be."

Faith was so startled by the admission that her eyes were drawn to him against her will. He was staring at the floor, the corners of his eyes and mouth tight with strain. His Adam's apple bobbed as he swallowed, then shook his head.

"I must apologize for my behavior," he said, still looking at the floor. His voice had turned crisp and businesslike, but not enough so to mask the turmoil in his expression. "It was . . . childish of me. His control was excellent for one so hungry. Had Lily been here, she would have been perfectly safe."

A lump swelled in Faith's throat, but she refused to cry. Armand had so much power over her, but in this one thing she would stand firm—she would not let him make her cry.

He sighed heavily. "I will return this young woman to where I found her. When I come back, we shall hunt Henri once more."

Faith's jaw dropped. "You're going to let her go?" She'd assumed the girl was doomed from the moment Armand had approached her.

Armand shrugged. "We fed last night. Her mind has been absent throughout. What reason have I to kill her?" Some of the usual steel returned to his voice and posture. "Have you ever known me to kill without reason? Is that the kind of monster you believe I am?"

She would never apologize for her opinion of him, but she knew that was one crime of which he was not guilty. "No, *Seigneur*."

He waited for the span of several heartbeats, perhaps hoping she would say something more. She stepped up to the window instead, looking out, reaching with her psychic senses, ignoring Armand while she searched for Drake. But he was long gone.

* * *

WHEN ARMAND RELEASED the whore from his glamour, she succumbed to the effects of the alcohol of which she reeked and collapsed onto the pavement. He coaxed her out of the way of the pedestrians, then tucked a bill into her exposed bra. She thanked him drunkenly, and he left her to sleep it off while he walked back to the house, trying to stay alert for Henri's presence while inside his thoughts flew and collided with one another.

He had made a complete and utter fool of himself tonight. He didn't even think he needed the mirror that was Faith's eyes to see that. Her heart would never be his. He knew that with unshakable certainty. Indeed, he wasn't even sure if it was her heart he wanted. Perhaps it was no more than her respect, or even her approval that he sought. If so, he had chosen a spectacularly bad way to go about obtaining it.

And since when did it matter to him what one insignificant woman thought of him? He was a *Seigneur*. It was his job to rule and control his people. It was not his job to be liked by them. A *Seigneur* couldn't afford sentimentality, couldn't afford softness of any sort. If he could cut himself off from his emotions completely, that would be best of all. Unfortunately, such was not possible.

His cell phone rang. His blood ran cold when he saw *La Vieille*'s number on the caller ID. He wasn't sure how he could maintain any hint of composure with the devil on the line, but he had no choice but to answer.

"I just got off the phone with my daughter," *La Vieille* said after Armand's cautious greeting. "She informs me that you've lost yet another of your entourage."

It wasn't something he could deny. "Yes, Your Excellency."

He felt the sizzle of her power all around him, making the air thin and hard to breathe.

"I am losing patience with you, *Seigneur,*" she said. "I did not send you to America to amuse my daughter with your comedy of errors."

"My deepest apologies, Your Excellency," he answered, trying not to gasp in the oxygen-starved air.

She made a rude noise. "Your apologies mean nothing to me! I grow tired of your incompetence. Tomorrow night at midnight your time, I shall call again. If you do not have concrete progress to report, I shall consider that a sign that you are a lost cause. Am I understood?"

"Yes, Your Excellency."

"And remember, dearest *Seigneur,* I have an insurance policy in place. Should you or your people attempt to flee my wrath, your punishment will be ever so much worse."

Armand tried to ignore the fear that chilled his spine, but between that and the thin air, he couldn't find the will to offer the polite response she awaited. But perhaps *La Vieille* understood the reason for his silence and was thus satisfied, for she didn't scold his lack of response. She simply hung up, leaving him alone to fight the demons of terror and despair.

By the time he'd reached the house once more, something vaguely resembling peace—or, perhaps more accurately, resignation—had settled over him.

There was still a chance that by *La Vieille*'s deadline, he would be able to report some concrete progress and gain a stay of execution. But once *La Vieille* decided he'd failed, there would be no hope for the survival of any of the delegation.

If Faith and Lily were to escape the price of failure, they would have to do so *before* he failed. And that left him but one option—he had to set them free.

15

DRAKE PUT AS much distance as he could between himself and the house, striding blindly down the street, still fighting to rein himself in. His glamour assured that he wouldn't be noticed by passersby, so he passed through their midst, an unseen presence.

The wounds where the glass had sliced his skin had closed up, though he could still smell the coppery scent of blood. That scent continued to stir his hunger, though he was at least marginally in control of himself. For all his hunger, for all his rage, he did not feel particularly tempted to drag a random pedestrian into a dark alley.

He kept his head down, his jaw clamped, trying to think through the fog that clouded his mind.

When he did manage to think, he was not at all happy with his thoughts, which hovered around the leaden moment when Faith admitted she wouldn't trust him with Lily. Not that he could blame her. His control had hung on the thinnest of threads, and there was no way she could have looked at him and not seen that. Why should she think he could resist the temptation of a helpless mortal victim when the predator inside him had so clearly been awakened?

There was no reason at all, and yet he couldn't help the ache in his heart, the sour taste of betrayal in his mouth. He had thrown himself out a second-story window to avoid killing a woman he didn't know, a woman whom some people would see as the dregs of society. How could Faith imagine he would harm an innocent child?

"You know," said a voice from behind his left shoulder, "if you're ready to pull your head out of your ass and come back to the real world, we have things to talk about."

Drake jumped and whirled around, not quite believing what he thought he'd heard. He stared at the spike-haired, leather-clad, baby-faced figure who stood grinning behind him, and blinked. The figure didn't go away.

"Gabriel?" he asked stupidly.

The grin grew wider. "Surprised?"

Drake shook his head in confusion. "But how . . . ?"

The grin faded, replaced with a much flatter expression. "Brigitte had me bricked up in a basement in the middle of bumfuck nowhere. There wasn't even a lock on the door I could use my telekinesis on. Eventually, a mortal wandered close enough to the property that I was able to snag him with my glamour and have him break me out with a sledgehammer."

Gabriel started walking, beckoning Drake to follow with a jerk of his chin. Drake stared at the pavement as he fell into step beside the older vampire.

"I assume you've spoken with Jez," Drake said.

"Yes."

"And she told you she wants me out of Baltimore."

"Yes. And I told her we'd talk about it later. We have more important things to think about right now than your feuding."

Drake cut him a sharp look. "I'm not the one feuding."

But Gabriel shook his head. "I told you, there are more important things to talk about. We'll talk about your future when we're not under invasion."

Drake came to a stop, unwilling to let the subject go. "You expect me to fight for you, to risk my life, when you might send me packing?"

Gabriel gave him one of his cold stares. "Yes, I do. Or are you so mercenary that you have to know what's in it for you before you agree to help?"

Drake winced and looked away.

"Sorry," Gabriel said with surprising gentleness. Gentleness was not ordinarily something he was very good at. "Spending several days bricked up in an eight-by-ten room hasn't exactly done wonders for my temper."

"No, you're right. I'm the one who needs to apologize."

Gabriel clapped him on the shoulder and they both started walking again. "Good. Now that we've got that out of the way, tell me what happened at the house tonight. Jez tells me there was a disturbance of some sort that apparently had nothing to do with Brigitte."

As quickly and unemotionally as possible, Drake told him what had happened. Afterward, they walked for a long time in silence. Drake was so lost in misery that it wasn't until they'd arrived in Gabriel's preferred hunting grounds that he realized where they were going. The hunger was a constant, tormenting ache in his chest and belly, but after his performance this evening, Drake could hardly bear the thought of feeding.

"Don't be a moron," Gabriel said sharply, easily reading Drake's expression. "You need to feed. You're no good to anyone if you can't control yourself."

"I know that!" Drake snapped back.

Gabriel gave a soft snarl, then grabbed Drake by the shirt and hauled him forward until they were nose to nose. Although Gabriel had stopped aging around the age of twenty, the steely expression of those gray-green eyes was not that of a twenty-year-old.

"I don't have the patience to deal with sulking and self-pity," Gabriel growled into his face. "If you'd like me to kick the shit out of you in punishment for your crimes, I'll be happy to oblige. And if that doesn't convince you to get your head back into the game, then I'll try again until it does."

Drake had taken too many beatings in his long life to be frightened by the threat—even though he knew Gabriel was dead serious—but he did take the point. Gabriel shook him when he didn't answer quickly enough.

"All right, all right!" Drake said. "I'll feed."

Gabriel released him, and Drake was sure he saw a hint of disappointment in his eyes. Apparently, Gabriel'd been eager for a fight, though Drake had learned in the past that if he managed to land a punch on Gabriel, it would be purely by accident.

They continued down the sidewalk as their surroundings rapidly deteriorated into the familiar gloom of the ghetto. Gabriel cloaked them both in his glamour—a pair of white men walking in this neighborhood at this hour would draw far too much attention. Each time they passed someone, Gabriel's nostrils would flare as he scented the air for what he called "corruption." When he found a suitable target, he steered the spellbound mortal into an alleyway, Drake following behind.

Never doubting for a moment that Gabriel's choice of victim was truly a person the world would be better off without, Drake forced himself to stop thinking about Faith, and made doubly sure his victim's mind was clouded by glamour. No matter how reprehensible his victims, Drake made sure they felt neither pain nor fear when he killed them.

Only then did he allow himself to sink his fangs into the mortal's neck.

* * *

ENSCONCED IN HER room, brooding and feeling dreadfully guilty, Faith at first didn't register the sound of the front door opening and closing. When she did come out of her funk and realize what she'd heard, her pulse leapt with the hope that Drake had returned from wherever he'd gone. She didn't know how she could apologize for the way she'd hurt him, but she was damn well going to try.

Wiping at her eyes to make sure no tear tracks remained, she stiffened her spine and crossed to her bedroom door as she heard footsteps approach. She swung the door open, rehearsing her apology. But it wasn't Drake who stood in the doorway.

It took every scrap of her will not to slam the door in Armand's face. Her fingers tightened on the door until her joints ached with the pressure, and instead of meeting his eyes she stared fixedly at his shoulder.

"I know how angry you are with me," he said softly, "and I know I deserve it. But we need to talk."

Something about his voice, a hint of roughness, made her look up. Never had she seen an expression so . . . vulnerable on the *Seigneur*'s face.

Her anger didn't exactly evaporate, but it dimmed from a roiling boil to a simmer. She stepped aside, silently inviting him into her room. Not that she could have kept him out anyway.

"What is there to talk about?" she asked when she closed the door behind him. "It's not like you've ever cared about my feelings."

She expected him to deny it, but he didn't, instead looking pensive. Finally, he said, "It was never that I didn't care. It was merely that in my arrogance, I assumed I would one day win you over."

She wanted to rage at him, tell him exactly what

she thought of him. She settled for thinking about the plan she had proposed to Drake. Perhaps Drake would no longer have any interest in helping her or Lily after this evening's display. Then again, perhaps he wasn't as petty as the *Seigneur*. She wondered if even now, Drake had found her a gun. She envisioned holding that gun to Armand's head and pulling the trigger.

The image was not as appealing as she'd expected, considering what he'd done tonight.

He licked his lips. "I never meant you ill, Faith," he said, startling her with his use of her name. "If . . . *When* I've treated you badly, it was never out of any malice toward you."

She raised her chin. She'd always known that, but it had never much mattered. "Do you think that made it hurt less when you hit me?" She wasn't sure where she was finding the courage to speak so boldly to him, and she half expected him to remind her of her place.

His eyes narrowed, but his tone remained mild. "I won't apologize for that. As a *Seigneur,* it has been necessary for me to be a harsh ruler. It would take someone far stronger than myself to rule vampires who did not fear me. And as you well know, even those stronger than I prefer to rule by intimidation, even if they don't need to."

She wanted to argue the point, but some small part of her knew he was right. She knew most, if not all, of the vampires who served him. Had they not feared him, he could never have controlled them. Even those who were mild mannered as mortals tended to become aggressive as vampires. Faith felt it herself, felt how once she'd turned vampire, her instincts urged her to choose "fight" over "flight."

"The point I'm trying to make," Armand continued, "is that whether you believe it or not, whether I've shown it or not, I do care about you, and about Lily." He moved closer to her, and though as usual her reflexes urged her to back away, she held still and met his gaze.

"You and Lily can do nothing to affect the outcome of our mission here." He closed the remaining distance between them, and when he reached up to cup her cheek in his palm, the expression in his eyes was so raw she didn't even think to pull away.

"I still hope and pray that Charles and I can prevail," he said. "But I can't risk the chance that we might not. I can't risk the chance that *La Vieille* would get her hands on you or Lily."

Faith's heart gave a thud behind her breastbone. She knew of only one way to keep herself and Lily out of *La Vieille*'s clutches. "Are you telling me you're going to kill us?" she asked, pleasantly surprised that her voice didn't quaver. It was a fate better than that which *La Vieille* promised, but Faith hated the idea that she and Lily could be so close to winning their freedom only to die before they had a chance to try.

Armand's eyes widened in surprise as his hand dropped from her cheek. "Of course not!" he said, and Faith let out a shaky breath. The corners of his mouth twitched into a wry smile. "*Ma petite*, if I were going to kill you to keep you from her, you can be sure you would never see it coming. I certainly wouldn't *tell* you about it beforehand."

"How comforting," she murmured, then winced because he might find the sarcasm insolent.

Instead, he ignored her words. "What I'm trying to tell you is that you and Lily are free to go."

Faith's heart gave another thud and her jaw dropped open. "What did you say?" she asked, her voice no more than a whisper through her constricted throat.

Armand had gone back to staring straight ahead, his eyes distant. "I know how little you think of me. I know you believe me a heartless monster. I bear little resemblance to the man I once was before I was turned, but no matter what you think, I'm not completely without honor. I can't risk what *La Vieille* would do to you just because I want you by my side. If I didn't need Charles to have any hope of success, I'd let him go, too. But everyone in Rouen who belongs to me will suffer if I fail, and I hope Charles will understand why he and I must continue to try."

Faith felt positively dizzy with the welter of emotions that whirled within her. Never for a moment had she considered the possibility that Armand might set her and Lily free for no reason other than to protect them.

Armand straightened his shoulders and faced her once again. The wry smile was back, though she detected a hint of bitterness in it as well.

"You thought my need to possess you was so great that I would allow you and Lily to risk death by torture before setting you free?" he asked, then shook his head. "Of course you did. But then, you've never really understood me anyway."

Faith couldn't help the derisive snort that escaped her. "This from a man who can't understand why forcing me to his bed with glamour is rape no matter how much pleasure he forces me to feel."

He grimaced. "I can't claim to understand. But I don't need to understand to apologize. It means nothing, I know, but I never meant to hurt you." The expression on his face turned closed and shuttered, and he abruptly changed the subject. "You must leave immediately. And you mustn't tell me where you're going. I would never willingly betray you to *La Vieille,* but I have no doubt she can do things to me that will suck every drop of honor from my soul. If I don't know where you are, I can't tell her."

The thought of what Armand would suffer if he failed made Faith's chest ache in distress. She had been willing—in theory, at least—to shoot him dead. But she wouldn't wish that kind of suffering on anyone, not even him. To her surprise, tears prickled her eyes.

"You'll still be in danger," Armand warned. "From what I've gathered, there aren't as many vampires in America as there are at home, especially in the more rural areas, but as long as you refuse to kill, you will be an easy target."

"I'm not becoming a Killer!"

He raised an eyebrow. "Even if that's the only way to keep Lily safe?"

She gave the idea a split-second's thought, then dismissed it. "No. If something were to happen to me, Lily would still survive. It would be hard on her, but she'd find a way."

Armand smiled at her. "I admire your principles, even if I don't share them." He sobered once more. "I suggest you pack the bare minimum of items you need and then leave this house within the hour. I want you as far away from us as possible, the sooner the better."

Once again, she felt the sting of tears. "Thank you, *Seigneur,*" she said, meaning it for the first time.

A tear escaped the corner of her eye. Armand smiled as he reached out to brush it away.

"I hope you will think better of me for this," he said softly. "And I am selfishly glad to know someone will shed a tear for me if the worst happens."

She sniffled and had to fight the urge to give him a hug. For six years, her life had revolved around him, and yet she'd failed to realize that she felt even the faintest hint of attachment. But for all his many faults, he could have been a lot worse.

Armand erased most of the emotion from his expression. "You'd better get packed. Remember, I want you out within the hour."

"Yes, *Seigneur.*"

He nodded curtly then strode to the door.

"Seigneur!" she said, just before he slipped out.

He turned back to her and raised an impassive eyebrow.

"Be careful." Her cheeks heated at her lame words, but Armand smiled faintly.

"Thank you. You, too," he said before slipping out the door. That was when she realized that if Drake didn't return to the house within the hour, she would never see him again. Would never have the chance to apologize. But that couldn't be helped. All she could do was hope he got back in time—and hope he was even willing to speak to her.

* * *

AFTER THE KILL, Gabriel helped Drake dispose of the body. They spoke very little, which, considering their mutual prickly tempers, was probably a good thing.

Feeding had calmed some of the clamor in Drake's body and mind, but he was still not himself. He kept thinking about how Faith had looked at him. The *Seigneur* had been determined to show her that Drake was as much a Killer as he. He had succeeded. And once again, Drake had to wonder if the cold-blooded Johnnie Drake had been more real than he wanted to believe.

"You're sulking again," Gabriel said when they left the crematorium.

Drake's lips curled back in a snarl. "I'm not sulking," he retorted, not entirely sure that was true. "It's been a rough few days."

Gabriel sniffed disdainfully. "Remember, I know what it's like to be judged by Saint Eli and found lacking. You can wallow in it, or you can admit he's a sanctimonious prick and get on with your life."

Drake couldn't help laughing. "And I thought you and your dad had patched things up."

Gabriel's grin was almost playful. "We're not trying to kill each other anymore. Surely that's an improvement?"

Drake acknowledged that with a nod. "Eli has nothing to do with the muddle I've got myself into."

"Like hell he doesn't."

Drake waved off the protest. "It has nothing to do with Eli," he repeated. "It has to do with my past. Which you know nothing about."

"Actually, that's not true. Brigitte dug up your past, and she shared some of it with me."

Drake's jaw tightened. "Why would she do that?" And what exactly had she told him? How much had *Padraig* told *her*?

"Like I said, we're going to have lots to talk about when this is all over. Now isn't the time. We need to rid ourselves of Brigitte and Henri while they don't know I've gotten free. Then we have to get rid of this damn delegation. Then we can handle the next set of problems."

"What next set of problems?" Drake asked, but wasn't surprised when Gabriel ignored the question.

"The good news is that Brigitte seems to be playing her little games every night. I want you to go back to the house—alone. Participate in whatever hunt the *Seigneur* has planned for the evening. I'll cloak my presence, but I'll be keeping watch. If Brigitte or Henri make an appearance, I'll be ready for them."

"I wish you'd tell me what else you know," Drake said.

"If I thought it would help, I'd tell you."

Drake laughed softly. "Now you sound just like your father," he said, knowing how much Gabriel appreciated any comparison with Eli.

"I could still kick the shit out of you on general principle," Gabriel mused, and Drake backed down.

"Fine. Keep your secrets. I'd better get back to the house. For all I know, they've gone out hunting without me."

"No, Jez says everyone's still there. And no sign of our friends yet. But you're right, you'd best get back."

They'd reached an intersection, and Gabriel peeled off to go wherever it was he planned to watch from.

"Oh, one more thing," Gabriel called before he was out of earshot. Drake turned and raised an eyebrow. "I know what corruption smells like. If you'd started to stink, I'd have killed you before you knew I was there."

Then he walked off without another word.

16

CHARLES WAS IN the downstairs den, trying not to think about how low he had sunk, when he saw Faith and Lily exit the house. They each carried a small, carry-on size bag, and they moved at a brisk pace just short of a jog.

He wondered how they could possibly think they would escape with both Armand and Charles in residence, and he expected to see Armand descend the stairs in a fury at any moment. But it didn't happen.

Charles didn't know what was going on, but he knew he didn't have time to alert the *Seigneur* to their departure if he didn't want them to get away. Faith not being the *Seigneur*'s fledgling, he would only be able to track her over a limited distance. If she jumped in a cab, she'd be out of range in a matter of minutes.

Charles hesitated only briefly in the foyer before he threw open the door and dashed outside. As he'd feared, Faith was hailing a taxi, though the cabbie drove past without stopping. Faith put a hand on the back of Lily's shoulder and urged her forward, and now they both broke into a jog. Where the hell was the *Seigneur*?

Cursing, Charles took off in pursuit, but they had more than a block's head start. He reached out with his glamour, trying to break through Lily's fragile mortal defenses. She faltered momentarily, then recovered when Charles's concentration broke. It was still relatively early in the evening, and there were too many pedestrians about. He could pass through them unseen in a cloud of glamour, but not if he was drawing attention to himself by chasing a pair of pretty women through the streets.

Faith waved at another taxi, and this time succeeded in hailing it. She looked over her shoulder at Charles as she pushed Lily in ahead of her.

To hell with the watching mortals! She was getting away, and that was unacceptable. All his hopes rested on being able to deliver her to Henri. And all of *Lily's* hopes, he reminded himself, because surely *La Vieille* would track them down if they escaped. He didn't particularly relish the idea of Faith in Henri's tender care, but he'd do anything to keep Lily safe. Faith would understand that, when the time came.

Faith's taxi pulled away from the curb, and Charles glanced frantically around. Directly in front of him, a mortal unlocked his car door and leisurely got in. Charles seized the mortal with his glamour and let himself into the passenger seat. Then, feeling faintly ridiculous, ordered the spellbound mortal to follow the cab.

He should be calling the *Seigneur,* letting him know that the girls were getting away. Should at least inform him that he'd left the house. But right this moment, he couldn't bear the thought of talking to the man he had betrayed. His stomach turned. Through his actions, he would survive this mission, and so would Lily. But he would never be the same afterward. Guilt and revulsion clawed at his belly, but even if he wanted to, it was too late to turn back now.

The cab carrying Faith and Lily eventually came to a stop in front of a train station. No way in hell was Charles letting them get on a train. He'd never find them again.

With a tug on the psychic leash, he made his driver come to a screeching stop, then dove out the car door, keeping Faith and Lily in sight. The station was busy, still bustling with commuter traffic from the tail end of rush hour. He lost sight of his quarry, so he reached out with his psychic senses in search of Faith's vampire aura.

He found her quickly. But hers wasn't the only vampire aura he sensed. And the second aura looked to be about two-hundred and fifty years old.

Henri!

What the hell was he doing at the train station? Charles didn't have time to worry about that. He had to catch Faith and Lily, not let Henri find them. Somehow, he didn't think Brigitte would consider his end of the bargain complete if he weren't directly responsible for turning Faith over. And the thought of Henri putting his filthy hands on Lily . . .

Charles shoved his way through the crowd, using glamour when necessary to get people out of his way, desperate to get to Faith and Lily before Henri did.

* * *

DRAKE COULD NO longer blame hunger for the turmoil that swirled inside him. He stood on the doorstep of Gabriel's house, key in the lock, willing himself to turn it. His more cowardly instincts reminded him that entering the house meant facing Faith. He didn't want to see the condemnation in her eyes, wasn't sure he could bear it. Maybe Drake didn't show up as tainted on Gabriel's psychic radar, but he wasn't so sure about his own.

Disgusted with himself, he finally managed to open the door and step inside. The house was strangely quiet, feeling almost empty. He did a quick psychic scan that revealed four vampires in residence. No mortals. His heart clenched at the thought that something might have happened to Lily while he was gone.

While he stood rooted to the floor, dread creeping through his system, the *Seigneur* appeared in the doorway to the den. Drakc stiffened, even while he let out a breath of relief, for surely Armand would be in a towering rage if Brigitte had attacked again.

"Where is everyone?" Drake asked, pleased with how steady and mild his voice came out. The beast inside him wanted to tear the man's throat out for what he'd done.

The *Seigneur* smiled faintly. "You've fed."

"Answer my question," Drake said through gritted teeth, though he knew if the *Seigneur* didn't want to answer, there would be nothing Drake could do to force him.

"I let Faith and Lily go."

Drake had to replay the sentence in his head to assure himself he hadn't misheard.

"They left perhaps fifteen minutes ago," the *Seigneur* continued. "After your dramatic departure, I had a call from *La Vieille*. It became clear I couldn't keep them here any longer. I could not risk them falling into her hands."

Drake wasn't sure how he felt about this. On the one hand, he certainly didn't want them to return to France. On the other hand, sending the two of them undefended into the night seemed insanely stupid.

"You're risking them falling into Brigitte and Henri's hands!"

The *Seigneur* shrugged as if it hardly mattered. "There was risk either way. Charles and I couldn't go with them. We mustn't have the faintest idea where they could be going, or *La Vieille* will drag that information from us if we are forced to return home. If I had to choose between *La Vieille* and Brigitte, I'm afraid Brigitte will always be the lesser of two evils."

Drake pictured Henri outside the crematorium, jacking off to the thought of what he would do to Faith.

"You don't have to agree with my decision," Armand said. "It's too late to change it now, right or wrong. For what it's worth, I offer my apologies for my behavior earlier. Neither you nor Faith deserved that."

This was a night full of surprises. Somehow, Drake didn't think the *Seigneur* was a man much used to apologizing. Still, he didn't find himself particularly moved. "If you expect me to graciously accept your apology and forget it happened, you've got a long wait ahead of you."

Again, the *Seigneur* shrugged. His face gave away nothing, but his body language was more telling. He looked tired. And resigned. Drake might almost have felt sorry for him in another situation.

Drake swept the house with his psychic senses again, and realized there still weren't as many people in the house as there should be.

"Surely you haven't sent people out hunting without you."

The *Seigneur* shook his head. "We had another casualty during the day. Louis is dead."

No wonder the *Seigneur* looked so defeated. "Who else is missing?"

The *Seigneur* gave him a puzzled look. "What do you—" Then he must have performed his own sweep, because he cursed and reached into his pocket, pulling out a cell phone. "Charles isn't here," he said as he dialed. "I've been too preoccupied. I didn't notice him leaving, and I certainly didn't send him out."

Drake suddenly had a very bad feeling about this.

* * *

THE TRAIN STATION was loud, echoing with many voices, so Charles almost missed the sound of his cell phone ringing. He was sincerely tempted to pretend he didn't hear it, but he had probably already aroused Armand's suspicions by running off without telling him he was leaving.

He answered the phone, still moving toward Faith's aura. Every now and then, he caught a glimpse of her through the sea of people. He was catching up, but she hadn't seen him yet. Strangely, the aura that he assumed was Henri's had not veered in their direction, had in fact headed straight for the exit.

Charles listened with only half his attention as Armand explained that he'd freed Faith and Lily. He felt a moment of outrage that Armand hadn't given *him* the opportunity to flee *La Vieille*'s wrath, but he knew how his old friend's mind worked. Knew Armand needed him if he had any hope of fulfilling his mission. Unfortunately for them both, that hope had died long ago.

"Come back to the house now," Armand said, and Charles finally paid full attention to the situation.

He couldn't go back to the house. Not without . . . *securing* Faith and Lily first. The only place he could imagine securing them was in *La Vieille*'s jet, which would be standing at the ready at all times. Charles obviously couldn't take them there himself—as his maker, Armand would be able to sense where Charles was, and that he wasn't coming back as ordered. *La Vieille* had given him a number for some of her other minions, the ones who had come specifically to make sure the delegation returned in the event of failure. But it would take time for them to get here. Time that Charles would have to explain away.

"I can't come back now," he said, noticing for the first time the sweat that beaded on his upper lip. He hoped his voice didn't show how close he was to panic as he tried to think of an excuse to placate the *Seigneur*. Then he realized the vampire aura he'd sensed earlier was perfect.

"I followed Faith and Lily to the train station. I'm not sure, but I think Henri is here, too. I sense someone about his age. I haven't laid eyes on him yet, but I can't just leave Faith and Lily alone if he's around."

Armand made a sound of frustration. "If he's around, then Brigitte is there to hold his leash. You are no match for them."

"So you would have me just *abandon* them?" he asked, not having to fake his horror at the idea.

Armand sighed heavily. "No. No, of course not. Try to keep him in sight. I'll be there as soon as I can."

Then the *Seigneur* hung up, and Charles suppressed a groan. The aura he'd sensed was long gone, and if Armand got here before he could get Faith and Lily away . . .

Hastily, he dialed the number *La Vieille* had given him and prayed that her people would get to the station before Armand did.

* * *

FAITH CHEWED HER lip as she and Lily waited in line. The cavernous station echoed with the clamor of too many voices, and the crowd could camouflage any number of hostile vampires. She did a brief psychic scan, then cursed when she sensed a vampire presence almost on top of them. She whirled and put herself between Lily and the approaching vampire, then let out a breath of relief when she saw Charles.

She couldn't imagine why Charles was following them—unless the *Seigneur* had changed his mind—but better him than Henri.

He smiled reassuringly as he approached, but despite the friendly demeanor, Faith remained on guard. There was a sheen of sweat on his face, and his eyes darted nervously left and right.

"What are you doing here, Charles?" she asked as the ticket line inched forward.

"Armand failed to inform me that he'd freed you, so I followed you." He took a step closer. "I was going to leave once he called and told me, but . . . Please don't panic, but I think Henri is in the station."

Faith's heart skipped a beat, and Lily gasped. Charles patted the air soothingly. "Armand is on his way. We won't let Henri get you."

Faith reached out with her psychic senses, but she

felt no sign of another vampire in the area. "I don't sense anything," she said, wondering why she suddenly felt suspicious of Charles, of all people.

He swallowed hard, his eyes a little too wide. "I don't, either. Not anymore. He just kind of . . . disappeared."

Now Charles's fear became more understandable. "You think Brigitte's here, too, and that she can mask his presence as well as her own."

Sweat beaded on his upper lip as he nodded. He reached for her arm and drew her out of line. "Let's head for the exit," he said. She noticed the hand on her arm was cold and clammy. "The faster we can meet up with Armand, the better."

Faith still felt a disturbing undercurrent of suspicion, but since she could think of no good reason to justify it, she allowed Charles to lead her and Lily back the way they had come. They were almost to the exit when Charles turned to her with a pleading look in his eyes.

"I'm very sorry about this, Faith," he said.

Her brows drew together in puzzlement as Lily continued past her to Charles's side.

"What—" she started to ask, but her jaw snapped shut and her voice died in her throat. She tried to force a sound out, but glamour held her silent.

Charles put his arm around Lily's shoulders and drew her close. Her eyes stared vacantly ahead. Faith's chest lurched at the proprietary way Charles looked at her sister. All this time, she'd worried about what Armand might do, but it looked like Charles had been the threat all along.

"I will do everything in my power to keep her safe," Charles vowed, though he seemed incapable of looking Faith in the eye. "If I could have saved you both, I would have, but I know you'd prefer I save Lily since I have to choose."

Tears of anger and frustration burned in Faith's eyes. How could Charles do this to them? But since he held her voice captive, she couldn't ask.

"Let's go," he said, and Faith's feet started moving against her will. "I have to get you out of here before Armand arrives."

Unable to resist the pull of his glamour, she followed him out of the station.

* * *

AT FIRST, THE *Seigneur* had balked at the idea of letting Drake accompany him to the train station. But when Drake had pointed out that he'd simply take the next cab if the *Seigneur* went alone, Armand had reluctantly agreed.

So far, Drake hadn't found it necessary to buy a car, although he knew how to drive. Gabriel and Jez owned one, but Drake decided not to point that out to the *Seigneur*. It was best to leave the car so Gabriel could follow them. Drake did a quick psychic scan as he and the *Seigneur* slid into the cab, but he sensed no vampires other than the Guardians.

When they were about halfway to the station, Charles called and said he'd lost the trail, claiming Henri must have taken a cab. Armand decided to pick him up at the station anyway. But when they arrived and Charles opened the door to get in, both he and the *Seigneur* suddenly tensed, and their eyes met. Drake didn't sense anything, but then his range was considerably shorter than theirs.

"What is it?" he asked.

Charles reached into his wallet and threw some money at the driver, while the *Seigneur* slipped out of the cab without answering. With a shrug, Drake exited, too, hoping Gabriel had managed to follow them.

The *Seigneur* was staring at Charles with narrowed eyes, and Charles looked pale.

"I thought you said you'd lost him."

Charles stared at the sidewalk with scared-looking eyes. "I had, *Seigneur*. He disappeared so fast I thought he had to have gotten into a car."

"And now he's come back? Is that what you're telling me?"

Once again, Drake performed his psychic sweep, and this time he thought he caught the faintest glimpse of a vampire aura at the periphery of his range.

"I don't know what's going on, *Seigneur*," Charles said, sounding desperate. "I don't know why he's come back." He raised his head and squared his shoulders. "But he's getting away."

The *Seigneur* gave his fledgling another long, hard look, then shook his head and without another word started jogging in the direction from which Drake had sensed the fleeting aura. Charles and Drake followed close behind. Drake's heart lurched a bit when he realized that he couldn't sense Faith's presence in the looming terminal. If she were inside, she should have been within his range.

But then, that was good news. It meant she and Lily had gotten on a train, and with Henri in the neighborhood they would have been in danger if they'd still been here.

As the three of them ran, Drake kept his senses stretched for the aura they were following, feeling it growing stronger in his mind. They were gaining, though their quarry had to be moving at a brisk pace or they should have caught up with him by now.

A flicker of unease prickled the back of Drake's neck. "Surely he senses us," he said. "With this big a head start, he could lose us easily if he wanted to."

The *Seigneur* glanced over his shoulder, frowning, but didn't slow down. "That may be, but Charles and I have no choice but to follow. You can go back to the house if you'd like. You'll be no help against Henri or Brigitte anyway."

Undoubtedly true, and if the four of them decided to battle to the death, Drake wasn't sure he cared who won. But he kept following anyway. Maybe it was pride, maybe it was sheer stupidity, but the last thing he wanted was to run from a fight in front of the *Seigneur*.

They all came to a sudden halt when a figure stepped out of the shadows and blocked their path.

Charles cried out in alarm, his hand plunging under his jacket after the tranquilizer gun.

Drake realized just in time that it was Gabriel who'd blocked their path and reached out to grab Charles's arm. "Wait!" he barked, and though Charles could easily have broken his grip, he listened.

The *Seigneur,* panting faintly from the exertion of their jog, drew himself rigidly upright and took a step forward.

"Gabriel, I presume?" he asked, giving Gabriel a once-over that managed to look both contemptuous and cautious.

"In the flesh," Gabriel responded. "And I thought you might want to think for a moment before you run headlong into such an obvious trap."

Reaching out with his psychic senses yet again, Drake realized that the aura they'd been following was still in range—no doubt slowing when he realized the pursuit had come to a halt. And he also noticed that Gabriel was still masking his psychic presence.

The *Seigneur*'s lip curled. "If I kill you now, I'll have some concrete progress to report to *La Vieille*."

"First of all," Gabriel said with a malevolent grin, "you'd find me harder to kill than you imagine."

Drake knew that was at least partially a bluff. If Gabriel hadn't been weakened by whatever he'd done to restore Jez to herself after their last encounter with Brigitte and Henri, there was no doubt he'd be able to win a battle, even against two vampires of such age as Armand and Charles. After all, he'd easily defeated his own eight-hundred-year-old mother and her flock of fledglings. But with his power as spotty as it was now, there was no guarantee.

"Secondly," Gabriel continued, "even if you succeeded in killing me, Brigitte would tear your guts out at her leisure without breaking a sweat."

The *Seigneur* held himself even more stiffly upright. "We are not newly created fledglings, Charles and I. Brigitte is *half* our age, and—"

"And a born vampire. From what I've heard, she's run circles around you from the beginning. I can help you capture her."

The *Seigneur* raised an eyebrow. "Why should I believe you'd want to? Your second led me to believe you were imprisoned, and now I find that is a lie. Your credibility is not high."

"I *was* imprisoned," Gabriel said, talking with exaggerated care. "The reason I can help you capture Brigitte is that she doesn't know I've escaped. She'll know *you're* coming, but she won't sense *me*. Surprise can be a powerful tool."

Drake cleared his throat. He was only halfway paying attention to the conversation, instead keeping most of his concentration on the vampire they'd been following. The vampire who was now moving in their direction.

"Uh, I think Henri is wondering why we've stopped," Drake said, and the three older vampires immediately took the point and started moving forward again, more slowly than before. Perhaps it wasn't unreasonable for them to have slowed down, considering they would have to be complete morons not to recognize this as a trap.

"If you'll give me one of your tranq guns," Gabriel said as they walked, "I'll take a shot as soon as we catch up with them, wherever they're leading us."

The *Seigneur* laughed. "I don't see myself handing a gun to you. We may at the moment have a mutual enemy, but that does not make us friends."

"No, it doesn't. However, Brigitte will have a harder time overcoming me with her glamour than she will you."

"Oh? If that's difficult for her, then how did she manage to imprison you?"

Gabriel gave him a disdainful look. "A tranq gun of course. And the element of surprise."

The *Seigneur* seemed to believe that explanation, but he didn't hand over his gun. With a shrug, Gabriel accepted the verdict and dropped back, allowing Armand and Charles to take the lead. He fell into step beside Drake as they continued to follow the elusive psychic presence that continually darted around corners and changed directions, leading them on a merry chase.

Eventually, the distance between them and the supposedly fleeing vampire closed. And then the vampire came to a stop. Drake exchanged a concerned look with Gabriel, but since they already knew they were walking into a trap, he supposed there was no reason not to keep going forward.

The vampire they all assumed to be Henri was by now little more than a block ahead of them, around the corner. Assuming Brigitte was on the lookout somewhere, she probably knew by now that Gabriel was with them. But Henri was nevertheless holding still, waiting for them to catch up.

They approached the mouth of what looked to be a narrow alley. Henri had led them to a commercial district, where most buildings were shut up for the night, so there were few people to see them. Charles and Armand held their guns at the ready, but waited for Drake and Gabriel to close the distance between them before they all turned the corner together.

* * *

FAITH HAD AT one time doubted her ability to kill another living being. That doubt was now thoroughly extinguished.

Hogtied, she lay in the darkened luggage compartment of *La Vieille*'s private jet and knew she would sink her teeth into the throat of Charles or any of his cronies without the slightest hesitation. She squirmed, trying without success to find a more comfortable position. She doubted she'd been tied for more than fifteen minutes, but already the strain was turning to agony.

"Lily?" she called into the darkness, her voice echoing against the metal walls.

Lily's only answer was a soft groan. The sound caused Faith's fangs to descend, and she struggled against her bonds despite the pain. When Charles's accomplices had tied Faith, Lily had unwisely protested. One of them had backhanded Lily hard enough to knock the poor girl out.

Tears blurred Faith's vision as her mind frantically sought an escape. But she and Lily were tied and sealed in this compartment, and outside lurked two vampires and two mortals, all of whom were loyal to *La Vieille*.

She suppressed a scream of frustration. She didn't care how many people guarded the plane, or how unlikely an escape might be. She would fight with every breath that remained in her body, and if she found a way to get Lily out, she'd take it, whatever the cost to herself.

Lily groaned again, and Faith slowly, painfully started wriggling in that direction. Every inch was a battle, but she would get to her sister's side if it killed her.

After what felt like an hour, her body was drenched in sweat and the muscles in both her arms and legs were cramping viciously, but she'd reached Lily.

"Faith?" Lily whimpered, the fear in her voice more than Faith could bear.

"It'll be all right, sweetie," she said, no matter how much she doubted her own words. "We're going to get out of this."

"How?" Lily asked, and the word was just short of a wail. Faith could smell her terror in the air. Once upon a time, she'd thought she hated Armand. Her anger at him had been but the palest shadow of what she felt now for Charles.

More pain lanced through Faith's strained muscles

as she shifted position and tried to find the knots that bound Lily's wrists. Lily tried to help, but let out a muffled shriek as soon as she moved, her mortal body reacting even more strongly to the bondage than Faith's.

"Just hold still, sweetie," Faith urged through gritted teeth. "Let me do the work."

Lily obeyed, and eventually Faith found a knot her fingers could pry at. The extreme awkwardness of her position made it almost impossible to get a secure grip on the rope, but Faith's vampire strength helped her begin to loosen the knot.

A jolt of adrenaline shot through her at this tiny success, but she reminded herself how far they still had to go. Even if she managed to get both of them free, they still had to get out of this compartment and escape their guards. And she had no idea how long it would be before someone felt the need to check on them.

Trying not to panic, Faith told herself to take one problem at a time as she continued working on the stubborn knot.

17

NEITHER DRAKE NOR his companions were surprised to see Brigitte and Henri, arm in arm, waiting for them at the back of what turned out to be a dead-end alley. What did surprise them was that neither vampire made a hostile move.

Without speaking, Armand fired at Brigitte, but she merely laughed as her telekinesis stopped the dart in midair. Charles was standing in a shooter's stance, but he didn't fire. Brigitte's eyes widened just a bit when she caught sight of Gabriel, but she recovered almost immediately.

Suddenly, the dart that had been hovering turned around and hurled itself into Gabriel's shoulder. Drake could see the effort Gabriel expended trying to stop it, but though he seemed to slow the dart's trajectory, its point still pierced his leather jacket. With a curse and a growl, he went down.

The gun that Charles failed to fire wrenched its

way out of his fingers and flew to Brigitte's hand. Drake, ignored by everyone, saw Henri's eyes start to glaze over as if he were succumbing to the *Seigneur*'s glamour—Charles looked far too unnerved and indecisive to be the source—but Brigitte fired the gun she'd snatched, and within seconds of the dart lodging itself in the *Seigneur*'s chest, Henri's eyes cleared.

Brigitte laughed again. "Would anyone else like a shot?" she asked. "I have some spare darts right here." She patted the pocket of her jacket.

Gabriel and Armand were both in too much pain to respond, and neither Drake nor Charles seemed up to a convincing quip.

"No?" Brigitte asked, sticking her lip out in an exaggerated pout. "What a shame. It's so much fun to shoot. And I *never* miss."

No, not when she could use her powers to guide the dart if it went astray.

"So what happens now?" Drake asked, because Charles seemed too dumbfounded to talk.

Brigitte sauntered forward, Henri at her heels like the faithful dog he was. "I've grown exceedingly bored with this game," she said, smirking at Armand. "Do you know that I sent Henri into that house *twice,* and no one so much as noticed he was there, much less laid a finger on him?" Her nose wrinkled. "I love to play games, but I like there to be at least *some* challenge."

Drake frowned. "Henri was in the house twice?"

"Yes. He took care of that strumpet Armand was

so enamored of. And then he finished off the cannon fodder. Er, that is, the mortals." She smiled brightly. "I'll have you know, Gabriel, that I forbade Henri to hurt the mortal child. I thought you might appreciate my restraint."

Gabriel said something unintelligible that didn't sound in the least appreciative.

The explanation didn't make sense to Drake. "How could Henri kill the mortals when he was busy attacking us and killing Jacques?"

"Henri *couldn't* have killed those mortals," Charles agreed, and Drake's nostrils flared at the stink of fear he emitted. A sheen of sweat coated his brow.

"He can't?" Brigitte asked innocently.

"No! One vampire couldn't drain four mortals dry all by himself."

A look of cunning entered Brigitte's eyes as she smiled once again. "Now did I say he was all by himself? I don't remember saying any such thing. And no, it wasn't Henri who killed your friend Jacques. Perhaps it will begin to enter your minds now that Henri and I might not be alone?"

Now it was Drake's turn to curse. "Padraig!" he spat. He was a fool not to have realized it earlier. He knew Padraig was Brigitte's ally, and that he still hoped to win Drake to his side. The note and the phone call hadn't worked, so he'd decided to try the in-person approach. "He's about the same age as Henri. Their auras would look the same." Although Padraig's glamour shouldn't have been strong enough to hold Charles, Drake, and Eric spellbound while he killed Jacques.

But he stopped questioning the idea when some instinct prompted him to do another psychic sweep. Slowly, dread rising from his toes and sweeping up his body, he turned to look behind him.

Padraig was almost close enough to touch. He had done away with the dramatic handlebar mustache that had once adorned his face, and his coarse red hair was longer and far less greasy than when Drake had last seen him, but the jaunty, friendly grin that hid the heart of a Killer remained exactly the same. Behind him stood five more vampires, four men and a woman, none of whom Drake recognized.

"Happy to see me, Johnnie-boy?" Padraig asked, and Drake could only scowl at him. The vampires behind him pressed a little closer, one of them staring at Gabriel with bared fangs.

Brigitte made a tsking sound, and the hostile vampire looked toward her. "Now, now, Luke. We've talked about this. Gabriel is under my protection."

It took a moment for Drake to make the connection, but he finally remembered that the Master of Washington was named Luke. He very much doubted it was a coincidence.

Brigitte continued. "These are the Masters of Richmond, Boston, Trenton, and Toronto. You already know the Master of New York, and Gabriel is well acquainted with the Master of Washington."

The last thing Drake wanted was to have Padraig at his back, but he forced himself to turn to face

Brigitte. Armand and Gabriel were incapable of speech, and Charles apparently had nothing to say.

"What do you want?" Drake asked, speaking for all of them.

"To be left alone," she answered. "I knew my dear mother would be sending people after me. Gabriel is still being difficult, but I thought some of the other masters in the area might be more . . . amenable to a strategic alliance.

"I am declaring myself the *Seigneur* of the Eastern Seaboard," Brigitte said, affecting a haughty pose. "And now, it is time for a quick phone call to Mama." She pulled out a cell phone, her eyes almost glowing with pleasure. The voice that answered was too low for Drake to hear.

"*Bonjour, Maman*," Brigitte said, before switching to English, for her audience's sake. "I hope I didn't wake you. But I thought you'd like to know that your dear Armand is curled into a whimpering ball at my feet, and that Charles appears to have misplaced his tongue."

Drake couldn't understand the voice on the other end of the line, but he could hear the fury in it.

Brigitte laughed. "You'll have to do much better than that, *Maman*. Shall I kill them and put them out of their misery? Or would you prefer to do the honors yourself? I wouldn't want to deprive you of that pleasure."

The hair on the back of Drake's neck prickled at the sounds that emanated from the phone, but Brigitte just smiled as Henri slipped his arms around her from behind and nuzzled her neck. When the tirade ended, Brigitte's smile widened even more.

"*À bientôt, Maman,*" she said, then closed the phone. Her glance swept the assembled vampires. "I believe we're finished here." Her gaze then focused first on Charles, then on Drake. "Unless one of you would like to provide some entertainment? No?" She sighed dramatically. "What a shame." She approached Charles and patted him on the cheek. "I'll give you a call sometime," she said cryptically, then headed toward the mouth of the alley.

Most of her pet masters followed her, but Drake wasn't surprised when Padraig stayed behind.

"Might I have a word with you, Johnnie?" he asked.

Drake looked at Charles. "Padraig's my maker, so I can't fight him. But *you* can take him."

"Why should I?" Charles asked, and Drake had no answer for that. Charles knelt at his maker's side and dragged Armand's arm over his shoulders. "We need to get out of here while we can," he said, though he didn't sound terribly hopeful.

If Gabriel weren't incapacitated, no doubt he would have killed both of them, either out of mercy, to spare them the wrath of *La Vieille,* or just to prevent them from taking up residence somewhere in the U.S. and wantonly preying on the population. But Gabriel still lay on the pavement, teeth gritted and face contorted with the pain of the drug. And Drake was no match for Charles.

"Come now," Padraig urged. "Talk with me. What can it hurt?"

The question made Drake laugh. "I have nothing to say to you." He turned, meaning to help Gabriel up, but suddenly he found himself in the grip of his maker's glamour.

"It wasn't a request," Padraig said. "Now come along."

Helpless to resist, Drake followed his maker out of the alley, leaving Gabriel lying on the pavement.

* * *

WITH ARMAND'S ARM slung over his shoulder, Charles made his way down the street, using his glamour to turn the attention of the few mortals they passed. He wasn't sure what Brigitte expected him to do now, but he couldn't imagine what alternative he had but to go to the airport. Surely if she had other plans, she'd call and let him know.

When Charles spotted a parking lot on his right, he dragged Armand into a pool of darkness and waited until a lone mortal parked his car. Impatient to get away, to have this all over with, Charles quickly killed the man and appropriated his car keys. Armand managed a feeble protest, but the tranquilizer still held him powerless.

"I'm sorry, my friend," Charles said as he popped open the trunk. By now, a lot of the guilt had faded, replaced by a soothing numbness. Charles was doing what was necessary to survive. Why should he feel guilty for preserving his own life? He doubted the numbness would last, but at the moment he was thankful for it.

The look in Armand's eyes said he'd finally realized that Charles was betraying him, but Charles hardened his heart even further as he heaved his maker into the trunk of the car then slammed it shut. Soon, all this unpleasantness would be nothing but a memory, one he would lock away in the corner of his mind where it couldn't hurt him. It was a lie, and he knew it, but he clung to it in desperation.

Thinking about what it would be like to bite into Lily's throat, to grant her immortal life while binding her to his will, Charles drove to the airport where *La Vieille*'s private jet awaited him.

* * *

DRAKE CONTINUED STRUGGLING against the pull of Padraig's glamour, but it was far too strong for him to overcome. So when Padraig opened the door to a car and gestured him in, he had no choice but to obey.

"Where are we going?" he asked as Padraig pulled out into the sparse traffic.

"Just putting some distance between us and your new master. I don't wish for us to be interrupted, so I'm taking you outside the range of Gabriel's senses."

Like Gabriel was capable of interrupting while the "tranquilizer" was in his system. "Why are you doing this? What do you want from me?"

"Patience, Johnnie-boy. We'll have a chance to talk soon."

Drake sat in stubborn silence as Padraig drove through the city streets. At his hip, his cell phone buzzed, but Padraig held him immobile and he couldn't answer.

Eventually they pulled into a large parking garage. Padraig drove until the lines of cars became scarce, then pulled into a spot in a dark and shadowy corner. He put the car in park, then turned to face Drake, finally letting up on the glamour.

Drake sat stiffly and looked straight ahead, trying not to grind his teeth. "Now will you tell me what you want?"

"I already told you."

Reluctantly, Drake turned to look at his maker. "You really want me to come back to New York?" he asked, but he couldn't imagine why Padraig would be so adamant about it. Why should he want Drake back after more than a century of exile?

"I was the first master that Brigitte and her friend approached. I'd never heard of a born vampire, and I was not about to bow down to a slip of a girl only a little older than I. She made an example of me that she could use to bend the others to her will. When she was finished, more than half of my fledglings were dead." He looked into Drake's eyes with utter sincerity. "I need you. I'm vulnerable now. Our fine lady talks as if she is to become both our queen and our savior, but I'm not buying what she's selling." He shook his head. "She doesn't give a damn about any of us."

Drake was unmoved. He crossed his arms over his chest. "You can kidnap me and drag me up there if you'd like, but that doesn't mean I'll work for you." But even he heard the doubt in his words.

Gabriel had said they'd talk about his fate later, but if Jezebel still wanted him gone, he was history. He couldn't return to Philadelphia. Any other city of any size would already have vampires who would object to his presence. And out in the country or the suburbs, the population wasn't dense enough for him to find the kinds of victims he could live with himself for killing. Assuming he could get himself to feed without Gabriel to vet his victims.

How easily Padraig could seduce him, given just a little time. He wasn't some terrible, cackling villain who repelled anyone who came near him. Drake could never have fallen under the sway of someone like Henri, whose evil nature was always on display. But Padraig's evil was far more subtle, masked behind a warm and friendly demeanor that could make someone forget the cold and calculating heart that lay beneath. He didn't go out of his way to be cruel, but he would never let a matter of conscience stand between him and what he wanted. He was a prince among gang lords, but that wasn't saying much.

"My people are no longer the Blood and Death gang," Padraig continued. "We have grown far more civilized since last you and I met. I might on occasion need to use you as muscle, but it would not be your full-timc job. I would do my bcst to accommodate some of your more inconvenient moral qualms."

Drake couldn't help snorting at that. "You were a murderous, conniving bastard a hundred years ago, and you're a murderous, conniving bastard now. If I allowed you to lull me into some sort of false sense of security, you'd have me separated from my humanity before I knew what hit me."

Padraig grinned at that. "Perhaps. But you're a vampire, lad. A Killer. Have you any idea how silly you look riding on that moral high horse?"

Drake reached for the car door and was surprised when Padraig didn't stop him. Trying not to let the surprise show, he shoved the door open and stepped out. Still his maker didn't stop him, so Drake started across the garage toward the lighted exit sign.

By the time he reached the door, Padraig had appeared at his side as if by magic.

"Fine night for a walk, Johnnie-boy," he said with another one of his grins.

Drake sighed, stepping into the stairwell with Padraig on his heels. "Are you going to let me walk away, or are you going to drag me back to New York against my will? Make up your mind."

Padraig ignored the question. "There's so much anger in you. But why should you be angry with me, Johnnie? Did I wrong you?"

Drake shook his head. "You wouldn't understand."

"Try me."

This evening was just getting better and better. Drake reached the doorway at the bottom of the stairwell and yanked the door open with far more strength than necessary. Perhaps if he simply refused to speak to Padraig, he'd go away.

Drake didn't really believe that, but at this point anything was worth a try. He stepped out onto the sidewalk and looked both ways, but the truth was, he'd paid little attention when Padraig was driving and had no idea where they were. Which way was home? Assuming he *had* a home.

He picked a direction at random and wasn't in the least surprised that his maker fell into step beside him.

"Ah, now we're trying the silent treatment, are we?"

Drake gritted his teeth against the urge to retort.

"Why are you in Baltimore?" Padraig asked, changing tactics. Drake gave him a sidelong look but still refused to answer. "The last I'd heard, you had joined forces with the Master of Philadelphia. He and his Guardians are quite famous in some circles, you know. It always surprised me that a man of his sterling character would take in a Killer, but I suppose those inconvenient morals of yours served you well."

Temper sizzled through Drake's nerves, and he shot his maker a murderous glare. Clearly Padraig knew he was touching a sore spot, for he continued hammering on it.

"You were with him for a century, and now you're here. One can't help but be curious why the change."

"Be as curious as you like," Drake snapped, then bit his tongue.

"I'll venture a guess. According to the self-proclaimed '*Seigneur* of the Eastern Seaboard,' the

Master of Philadelphia has made a considerable leap in power lately. Perhaps he has grown too powerful to need his hired muscle anymore."

Drake knew his face was showing too much reaction, but he couldn't control the pulse of pain within him.

"You never belonged in Philadelphia," Padraig said. "You were never one of them. And you'll never be one of these Baltimore Guardians, either."

"Shut up!" Drake snapped. "You don't know anything about it."

Padraig just laughed. "If I were off base, my lad, you would be shrugging off my words." He came to a stop, grabbing Drake's arm and jerking him around so that they were face to face.

"Johnnie Drake was never meant to be a benevolent pet on a leash. He's a predator, a Killer. And the longer you pretend otherwise, the more you will hurt yourself. For all your fine morals, have you been happy in the years since you left me? Would you say that yours has been a life filled with contentment?"

Drake snarled and jerked his arm out of Padraig's grip. He'd never particularly thought of himself as unhappy. Yes, there'd been a sense of loneliness that had clung to him, the sense of being on the outside looking in. But he'd always accepted it as the status quo, never questioned if his life could be better.

"I'm not Johnnie Drake," he told his maker through clenched teeth. "I haven't been for over a century, and I'll never go back. I'd rather die."

Padraig grinned crookedly. "That can be arranged, boyo."

Once again, Drake turned away and started striding down the sidewalk, heedless of where he was going. If Padraig was going to kill him, there was nothing he could do to stop him.

Padraig's glamour stopped him in mid-stride.

"Still uncommonly stubborn, I see," Padraig said, stepping in front of him. "I won't force you to come with me. If you're to work for me, I want you willing."

"That'll never happen."

Padraig shrugged. "We'll see. Perhaps for now you'll choose to stay with your friends in Baltimore, but you may soon find life here . . . difficult."

"What do you mean?"

For once, Padraig was not grinning. "Our dear Brigitte will not be content to leave Baltimore or Philadelphia outside her influence. Johnnie, she's tamed every master from Toronto to Richmond. She chose a small entourage today, but she could have called in many more. I know she still has some hopes that she will win your Gabriel's allegiance, but she's already planning alternatives."

A chill of unease shivered down Drake's spine at the news. "What kind of alternatives?"

Padraig shrugged. "Did you know that your time as interim Master of Baltimore was a test of sorts?"

"What?"

"If she decides to dispense with Gabriel, she'll

need someone to run Baltimore for her. I know Luke has hopes that she'll merge the Baltimore and Washington families—under his rule, naturally—but she feels that's too large a territory. The last few days have been an audition, and I believe my lady has been pleased with what she's seen."

Drake curled his lip in a snarl; Padraig laughed and clapped him on the shoulder.

"I told her you were a practical man," Padraig continued. "That you would accept her rule even if you didn't like it because you knew you had no choice. Would you rather serve *her* than serve me?"

Drake's hands were fisted at his sides, and even without the hunger to spur his temper he felt tempted to throw a punch. One that no doubt would never make contact. Unless Padraig thought there was some advantage to allowing him to land it.

"You might want to consider abandoning the sinking ship, Johnnie. All the honor in the world won't keep it afloat."

Drake met his maker's eyes. He had no doubt that given a few months under Padraig's influence, he'd find himself transforming back into Johnnie Drake. And when he'd shrugged off his humanity and embraced himself as a Killer, he would be a bona fide member of Padraig's "family." Never again would he be on the outside looking in. Never again would guilt and doubt gnaw at his conscience.

But the price was too high, tempting though the idea of that oblivion might be.

"If the ship sinks," he said, "I'll go down with it."

Padraig gave a derisive snort. "Have it your way, then. If you live through this mess and want to reconsider my offer, give me a call." He glanced at his watch. "Well, it's been lovely catching up with you, lad. I'd love to stay and chat, but I've got a train to catch."

Drake frowned. "A train? What about your car?"

He laughed. "Not mine, boyo. There was such a rush-hour crush at the station I didn't feel like fighting for a cab."

"Or *paying* for one," Drake muttered under his breath, but of course Padraig heard him and laughed again.

"Indeed. Why pay when I could so easily persuade a lovely lady to lend me her car for the duration of my stay?"

Drake resisted the urge to ask whether said lovely lady had survived the persuasion. Sometimes it was better not to know.

But something other than Padraig's thievery was bothering Drake, something about what he'd just heard that set alarm bells jangling through his system. He frowned fiercely, not immediately able to pinpoint the source of his unease.

"Something wrong, boyo?" Padraig asked.

Drake grimaced. He could hardly count high enough to number all the things that were wrong. "You were at the train station earlier this evening."

Padraig raised an eyebrow. "Aye. What of it?"

"Charles was at the train station earlier and said he sensed Henri there." He regarded his maker, and the alarm rose a notch. Something about this was striking

Drake as terribly wrong. If only he could figure out what.

Padraig shook his head. "I did not warrant a welcoming committee, I'm afraid. 'Twas only me at the station. Why does it matter?"

Drake remembered how Charles had looked when Brigitte had discussed her tactics. How he'd smelled scared. Of course, considering the circumstances, he'd had a right to be scared, but still . . . Something had seemed off about it.

Padraig prodded his shoulder. "What's eating you, lad?"

"Something about Charles just isn't right," Drake murmured, more to himself than to Padraig.

Padraig chuckled. "Aye, that's a fact."

"What do you mean?"

"I mean our lovely Brigitte has found the key to buying his loyalty. You can be certain that he was not taking the *Seigneur* to safety when we parted ways."

Charles had claimed he'd chased Henri until Henri had driven away. True, he might have mistaken Padraig for Henri, given the similarity in their ages, but considering how long Charles had been tailing Henri before he lost him, surely he should have caught sight of him.

"What was the key to buying his loyalty?" Drake asked.

Padraig made an expansive gesture. "A woman, naturally."

Drake's blood ran cold. The woman had to be either Faith or Lily, and neither option was acceptable.

And then his blood turned to ice water when he remembered how Henri had coveted Faith. Had Charles delivered her into Henri's hands?

"Do you still need that car you borrowed?" he asked his maker, trying to keep calm, though he knew there had to be at least a hint of panic on his face.

Padraig laughed. "You refuse my kind offer and then expect a favor?" He shook his head. "I'm not walking to the train station from here, Johnnie. What bee's gotten in your bonnet?"

But everything in Drake's body told him time was of the essence, even if he didn't yet have the faintest idea where Charles might have taken Faith and Lily. "You wouldn't understand," he barked at Padraig, then began sprinting down the sidewalk, looking for a mortal whose car he could appropriate without drawing too much attention to himself.

Once again, Padraig's glamour seized him, and Drake almost howled in frustration.

"An emergency, Johnnie-boy?" Padraig asked with one of his infuriating grins.

Fury and fear for Faith's safety frayed the edges of Drake's temper. If Padraig's glamour had been even slightly less powerful, Drake would have shaken it off and attacked. As it was, Padraig merely regarded him with an expression of curiosity.

Then he smiled and reached into his pocket. "Perhaps a goodwill gesture will help you make the right decision down the road," Padraig mused half to himself. He dangled a set of car keys from the ends of his fingers and released Drake from his hold.

Drake hesitated a moment. "This doesn't mean I'm agreeing to come to New York."

Padraig inclined his head. "Understood."

Drake snatched the keys from his maker's hand and hurried back toward the garage where the stolen car was parked.

"Johnnie!" Padraig yelled when Drake had gotten no more than ten yards away. Some instinct he didn't understand made him look back over his shoulder at his maker.

"If you've got a small airport in the area, you might want to check there. I believe our lady plans to rendezvous with Charles at a jet."

Despite the ticking clock, Drake couldn't help giving Padraig a challenging stare. "You knew all along that he had the girls. And you knew I wouldn't stand for it. You thought I'd be grateful to you for letting me take the car."

Padraig shrugged. "I'll neither confirm nor deny it. You'd better hurry, though. You wouldn't want to miss the excitement."

Knowing Padraig was right, Drake dismissed his anger and ran for the car.

18

Drake speed-dialed Gabriel's number as he took the stairs in the parking garage two at a time.

Gabriel answered on the second ring. "Where the fuck are you?" he snarled, proving that he'd at least partially recovered from the tranquilizer.

"Long story," Drake said, bursting through the door of the stairwell and into the darkened garage. He hoped he wouldn't lose the signal as he hurried toward Padraig's stolen car. "Is there a small airport around here somewhere?"

"Why?"

"Just tell me, dammit!" He jerked open the car door and threw himself in.

"Well, there's Martin State Airport on Highway 150, but—"

"Charles is a traitor." He put the car in reverse and stomped the gas pedal, filling the echoing garage with the squeal of rubber on concrete.

"And I care about this, why?" There was a certain tightness to Gabriel's voice that said he was still in pain, but Drake knew he'd be capable of sarcasm even in the midst of being flayed alive.

"He has Faith and Lily." Drake remembered suddenly that Gabriel had no idea who Faith and Lily were, but before he could explain, Gabriel interrupted.

"Don't be an idiot. Jez told me you're involved with this Faith person, and I can certainly understand your need to mount your white horse and ride to the rescue, but—"

"I'm not abandoning them." Drake slowed down only marginally when he burst through the gate at the garage exit.

"I didn't say you should. If you hadn't interrupted, I was going to suggest you come to the house and pick me up."

But Drake shook his head. "You're in the opposite direction from the airport," he said, finally seeing a landmark he recognized so he could orient himself. "And you're shot full of tranquilizer."

"It wasn't a request, Drake. Get your ass back to the house. Now."

Drake hesitated only a moment before snapping the phone shut and throwing it carelessly onto the passenger seat. He didn't have time for this. Gabriel wouldn't want any harm to come to Faith and Lily, but having never met them, he had no personal stake in this. Drake's stake was very, very personal.

He didn't have the faintest idea what he was going to do if and when he caught up to Charles. All he knew was that he had to do something. He remembered how Jez had scorned him for giving up too easily when he knew he was outmatched. He smiled grimly. Well, now he was going to try it her way—and hope that he and those he cared about lived through the effort.

* * *

ADRENALINE SURGED THROUGH Faith's system as the final knot binding her legs came loose. Lily sat beside her in the heavy darkness, trying to rub some life into her blood-starved legs. Faith's own legs screamed with the pins and needles of returning blood, but she would recover quickly.

"Can you walk?" she whispered to Lily as she did a psychic scan to see where their captors were. It seemed there were two in the plane above them, and two outside. Surely they couldn't be expecting too much trouble from a six-year-old vampire and a mortal teenager who'd been thoroughly trussed.

"I'll try," Lily whispered back, sniffling.

Faith touched her sister's leg and felt the rope burn around one ankle. For a moment, a red haze filled her, and she wanted to kill everyone who had conspired to hurt Lily. Charles most of all. But she couldn't afford to indulge in revenge fantasies now. She had to get Lily out of here.

Her glamour was nowhere near as strong as a Killer's, but nonetheless Faith touched her sister's mind with it to try to ease the pain.

"Did you do that?" Lily asked, proving that the glamour was working.

"Yes," Faith answered. "I don't know how long I can keep it up. I have to concentrate a lot to do it. Now do you think you can walk?"

"Yeah."

Fumbling in the dark, Faith helped Lily to her feet and guided the two of them to where she remembered the door to be. She had to feel along the wall a while to find it, and she heard Lily's faint groan when the glamour slipped.

"It's all right," Lily hastened to assure her. "I can walk. Just concentrate on getting us out of here."

Grimly, Faith complied, her hands exploring the seam of the door until she figured out how to open it. Her psychic probe told her that two of their captors were still above them in the plane, but that one vampire and one mortal were at most ten yards away from the door. She bit her lip.

How old was their vampire guard? She'd never met him before, and she couldn't tell by his aura. Certainly he was capable of overpowering a fledgling like herself, but if he wasn't too old and she could take him by surprise, she might be able to delay him long enough for Lily to get away. And it would take a relatively mild glamour to lure the mortal close enough for her to make a quick kill.

A shiver traveled down her spine at the thought of killing someone, especially a mortal. But she didn't have a lot of options.

"What's the plan?" Lily whispered when Faith hesitated too long.

Faith took a deep breath and reached for Lily's hand in the darkness. "I'm going to use my glamour to get the mortal guard to come close to the door. Then I'm going to pop the door open and kill him." Her voice choked a bit on the words, but she forced herself to continue. "And you're going to jump out and run like hell."

Lily's hand tightened on hers. "That's a rotten plan. There were at least four guys when Charles brought us here."

"Yes, and two of them are in the plane. There's only one vamp on the tarmac, and as soon as the mortal's out of the way, I'll do my best to take him down."

Lily snorted softly. "Like I said, it's a lousy plan. I'm not stupid. You can't fight off one of *La Vieille*'s vamps."

"Maybe not, but I can delay him enough for you to get away." At least, she hoped she could.

"No way!"

"Shh," Faith reminded her, and Lily's voice dropped back to a whisper.

"No way. I'm not going to run away and leave you here."

"Yes, you are. You can't help me by staying here. You *can* help me by getting to a phone and calling Armand." Faith wasn't sure that even Armand could help her, if he had to fight Charles and *La Vieille*'s two vampire cronies to get to her, but she thought he might try. And at least if she gave Lily hope, she might actually go along with Faith's plan.

"But they could kill you before he gets here," Lily protested, a hint of tears in her voice.

"They won't," Faith said grimly. "Remember, *La Vieille* wants me alive. And anything they do to hurt me, I can heal from. Please, Lily. This is our only hope."

Lily threw her arms around Faith's neck and hugged her fiercely. "I love you," she said. "I'm sorry I've been such a pain in the butt."

Faith's own eyes burned with tears as she returned her sister's hug. "That's what little sisters are for. And I love you, too." She gave Lily one more squeeze, then pushed her away, wishing she could see in this inky darkness. "Now, are you ready?"

"For the record, I still think this plan sucks. But yeah, I'm ready."

After one more deep, calming breath, Faith very slowly cracked the door open. She winced at the noise it made, but when she peeked through the crack, she saw that their captors were engrossed in conversation with each other. Good, because their distraction covered the noise. Bad, because Faith couldn't lure the mortal toward her without the vamp noticing.

Patience, she told herself. She had to wait for just the right opportunity. Behind her, Lily practically vibrated with anxiety, but she remained still and quiet, following Faith's lead.

After a few minutes, the conversation finally died down. The sound of footsteps on metal stairs made both the mortal and the vamp look toward the plane. Caught by surprise, Faith could do nothing but hold her breath and hope they didn't notice the door was ajar.

She allowed herself to breathe again when she realized this was a changing of the guard, especially when it turned out this new pair wasn't as chatty. The vampire stood disturbingly still and quiet, while the mortal fidgeted and looked bored. This was Faith's chance.

She stared at the back of the mortal's head and reached out with her glamour. His fidgeting slowed, then stopped, but the vamp seemed to be completely ignoring him and didn't notice. Slowly, Faith reeled the mortal in, drawing him closer and closer, trying not to think too hard about what she was about to do.

"Get ready," she said to Lily in the faintest of whispers.

The mortal was almost within reach, and Faith pushed the door open a little more. Then she drew on every scrap of will and courage she had, reminding herself that she would do *anything* to keep Lily out of *La Vieille*'s hands.

Swallowing the last of her reluctance, she shoved the door all the way open and leapt at the mortal. She lost control of the glamour at the last moment, and he started to turn, but she barreled into him before he got all the way around. She wrapped one arm around his neck and gave a hard jerk.

The feel of his neck snapping made her stomach heave, but she didn't have time for squeamishness.

The vampire had turned toward her, and she launched herself at him. Out of the corner of her eye, she saw Lily jump to the tarmac and start running like mad.

The vampire tried to call out some warning to his accomplices, but when Faith crashed into him, he fell to the tarmac. When they landed, her knee dug into his groin, and all the sound he could manage was the faintest gasp of pain.

In that moment, when the guard was too stunned with pain to summon his glamour or fight her, she could have made a run for it herself. But she feared he would recover too quickly, and she needed to give Lily as much time as possible to make her escape. So instead of running, she swung her fist at the vamp's head with all the strength in her body.

She felt bone give way, and the tantalizing scent of blood perfumed the air. Her fangs descended, and she fought the urge to tear into his throat, knowing a wound like that wouldn't kill him. She needed an instant death, like the snapping of a neck. Something he couldn't heal from. She grabbed his head in both her hands.

And then froze under the power of another's glamour.

The guards in the plane must have heard the commotion, for they were both running down the stairs toward her. She reached out with her senses, trying to find Lily, and was thrilled when she couldn't. Granted, her reach wasn't very impressive, but it meant Lily had a good head start. If these two guards took a little more time to realize she was missing, she had a chance of escaping.

The vampire from the plane grabbed her roughly by the arm and swung her around to face him. He bared his fangs at her. Then his fist crashed into her chin and she blacked out.

* * *

THOUGH IT WAS long past the airport's closing time, glamour ensured that the guard at the gatehouse let Charles drive his car, with Armand still and silent in the trunk, toward *La Vieille*'s jet. He'd been expecting a call from Brigitte, but so far his phone had remained silent. Uncertainty gnawed at his gut, but there was nothing he could do other than bring the *Seigneur* to the plane. If the plane took off before Brigitte contacted him, then he would just have to fall back on his original plan. The thought made him grimace as he now wondered if *La Vieille* would give him Lily as he'd so optimistically hoped.

His worries were interrupted when he caught a glimpse of movement out of the corner of his eye. Slowing the car, he squinted into the darkness, reaching out with his senses to help him locate the source of the movement. He picked up the aura of a mortal, running fast. The hangar blocked his view, but he could think of no good reason for a mortal to be running around a closed airport at this time of night.

When Lily emerged from behind the building, Charles slammed on the brakes. What was she doing running free? And where was Faith? With a curse, he put the car in park and reached out for her with his glamour. She came to a dead stop, and he called her to him. He opened the passenger door and gestured her in.

"Please," she sobbed, but his glamour had a firm hold, and she had to obey him.

He used his telekinesis to close Lily's door, and then drove back in the direction from which she had come. "I'm truly sorry, Lily," he said. "I can't allow you to run away." He risked a glance at her tear-ravaged face, and his heart constricted with pity. Yes, he wanted Lily to be his. But he wished there could have been some other way to win her. As it was, she was probably going to hate him for years.

"I promise I'll keep you safe," he told her.

"What about Faith?"

He had no answer for that. None she'd want to hear, anyway. There was nothing he could do for Faith. She'd go to either *La Vieille* or to Henri.

When he reached the plane, Charles saw the remains of a battleground. One of *La Vieille*'s mortals lay on the tarmac, his head twisted at an unnatural angle. One of the vampires limped over to the stairs leading into the plane, clutching his face and hunched over in obvious pain. And Faith lay facedown as the other vampire bound her hands behind her back. The bright white lights of the plane revealed a heavy bruise on the side of her face.

"Faith!" Lily screamed, but Charles wouldn't let her go dashing out of the car.

Instead, he pulled to a stop and parked, assuring himself that the situation was well under control. Then he turned to Lily, frowning at the rope burns that circled her wrists. He reached out to touch one gently. Lily tried to jerk away.

"I'm sorry they hurt you," he said, wishing he could kiss the wounds and make them better.

He realized with something of a shock that he could. All he had to do was bite her, transform her, and she would be unconscious for days as her body changed. Then when she woke up, all her wounds would be gone. He found himself staring at the pulse that throbbed in her throat. His fangs descended, and he leaned toward her without even meaning to.

He stopped himself before she had a chance to guess what he'd been about to do. Now was hardly the time for him to transform her. He couldn't *force* her to become a vampire—she'd have to accept the lifeline he offered her when he took her to the brink of death, and he feared right now she wouldn't do it. Somehow, he was going to have to win her over, and that was going to take time.

He sighed. "Behave yourself and you won't need to be tied again," he said, getting out of the car. He popped the trunk, then came around to Lily's side and opened her door.

For a moment, she just sat there with her arms crossed over her chest and a stubborn scowl on her face.

"You're not a child anymore, Lily," Charles scolded, a little more sharply than he meant to. "Stop acting like one. You're only making this more difficult for yourself."

She glared at him through damp lashes and red-rimmed eyes. "I don't see how things could possibly get worse."

The vampire who'd just finished trussing Faith laughed, and it was not at all a pleasant sound. But he was a relative youngster, only about a hundred and fifty. Charles could destroy him easily, and he let that thought show in his steady stare. The vampire stopped laughing and shrugged.

"Get the body out of sight," Charles snapped. His senses told him there were no security personnel close enough to see the dead man lying on the tarmac, but there was no point in taking chances.

La Vieille's minion left Faith where she was lying and slung the dead man over his shoulder. He headed for the hangar, and Charles figured that was as good a place to stow the body as anywhere. By the time anyone found it, the plane would be long gone.

He snapped his fingers at the wounded vampire who sat moping on the stairs. "Come take the girl," he said, grabbing Lily's arm and pulling her out of the car. "Hurt her, and I'll tear out your tongue."

The man snorted, but used his glamour to call Lily to him and didn't touch her when she was within reach. Charles nodded his approval. Then he drew the tranq gun once more and moved to the back of the car, carefully opening the trunk.

Armand lay there curled in fetal position, his body drenched with sweat, his face a mask of pain. Charles lowered the gun, reassured that Armand wasn't close to needing another dose yet. He tucked the gun back into its holster, then dragged Armand out of the trunk.

Armand's eyes had been closed when Charles first hauled him out, but when he let go to close the trunk, he heard a pained moan and saw that Armand was looking at Faith and Lily. Charles slammed the trunk and squatted near his friend, trying to harden his heart.

"I'm sorry, Armand. I owe you . . . everything. But I haven't your courage, I'm afraid. *La Vieille* offered me immunity if I would bring the surviving members of the delegation home." He shook his head and stared at the ground beneath his feet. "I couldn't refuse her. Not even for you."

The look in Armand's eyes was positively murderous, but he said nothing.

"There's a car coming, boss," *La Vieille*'s surviving mortal said.

Charles shot to his feet, but he knew as soon as he caught sight of the little red sports car just who it would be. Brigitte pulled her car to a stop beside Charles's, then waited for Henri to come around and open the door for her.

La Vieille's minions stood there looking dumbfounded. Brigitte smiled and waved at them one at a time, then turned that smile to Charles.

"Were you beginning to worry about me?" she asked.

"I was beginning to wonder," he said warily. He

might have allied himself with her, but he couldn't exactly say he trusted her.

She reached out to pat his cheek, and he had to check his urge to jerk away. "I wouldn't miss out on this for the world. Now, why don't you explain to my mother's friends just what's going on here?"

He looked at *La Vieille*'s people, and his heart quailed at the thought of them reporting his actions to *La Vieille*. All hope of clemency would be gone—which, of course, was why Brigitte wanted him to do this and cement his loyalty to her.

He had already made his decision when last he'd talked to Brigitte. Now it was time to make that decision irrevocable. He straightened his spine and tried to look dignified.

"I will not be returning to France with you," he told them. "I have decided to stay in America with Brigitte." They stared at him in open shock.

Brigitte prodded him with her elbow. "Go on. What else?"

"The girl is mine," he said, reaching out a hand toward Lily. *La Vieille*'s vampire grabbed her arm. "Don't be a fool," Charles told him. "You couldn't overpower *one* of us, much less all three." He indicated himself and Brigitte and Henri.

The vampire let go of Lily's arm and gave her a shove toward Charles. "*La Vieille* will eat your liver every night for this."

Charles ignored the threat as best he could, guiding Lily so that he stood between her and *La Vieille*'s men.

"Henri will be taking Faith," Charles said, before Brigitte could prod him again.

Lily gasped, and before Charles could turn to apologize to her yet again, she delivered a sharp kick to his shin. He winced and jerked away, then stilled her with glamour before she could do it again.

"Very good," Brigitte said, sounding like she was praising a well-behaved dog. "But really, Charles, you are too stupid to live."

There was a popping sound, and then a sharp sting in his shoulder. He blinked in confusion until he saw the little dart sticking out of his flesh.

His knees gave way without warning and he fell to the tarmac as pain spread with lightning speed from the injection site.

Brigitte tucked away her gun and came to stand over him, shaking her head. "You betray your friend and maker, then you betray my mother, and you expect *me* to trust you?" She laughed. "I'm afraid I'm not hiring at the moment. But thank you very much for applying for the job. It's been most entertaining."

Through the haze of pain, Charles realized the real reason she had forced him to declare himself in front of *La Vieille*'s people: to entertain herself, and to condemn him to a traitor's fate. The terror that struck him was worse even than the pain, and a scream tore from his throat.

19

DRAKE TURNED OFF his lights the moment he passed through the gates into the airport. Even a small airport was a large area to search, but a psychic probe located seven vampires off to his right somewhere. He tried not to let his heart sink at the hopelessness of his cause.

Gabriel had taken to dialing Drake's cell phone repeatedly, so Drake had turned the damn thing off. Maybe Gabriel would show up in time to help—and be recovered enough from the drug to be useful—or maybe he wouldn't. Drake didn't dare depend on him.

He drove slowly toward the congregation of vampires, his head whirring through possible plans, none of which had a prayer of succeeding.

He considered parking the car and then sneaking up on foot, but rejected that as useless. They would no doubt be on alert and sense him coming. If stealth wasn't an option, he might as well use the car to reach them as quickly as possible.

He turned on the lights and sped up, trying not to think about the last time he'd tried to save someone he loved against terrible odds. When he'd tried to save Eamon, he'd done nothing but cause his brother more pain. But considering what he'd heard of *La Vieille,* nothing he could do could possibly make it worse for Faith or Lily.

When the plane came into view, the first thing Drake noticed was the pair of cars parked just out of the brightest glow of the plane's lights. Then he saw the gathering of vampires, only two mortals in their midst. Charles was standing by the open trunk of one of the cars with a figure huddled on the tarmac at his feet. The *Seigneur,* no doubt. Next, Drake caught sight of Brigitte, with Henri glued to her side as usual. He cursed and hit the steering wheel, hardly believing his odds of success had gotten worse.

Still, when he saw Faith swaying on her feet, her arms bound behind her, a strange vampire holding her, his will steadied. It didn't matter what the odds were.

No one seemed to be too worried about him when he pulled his car up beside the red sports car he presumed belonged to Brigitte. By the time he got out, Charles had dropped to the tarmac himself and was howling in pain. Drake saw the tranq gun in Brigitte's hand and knew what had felled Charles.

He held his hands out to his sides and approached slowly, still having no plan. The only thing he had going in his favor at the moment was that one of the oldest of his adversaries was down for the count. He glanced from Charles to Brigitte, wondering what she was up to. If she'd wanted to kill him, she could easily have done it in the alley.

"How good of you to come and see your friends off," Brigitte said. She kept the tranq gun trained on him, and though he knew she didn't need it to stop him in his tracks, his muscles tensed in anticipation.

"I wasn't expecting to see you here," he said, his voice calmer than he'd dared hope it would be.

"The feeling is mutual," she assured him, cocking her head. "Why *are* you here, I wonder?"

"He wants the girls," Henri said, looking over his shoulder at Faith and Lily, then turning back toward Drake and licking his lips.

"Ah!" Brigitte said. "Of course. I've heard you fancy yourself something of a gentleman."

Drake looked at Faith and Lily as Brigitte and Henri gloated. There was a bruise on Faith's chin, and angry red welts circled Lily's wrists and ankles, but otherwise they seemed unhurt. So far.

"What would you offer me in exchange for these lovely ladies?" Brigitte asked.

Drake wracked his brain for something he could offer, but he couldn't think of a single thing he had that Brigitte might want. He dropped his gaze, and noticed the *Seigneur,* lying in the shadow of the trunk of the car, had his eyes open and was staring at him.

Instinct warned him to look away before anyone

noticed the direction of his gaze, and he did. But he wondered if that stare meant the *Seigneur* was beginning to recover from the drug. Drake's sense of time was completely out of whack with all the adrenaline that had been pumping through his system since the confrontation in the alley, but he remembered that Gabriel had been feeling better—if not exactly *well*—when they'd spoken. Perhaps he had an ally here after all.

The one thing he knew was that the longer he managed to stall, the more Armand would recover, and the more likely that Gabriel would catch up with him—assuming Gabriel cared enough to come after him.

He shook his head and met Brigitte's curious gaze. "Why don't you tell me what you would like in exchange for them?"

"Hmm," she said, tapping her chin with her index finger. "I've promised the lovely Faith to Henri. But I can let you have the mortal." She turned to the vampire who had hold of Lily. "Let her go."

"I can't!" the vampire protested. "*La Vieille* would kill me for giving up one of her—"

Brigitte laughed. "As if you have any choice in the matter. You know how easily I can force you to let her go, so why don't you stop acting the fool?"

Reluctantly, he released Lily, but she stood frozen to the spot, her eyes glazed. Drake might have thought she was under the influence of glamour, but the scent of fear that emanated from her suggested it was more shock and terror than anything.

"Go on, Lily," Faith urged. "Go with Drake." She hiccupped slightly, and a tear snaked down her cheek.

There was no way in hell he was leaving without Faith, but if Brigitte was willing to give up Lily without a fight, he'd take her. He held out a hand to Lily.

"Come on," he said, checking on Armand's condition out of the corner of his eye.

The *Seigneur* was still watching him, but when Drake caught his eye he gave a slight shake of his head. Drake took that to mean he wasn't up to a credible attack yet.

Lily still hadn't moved, though her eyes had cleared somewhat, a hint of intelligence returning to her expression.

Drake beckoned with his outstretched hand. "Come here. Let's get you taken care of first, then we'll see what we can do about Faith, okay?"

She blinked, then glanced at her sister. "Faith?" she asked, sounding suddenly younger than her sixteen years.

"Please go with him, sweetie," Faith begged, desperation clear in her voice and face.

Lily swallowed hard, then began to move cautiously toward Drake, her eyes darting from one vampire to another, as if she could prevent them from jumping her if she could just keep them in sight.

When she took Drake's outstretched hand, he sighed in relief, then reached into his pocket with his free hand and pulled out the car keys.

"Take my car," he said, "and get out of here. The

car is stolen, so you'll want to abandon it as soon as you're far enough away." He pushed the keys into her hand when she didn't immediately take them. Then he pulled out his cell phone and handed it to her. "You can speed-dial Gabriel when you're out of here and he'll send someone to come pick you up."

She took the phone, but looked over at Faith once more. Drake's heart broke at the raw emotion on the girl's face. Drake reached out and turned her face toward him, making her look into his eyes.

"The best way to help your sister right now is to get to safety," he told her. "Her fear for you hurts worse than anything they can do to her."

Lily's lip quivered, and she looked at the keys in her hand. Then she stood up a little straighter and glared at him. "You'd better get her out of here," she snarled. Then she got into the car, not even bothering to adjust the seat before she shoved the keys in the ignition and stomped on the accelerator.

Drake held his breath as he watched the lights of the car recede. When he couldn't see the lights anymore, he tracked her with his psychic senses and was relieved that she continued toward the exit. He wasn't sure what would happen when she reached the gates and the security guard—especially considering that she was driving a stolen car without a license—but he'd done what he could for her. Now he had to figure out what he could do for Faith.

He turned back to Brigitte, who was smirking at him. "Now, let's talk about what you're going to give me as a reward for freeing the little mortal girl," she said.

Drake snorted. "You were going to free her anyway. You know Gabriel would never forgive you for hurting a child."

She shrugged. "All I'd have had to do is kill you, and he'd never have known."

"If you were planning to keep her, you never would have let her go without getting your pound of flesh first."

She stuck out her lower lip. "I suppose that's true." She dispensed with the pout and became all business again. "Are you satisfied now that I've let the little girl go, or are you still hoping to bargain for Faith?"

"What do you want for her?" he asked, feeling like a slaver at an auction. And he had a bone-deep conviction that Brigitte was just toying with him. She'd promised Faith to her boy toy, and Drake doubted there was anything he could offer that would make her break that promise. However, she'd probably enjoy giving him hope and then snatching it away. Every moment he kept her talking was another moment for the *Seigneur*'s strength to come back and for Gabriel to catch up.

"Make me an offer," Brigitte said.

He thought furiously. Then he realized he already had part of his answer. Brigitte wanted to be "entertained." And she was entertained by strife, despair, and pain.

"I'll fight Henri for the right to take her," he said, and saw the interest that kindled in her eyes.

"Henri is more than twice your age. Even without my help, he's more than a match for you."

"Not if we agree not to use glamour." Henri was no doubt physically stronger than Drake, but the difference in physical strength that came with age was nowhere near as prominent as the difference in psychic strength. Theoretically, Drake should have a chance against the older vampire in a good, old-fashioned fistfight. And Drake might well have the advantage of experience in street fighting.

Brigitte looked thoughtful, and Drake's hopes surged. He had no illusions that Henri would refrain from using glamour and fight fair, nor did he believe that Brigitte would hand Faith over even if Drake managed to prevail. But if he could use the fight to maneuver Henri toward Armand . . . The *Seigneur* didn't seem to be anywhere near strong enough yet to attack, but if Henri were to fall in his lap, he might be able to summon one burst of strength. Brigitte was a significant threat on her own, but Drake suspected she'd be severely weakened without Henri.

"I have to admit," she said, "your offer is tempting. But only if Henri agrees." She smiled at him. "What do you think, dearest?"

He gave Drake a disdainful look. "She's already been promised to me," he said. "Why should I have to fight to keep her?"

"Are you afraid you'll lose?" Drake retorted. It was an obvious ploy, but with a predatory creature such as Henri, it might work. At least, that's what Drake told himself until Henri laughed.

"I would not lose," he said, still chuckling. "I simply see no reason to exert myself. I believe you Americans would say, 'What's in it for me?' "

"The chance to impress your maker."

He raised an eyebrow. "You think she would be impressed that I could defeat you when it's a foregone conclusion?"

Drake found himself more eager for the fight now—he itched to prove the bastard wrong, even while he doubted his ability to do so. "All right, then—the chance to entertain her."

Henri paused at that, then turned to Brigitte. "Is this true, *ma déesse*? Would you enjoy watching me fight him?"

Brigitte's eyes twinkled as she smiled at him. "Yes, I believe I would. Especially if you were both to remove your shirts. I so admire the sight of solid male muscles."

Henri put one hand to his heart and bowed. "Then for your pleasure alone, I will accept the challenge." He began removing his expensive silk shirt, but considering it was already unbuttoned halfway to his navel, it didn't take long.

Drake felt mildly ridiculous taking off his shirt, but he did it anyway, ignoring the ooh of pleasure from Brigitte. Henri's eyes hardened when he heard it, and Drake knew that jealousy would feed into his ferocity.

They began to circle each other, Drake trying to draw Henri closer to where Armand lay. Henri charged before Drake got him where he wanted him. He met the charge with an uppercut that "mysteriously" missed its mark. Drake knew it was glamour that had caused him to miss, but he was in no position to protest. Henri plowed into him, and they both fell to the tarmac, Henri on top.

A crushing punch landed on Drake's jaw, but he ignored the pain and concentrated on pitching Henri off of him, knowing he was neither winning the fight nor moving it where he wanted it to go. He kicked upward with both legs, catching Henri right about hip level and catapulting him up and over Drake's head.

Drake immediately rolled to the side and got to his feet. Unfortunately, his throw had moved Henri even farther from Armand. Henri flashed fangs as he picked himself up off the tarmac and stalked closer. Drake backed up, leading him toward the cars—and the *Seigneur*.

Henri stopped and gestured for Drake to take a swing. Drake knew he couldn't refuse the challenge without someone wondering about his true motives. Telling himself to be patient, he stopped his retreat and looked for an opening.

Henri gave him that opening, and though Drake knew he'd done it on purpose, he swung anyway. His fist glanced off Henri's shoulder as the older vampire dodged at supernatural speed and kicked out at Drake's knee. Drake saw the kick coming and managed to twist enough to take it on his calf instead of his knee, but the pain that shot through his leg felled him anyway.

Instinct made him roll as soon as he hit the ground, avoiding Henri's pounce, but when he got to his feet he could hardly put any weight on his left leg. He smelled blood on the air, and that's when he noticed the abrasions the tarmac had left on the bare skin of his chest and back.

Henri grinned at his wounded prey. "You've had enough?" he asked, sounding like he knew better.

Drake didn't answer, instead trying to put a little more distance between them while he waited to see if his leg would recover enough to hold his weight. It didn't seem like it was going to anytime soon, so he ended up practically hopping on one leg. But he'd moved closer to Armand. He didn't dare look, but a quick psychic scan told him he was about ten yards away. If he could get Henri to charge him again, he might be able to use the older vampire's momentum to shove him straight into Armand's path. Then he just had to hope that Armand had enough strength and quickness to make the kill.

His leg throbbed and his skin burned from the abrasions, but Drake tried his best to brace himself. With his leg unable to hold his weight, he wasn't going to have much leverage, but if the fight went on much longer, he was going to be too banged up to exert even a small amount of control. If he was going to win, it had to be now.

Steadying himself, rehearsing in his mind what he needed to do, he crouched. This time, it was his turn to invite Henri to take a swing. Henri grinned eagerly and cracked his knuckles. Then he charged.

Drake made no effort to duck or dodge, nor did he try to land a blow himself. He merely waited until Henri's fist made contact with his face, then allowed himself to fall backward, his arms by his sides. As Henri came down on top of him, Drake used his good leg and both his arms to once again flip Henri over his head. The idiot shouldn't have fallen for it twice, but he'd been too cocky, too sure Drake's wounds would debilitate him.

Henri grunted when he landed, and Drake rolled to see where he was. A trickle of blood obscured his vision, but Drake hurriedly wiped it away.

Henri was sitting on his ass not three feet from the *Seigneur,* shaking his head as if to clear the cobwebs. For a moment, Drake thought his plan had failed as the *Seigneur* lay motionless. Then, just as Henri was starting to rise, the *Seigneur* surged to his feet with a roar.

Before anyone was able to move or react, the *Seigneur* grabbed Henri by the neck and jerked. Drake heard the telltale crack of breaking bone. Brigitte screamed, an ear-splitting sound that sent a spike of pain through Drake's head. He started to rise, but then something inexplicable happened.

Something resembling a shimmering heat wave emanated from Brigitte's body, then expanded away from her like a ripple of water. The ripple hit Faith and her captor, and both of them were thrown several feet back. Then it hit *La Vieille*'s other vampire, and threw him. The ground beneath him seemed to rumble as the wave advanced, and Drake was too badly hurt to do anything but brace himself and hope for the best.

It crashed into him with bone-jarring force, sending him flying through the air. Then he hit the ground, his head smacking firmly into the pavement, and everything went black.

20

FAITH LAY ON her back, staring at the stars in the night sky. For half a second, she couldn't remember where she was or what was happening. Then her brain seemed to pop back into place and she remembered. With a lurch, she dragged herself up into a sitting position and looked frantically around.

Everywhere around her, bodies lay strewn on the tarmac, felled by the wave of power that had emanated from Brigitte when Henri had died. There was no sign of Brigitte. Faith shuddered when she saw that both cars had been thrown backward by the wave. Brigitte's lightweight sports car had flipped over, its roof crushed by the impact. Charles's car had merely rolled backward several yards.

Faith ached all over, but she had landed on top of her guard when they'd fallen, and he appeared to have gotten the worst of it. She could see that he was breathing, but he lay still. Barely even thinking about what she was doing, she bent down and twisted his neck until it snapped.

Then she staggered toward Drake, who lay on his side near the cars. She knelt beside him, wincing to see how much skin had been scraped away by the rough tarmac, and gently turned him over onto his back. Relief flooded her when she saw his chest rise and fall. Tears dribbled down her cheek as she wiped the blood from his face with the corner of her shirt. His eyes fluttered open at her touch.

"Are you all right?" she asked. It was a foolish question, but it was all she could think of to say at the moment. Her mind remained sluggish, overwhelmed by everything that had happened.

He managed a strained smile. "I'm not dead." He started to sit up, and she slipped a hand under his shoulders to help him. The effort seemed to exhaust him.

As she waited for Drake to recover, she took another look around, reminding herself that the danger wasn't over. She'd killed one of *La Vieille*'s vampires, but she didn't see the other one. A psychic probe showed he was on the other side of Charles's car and so far wasn't moving.

Armand lay on his stomach not far away, Henri's body draped over his back. And the glaring white lights from the plane spotlighted Charles, who was curled up in a ball and moaning piteously. Faith tried to imagine walking up to him and snapping his neck as she had *La Vieille*'s vampire, but her stomach curdled in fear at the idea. Even in his current condition, he could be dangerous to someone as weak as she.

Armand caught her attention when he rolled over and shoved Henri's body away. Their eyes met across the short distance, and Faith realized she no longer had the faintest idea what she felt about him. He tried to stand up, but he swayed on his feet and fell back to the tarmac.

Drake took her hand and gave it a squeeze. "We've got company," he said, and she followed his gaze to see a pair of headlights coming straight toward them. She couldn't seem to summon the energy to be alarmed. She shaded her eyes from the glare as the car rolled to a stop in front of them.

The driver's door opened, then slammed shut, and a voice she didn't know said, "What the fuck happened here?"

Someone—not the driver—turned the lights off, and Faith looked up to see an unfamiliar vampire staring down at her and Drake. The stranger was dressed entirely in black leather decorated with silver studs, and his white-blond hair stood in stiff spikes at the top of his head.

"I'll let you know when I figure it out," Drake said, not sounding in the least alarmed. Faith made a wild guess that this scary-looking guy was Gabriel. "Are you really up to driving?" Drake continued, and Gabriel's eyes narrowed.

"Jez drove most of the way here." For the first

time, she noticed Jezebel, leaning against the passenger side door. "We ran into the mortal girl being given a hard time at the exit."

Faith gasped. "Is she okay?"

Gabriel gave her a cautious look, but nodded. "She's fine. I convinced the guard to let her go. Eric and Harry are taking her back to the house as we speak. You must be Faith."

She nodded, not at all sure of her welcome in the Master of Baltimore's eyes. After all, she'd been part of the delegation, the enemy. And Jez hadn't seemed to like her much.

"Pleased to meet you," Gabriel said, not sounding like he meant it. But he turned his attention to Drake immediately afterward. "You look like you're in rough shape at the moment, so I'm going to let you heal up before kicking your ass."

Faith bristled and opened her mouth for an unwise retort, but Drake silenced her with a hand on her shoulder. Gabriel squatted to put himself at eye level with Drake.

"While we're waiting, care to tell me what happened here?"

Drake gave an abbreviated version of the events, his voice gaining strength as he went. When he got to the part where the *Seigneur* killed Henri, he pointed to Armand, who was still seated on the tarmac. His eyes were clear, his breathing easy, and Faith guessed he was almost completely recovered from the drug. But he neither tried to run nor attack.

Gabriel stood and offered Drake a hand up. Drake regarded that hand suspiciously, and Gabriel laughed.

"It's safe, for the moment," he said. "I need to grill you some more before I decide how hard to thrash you."

Drake grimaced and took Gabriel's hand, but he looked relatively steady when he got to his feet. He then extended his hand to Faith, and she allowed him to help her up as she wondered what she could possibly say to thank him for what he'd done.

* * *

ARMAND FELT STRANGELY numb, considering all that had happened, all that would soon happen. His head still spun from the aftereffects of the tranquilizer, and every beat of his heart pushed the burn of it through his veins, but the pain had become manageable. He sat calmly on the tarmac, keeping both hands splayed on his knees so everyone could see he was unarmed.

As the Master of Baltimore turned his attention away from Drake and approached, Armand thought fleetingly that he should be afraid. There was death in Gabriel's eyes, and, outnumbered and still weakened, Armand was helpless to defend himself. However, the numbness shielded him from the fear, and he boldly looked his death in the face.

"May I make a final request before you kill me?" he asked, and Gabriel stopped short.

"What's your request?" Gabriel asked. His expression didn't change, but at least he allowed Armand to speak.

Armand's throat tightened as he looked over at Charles, who still lay on the tarmac in fetal position. Occasionally, a faint whimper of pain escaped him. Charles had betrayed him, after six hundred years of friendship and loyalty. Armand should be hurt, furious, vengeful. Instead, all he felt was a pulse of pity. "Allow me to kill Charles myself," he said, and knew from Charles's gasp that he heard. "I would not have him die at a stranger's hands."

Gabriel shrugged. "Be my guest. But I hope you're not planning any tricks. I am capable of making your death most unpleasant if you piss me off."

"No tricks," Armand agreed quietly. He rose to his feet, moving slowly, keeping his hands away from his body. Gabriel shadowed him as he approached Charles. Armand knelt beside his friend and fledgling, putting a hand on his shoulder and turning him over onto his back.

Armand thought he'd never seen anything as desolate as Charles's face at that moment. His eyes squinched in pain, his jaw standing out in sharp relief, his breath coming in short gasps, he met Armand's gaze.

"I'm so sorry, Armand," he sobbed, then covered his face with his hands. "I wasn't strong enough to refuse her. I hated myself for it, but I couldn't do it."

Armand sighed heavily. "I should hate you for

what you've done," he said, "but I don't. You may not believe this, but I do understand." He drew his friend's hands away from his face. "It is *La Vieille*'s unique gift to draw out the worst in everyone she touches."

"Not you," Charles argued, blinking away tears. "She never managed to get to you."

The corners of Armand's mouth tightened. If only that were true. "Yes, she did, my friend. The damage was just more subtle. She changed me from the man I once was into what I am now." He smiled grimly. "It is not an improvement."

But Charles had a loyal heart, despite everything he'd done. "You were a good man. And you've been a good *Seigneur*. She did not corrupt you, no matter what you think."

Let Charles believe that if he wished. Armand knew the truth. Meeting his friend's eyes, he reached out with his glamour. Even with the debilitating effects of the tranquilizer, Charles could have tried to fight the glamour, but he didn't. His body slowly relaxed as Armand fogged his mind, blocking out pain, and fear, and thought.

When Charles was completely under, Armand put one hand on each side of his head. His body was rigid with conflict, his soul screaming at him that he could not kill his friend, no matter what Charles had done. But it was somehow fitting that Armand be the one to usher him out of this life, when it was Armand who'd made him in the first place.

He blew out a deep, harsh breath. "I forgive you,

my friend," he said, so softly no one could hear. And then snapped Charles's neck with one quick twist.

Afterward, he remained on his knees, his eyes closed, his head bent, trying to absorb the pain of what he'd just done. His only consolation was that he wouldn't have to live with it for long. He expected to fall under Gabriel's glamour at any moment, but excruciating minutes passed while nothing happened.

Finally, Armand opened his eyes and looked up at Gabriel. "What are you waiting for?"

"Is Brigitte dead, do you think?" Gabriel asked instead of answering.

Armand frowned, finding it hard to care one way or another. "I don't know. I would have thought she'd have killed us all if she were still alive. But I also wouldn't have thought Henri's death would kill her."

Gabriel nodded. "My thoughts exactly. But they'd been together for two hundred and fifty years. His death could have had dreadful consequences for her without killing her. My gut tells me she's alive. I hope I'm wrong, but if I'm not, it means this unholy alliance of hers is still alive and well."

And still, Armand couldn't muster up the energy to care. "What is your point?"

"My point is it might be helpful to have a six-hundred-year-old vampire on our side."

"You can't be serious," Drake objected.

Armand was too stunned to say a word.

Gabriel gave Drake a cold look. "Neither you nor I have room to throw stones."

"Yes, we do! We don't kill or hurt innocents."

"If you'd be so kind as to let me finish, you'll see that I've taken that into account."

Drake looked like he was grinding his teeth, but he fell silent. When Gabriel seemed sure he would remain that way, he turned back to Armand.

"As I was saying, I have a feeling we might be in need of an ally. However, given your history, I have serious concerns over whether I can trust you."

Armand's head spun with confusion. He was prepared—in fact, *more* than prepared—to meet his death. He couldn't argue that it wasn't deserved, and right now it seemed more a mercy than anything else.

He glanced around at the assembled Guardians, acutely aware of how weak they all were, with Gabriel as the sole exception. If Brigitte was still alive, she would be more than a match for them. Especially if she had her pet masters at her beck and call.

Armand's gaze landed on Faith, who stood back in the shadows. And he realized that even though it might be easier to abdicate all responsibility and flee his troubles in death, that would be the coward's way out. He was many things, but a coward was not one of them.

Armand slowly rose to his feet, again keeping his hands clearly visible. "I am prepared to die," he said. "However, if by living I could help protect those I care about," his eyes darted quickly to Faith, "then I would do just about anything to stay alive. What must I do to gain your trust?"

"My father was a Killer," Gabriel said. "For over a

thousand years. But in a fit of remorse—otherwise known as a suicide attempt—he accidentally cured himself of his addiction to the kill."

Armand's jaw dropped. "I've never heard of such a thing!"

"Almost no one has. Eli managed to do it, but several of his fledglings tried it and they all died. The oldest of them was almost five hundred, but Eli was over a thousand when he did it. He thinks his advanced age may have been what made it work. I have no idea whether a Killer of your age could survive the process. The question is, would you be willing to try?"

Armand raised an eyebrow. "The alternative is you kill me now, right?"

Gabriel grinned. "I think you're beginning to see the advantages of my offer."

Armand couldn't fathom what Gabriel was thinking. They were enemies, he had to know that. If their positions had been reversed, Gabriel would have been dead ten minutes ago. "Why would you trust me, even if I went through this process of yours and survived? You've known me for all of ten minutes. And you know I came here to kill you."

"It's been a telling ten minutes. And I can't imagine after all that's happened you'd have any great desire to return to your homeland or team up with Brigitte, assuming she's still alive."

Armand suppressed a shudder. There was certainly truth in that. If he was actually going to live through this encounter, there was nowhere in the world he could go that would be safe if Brigitte or *La Vieille* knew he still lived.

"He might not team up with one of *them,*" Drake protested, "but what's to say he won't just skip town and set himself up as a master somewhere? He's old enough to take over any city in the U.S. except Baltimore and Philadelphia!"

Armand managed a strained laugh. "I'm not a fool, Drake. If Brigitte is alive, she's very, very unhappy with me. Whatever you may think of me, I am powerfully motivated to remain in your master's good graces."

Drake looked like he had much more to say, but Gabriel cut him off. "The subject isn't open for debate." He turned to look at Jezebel, who hadn't said a word throughout and whose face was studiously neutral.

"I'd like you to take Faith and Armand back to the house. Armand can have the, er, guest room in the basement." He looked at Armand. "You will be locked in. Sorry if that makes me seem inhospitable."

Armand doubted there was a lock that could hold him, but he declined to disabuse Gabriel of the notion. He was willing to call a truce with the Master of Baltimore, and he was even willing to team up with him against Brigitte. That didn't mean he completely trusted him. After all, Gabriel was a born vampire, and born vampires were known for mental instability.

"You're going to let Jez and Faith get into a car with him unprotected?" Drake cried.

"He won't harm them," Gabriel said calmly and with great conviction. "I doubt he needs to be told what would happen to him if he laid a finger on anyone under my protection."

Drake sputtered, and Jez finally spoke up. "If I'm taking Armand and Faith back to the house, what are *you* doing?"

"Drake and I are going to have a long talk," he answered. The tone of his voice suggested "long talk" was a euphemism.

"Please," Faith blurted, taking a step toward Gabriel and reaching out a hand, though she didn't quite dare touch him. "If he hadn't come, Lily and I would have been long gone before you got here and we'd be worse than dead."

"That may be," Gabriel said, "but he disobeyed a direct order. And there are other matters we need to discuss. I'm not going to kill him, if that's what you're worried about."

Faith stared at Drake, her expression stricken. Armand's heart gave a dull thump, and he looked away. In the course of a handful of days, Drake had melted her heart and won her love. And Armand would always wonder whether things would have turned out differently if only he'd treated her better from the beginning. But he'd been a *Seigneur,* and even if he'd recognized his feelings for her earlier, he could never have treated her as an equal.

Perhaps if he survived whatever the process was

that might cure the blood addiction, he would be able to start anew when it was over. Perhaps he could lay the *Seigneur* to rest and become just Armand Durant once more. Only time would tell.

21

DRAKE WATCHED THE car drive away and hoped like hell Gabriel knew what he was doing.

He heard a faint groan behind him and turned to see Gabriel walk around to the other side of Charles's car. The groan was cut off. Gabriel bent, and a moment later Drake heard the sound of breaking bone. The last of *La Vieille*'s vampires was dead. Drake scanned for the single mortal that had been part of the entourage, but couldn't find him. Then he peered into the darkness and saw a limp body just beyond the wreckage of Brigitte's car. Apparently, the mortal hadn't survived his encounter with the shockwave—or whatever that had been.

"What are we going to do about this mess?" Drake asked Gabriel, indicating the scattered bodies and overturned car.

Gabriel shrugged. "We take the vamps to the crematorium, and we let the mortal authorities be extremely puzzled as to what the hell happened here. Especially since we're going to appropriate the security tapes before we leave." He grinned. "I don't think vampires are going to be high on their suspect list."

Drake had to concede the point. But he supposed he'd only asked about it in an effort to put off the dreaded conversation. Now it was best to just get on with it.

"You said you wanted to talk to me," he said, his nerves making his voice sharp, "so talk."

Gabriel raised an eyebrow at the tone of voice but didn't go into aggression overdrive. "Care to make excuses for why you disobeyed me?"

Drake bristled and had to swallow the first couple of responses that came to mind. "I didn't have time to come get you first," he said simply. "Like Faith said, it would have been all over by the time we got here if I'd delayed."

"That may be true, but this isn't a democracy. You don't get to pick and choose which orders to follow. Either I'm in charge, or you are. There's no in between."

"I never wanted to be in charge, and I certainly didn't intend to challenge your authority." Drake stiffened his spine and blurted out the truth he'd barely been able to admit to himself. "Look, I'm at least halfway in love with Faith, and there was no way in Hell I was going to leave her at Charles's mercy. And if Jez had been in danger, you would have done the same thing, no matter what the consequences."

Gabriel grimaced. "True," he agreed. "I just don't like the precedent."

"What does the precedent matter if you're going to kick me out anyway?"

"If I'm going to kick you out, it doesn't. However, I haven't decided what to do with you yet, and if you stay, it's an issue."

"When do you think you'll reach a verdict?"

Gabriel ignored the question. "If I sent you packing, where would you go?"

Drake had already figured out his choices were New York or nowhere. For a moment, he thought longingly of what it would be like to set aside his humanity. To join with Padraig's "family," and for the first time in more than a century actually *belong* somewhere. It would be so much easier than trying to fit in with Gabriel's Guardians. It might not make him *happy,* exactly, but after the initial period of adjustment, he suspected he would at least feel . . . content.

And therein lay the problem. Much though he might long for a comfortable life, he couldn't bear the thought of becoming content with Johnnie Drake.

Secure in his decision, he met Gabriel's disturbingly intense stare. "If you want me out of Baltimore, you're going to have to kill me."

A long, tense silence stretched between them. Drake hadn't the faintest idea what Gabriel was thinking, for nothing showed on the older vampire's face.

Then finally, Gabriel shrugged as if his decision were inconsequential. "I don't suppose we can afford to lose you, so I guess I'll have to let you off with a warning this time. Disobey me again, though, and I promise I'll make you sorry. I am most definitely *not* Eli, if you get my drift."

Drake almost laughed. "Yeah, I get it. And I've noticed." The hint of laughter fled. "But what about Jez? She really, really wants me gone."

"She'll calm down in time. You didn't do anything I wouldn't have done, and she knows that, even if she doesn't want to admit it."

"And are you really going to let the *Seigneur* join us? He's been a leader, and a ruthless one at that, for six hundred years. He hasn't had our qualms about hurting innocents, and that's not going to change even if he ends up not addicted to the kill anymore. He may not be the Antichrist, but he's not exactly one of the good guys, either."

"You think people are incapable of changing?"

"A little change, I can imagine. Not something like that."

To Drake's surprise, Gabriel smiled. "What do you think Eli was like before he transformed himself?"

Drake had no answer to that, had never allowed himself to think too much about the unpalatable truths he'd learned about his mentor.

"He was never cruel," Gabriel continued, "and he had the guilt thing down to an art form, but he was never as picky about his prey as I was. He'd take people who were already dying whenever he could manage it, and scum when he couldn't, but if neither was available, he'd take what was. Prostitutes, beggars. Anyone on the fringes of society, anyone who wouldn't be missed. Which is what I suspect Armand does as well."

Drake shook his head. "Why would you suspect that? You don't know him."

"No," Gabriel said patiently, "but you're forgetting something important—like why it is you want me by your side when you hunt."

Drake's brain still felt a little foggy, and it took him a moment to understand what Gabriel was saying. When he did, his eyes widened.

"Even before Eli changed," Gabriel said, "there was always a difference between him and my mother. Because he was her maker, she made the same choices in victims as he. But if she could have gotten her hands on innocents, or if Eli would have let her get away with making her victims suffer, she would have done it. She always stank of corruption to me, and Eli never did. Nor do you. Nor does Armand."

"How can that be?"

Gabriel shrugged. "I don't have a good answer for that. My best guess is that what I pick up on has to do with intentions and conscience—or lack thereof—more than actions."

Drake looked at Charles's body. "What about him?"

"There was a whiff of it, but it wasn't strong. He might have been salvageable, but I couldn't chance it. He'd already proven himself to be weak, and I'd never have been able to trust him."

Drake gave him a knowing look. "Plus, you feel sure you have the upper hand against *one* six-hundred-year-old even in your weakened condition, but you couldn't be sure about *two*."

Gabriel laughed but didn't deny it. "Let's take care of the bodies and get home, shall we?"

* * *

FAITH SAT ALONE on the couch in the den, waiting.

Eric and Harry, no longer needing to act as Drake's entourage, had packed up and gone to their own homes. Armand was locked in the basement below, beginning the fast that would either kill him or cure him. Lily was in bed, exhausted from the ordeal. Faith had used a light pulse of glamour to help lull her sister to sleep, hoping she wouldn't have nightmares. And Jez was in the master bedroom, anxiously awaiting Gabriel's return in a black silk nightie she'd shown to Faith in a moment of camaraderie.

Faith's stomach knotted and unknotted, and she had to keep her hands clasped in her lap or she'd start unconsciously fidgeting with her hair and end up pulling most of it out. The danger was over, but she didn't feel any better. She was still haunted by the look on Drake's face when Armand had manipulated her into saying she didn't trust him with Lily. That look might well haunt her till the end of her days.

It was after midnight when the front door finally opened. Faith's heart leapt into her throat, and a feeling akin to panic crept over her as she imagined facing

Drake after everything that had happened. Perhaps he wouldn't even want to talk to her.

But when she stepped into the foyer, she saw only Gabriel. Her heart clenched in her chest as every terrible possibility flooded her mind. Gabriel had killed Drake for his disobedience. Or banished him from Baltimore, forcing him out of town without a goodbye. Or Drake was so angry with her that he'd refused to come back to the house and get his stuff until Faith was gone.

Gabriel's eyes were cold and flat as he gestured her back into the den. "Let's have a chat, shall we?"

She put a hand to her throat, feeling the frantic throb of her heart. "Please tell me he's all right!"

His expression didn't change. "Physically, he's fine." He strode toward the den, herding her in as she hastened to avoid physical contact with him. "Sit," he ordered, pointing at a chair.

But she was through taking orders and remained stubbornly on her feet. After all she'd been through, she refused to be a doormat ever again. "I'll stand," she said.

Gabriel smiled pleasantly while his eyes promised terrible things. "Either you put your ass in that chair, or I'll do it for you."

"I'm not afraid of you," she said, and was surprised to find that it was true. She knew of his fierce reputation, knew he could swat her like a fly if he wanted to. But after facing Henri, after facing the threat from *La Vieille,* she couldn't muster the appropriate terror.

Gabriel's smile didn't falter as suddenly an unseen

force flung her backward until she hit the chair with a thump. If the chair hadn't been nicely padded, the impact would have hurt.

"Maybe you should be," Gabriel said, looming over her. "You've done quite the hatchet job on my second-in-command, and I'm somewhat put out with you at the moment."

The starch left her spine, and she sagged in the chair. "He told you what happened."

"Yes. I caught up with him shortly after he threw himself out a second-story window to resist feeding on a bleeding mortal when he was half starved."

She winced.

"Did you really tell him you wouldn't trust him around your sister?"

She winced again, fixing her gaze on the floor. "It was stupid," she admitted. "I knew in my heart he would never hurt her, but Armand managed to scare me enough to make me ignore what my heart told me." She forced herself to look up and meet Gabriel's hostile gaze. "If I could take that moment back, I'd do it in a heartbeat. I'm more ashamed of myself than I can possibly say."

Gabriel rolled his eyes but finally stopped looming over her, backing off to slouch into a seat across from her. "My father will take excellent care of you and of your sister. He and I aren't on the best of terms, but I know he'll be happy to take you both in, and I know you'll find a place for yourself among the Guardians."

Faith's throat tightened at the thought. "Are you saying we're not welcome here?"

"You're not welcome here unless you can fix things with Drake. I've got enough tension in my Guardians already without adding more. Especially if Armand pulls through."

"Do you think there's a chance I *can* fix things?" she asked. "I've wracked my brain trying to think of what to say, and everything seems so lame."

"I'm not what you'd call an expert at romance," Gabriel said with a twist of his lips that wasn't quite a smile. "You'll have to figure that one out on your own. If you're willing to give it a try, I suspect he's currently moping around his house." Gabriel reached into his pocket and pulled out a piece of paper. "That's his address."

She bit her lip as she took the paper from his outstretched hand.

22

IN THE DAYS he'd been staying at Gabriel's, Drake had forgotten how much he disliked his own crappy house. Those memories came to life as he wandered restlessly through the rooms, at loose ends. His first order of business had been a long, hot shower, but after that, he couldn't quite figure out what to do with himself. He didn't want to sit around and *think,* but he wasn't sure he had the energy for much else.

Finally, he decided that physical labor was the best way to keep his thoughts at bay, so he started working on the ugly downstairs bathroom again. He spackled and sanded the spots where he'd pulled the paint off when removing the wallpaper, then rooted around the attic until he found the dregs of a can of off-white paint he'd bought to cover the numerous scuffs and stains in the upstairs hallway.

The rhythm of dipping the roller in the paint and

then rolling it onto the wall helped lull him into numbness, but he knew it was a temporary reprieve.

Faith and Lily would be on a train to Philadelphia as soon as the sun set tomorrow night. He was glad he'd been able to save them from whatever fate Brigitte and Henri had planned, but how he wished he could have done it *before* he'd let Faith see the fragility of his self-control. He'd decided to spare her—and himself—the awkwardness that would arise from saying goodbye. So he would wait until she was gone before he returned to the house to gather his belongings. And he'd settle for being happy that Faith was finally free of Armand—no matter what redeeming qualities the *Seigneur* may or may not have.

He had just started on the second coat when the doorbell rang. He was seriously tempted not to answer—he wasn't exactly feeling sociable at the moment. However, not answering would feel too much like sulking, which he wouldn't allow himself to do. At least, that's what he tried to tell himself even though he had the uneasy impression that might be exactly what he was already doing.

When he discovered Faith standing on his doorstep, he stood dumbstruck in the doorway, unable to come up with a single thing to say. Hope tried to claw its way through the cloud of gloom that surrounded his heart, but he did his best to suppress it. No doubt Faith hadn't been willing to leave town without expressing her gratitude for his role in rescuing her and Lily. She was just here to say goodbye, and he wasn't sure he could bear it.

"May I come in?" she asked tentatively.

He'd already let her in, way too deep, letting her penetrate the barrier of indifference he'd built around himself. She'd cracked the shields he'd used to protect himself from others' opinions of him, and he wondered what it would take to repair them. And he needed to, because even though Gabriel was allowing him to stay, Jez was no doubt still mad at him, and neither Eric nor Harry would ever look at him the same way they had before this debacle.

Fighting the cowardly urge to hide from this conversation, he swung the door open and allowed her to step inside. Her nose wrinkled at the stink of paint, and he realized he looked like some kind of street bum in his old, ragged T-shirt and paint-stained carpenter pants.

Faith smiled at him faintly. "This is a new look for you."

He grimaced and hoped he didn't have paint splattered all over his hair and face, too. He hadn't exactly been paying a lot of attention to how much paint actually made it onto the walls. "Sorry," he said. "I wasn't expecting company."

Faith wandered into his bachelor-pad living room, and he followed close behind.

"I've only been here a month," he hastened to explain as she looked around. "None of this stuff is mine, and I'll get rid of it all eventually." Damn, he sounded like a complete idiot, babbling at her like this. This was the reason he really, really hadn't wanted to play out the goodbye scene.

After a skeptical examination, Faith deigned to sit on the mustard-yellow couch with its sagging cushions. Not sure what he was supposed to do, he sat on the edge of the recliner beside her seat. She looked as uncomfortable as he felt, her eyes averted while her teeth worried at her lower lip. He found himself riveted to the sight, thinking about how that lip had tasted when he'd sucked on it. Thinking of the feeling of her mouth trailing kisses over his skin.

Don't go there, he ordered himself, forcing himself to remember much more recent events.

Faith clasped her hands together in her lap and huffed out a deep breath. "I know there's nothing I can say to make up for how I acted, but—"

"Please don't," Drake said, holding up his hands. Faith fell silent, her eyes full of hurt. Drake softened his tone. "I don't blame you for not trusting me," he said. She opened her mouth to say something, but he interrupted. "I was about as close to losing control as it's possible to be while still retaining any shred of humanity. I wouldn't have trusted myself with Lily at that moment, either."

"*I* would have," Faith said.

A muscle in his jaw ticked as he met her eyes. "But you didn't."

"Armand manipulated me into saying I didn't. But it was my judgment he made me mistrust, not *you*."

Drake smiled gently, no matter how badly his heart ached. "I appreciate what you're trying to do. I really do. But I have to cope with the consequences of my own actions, including losing my self-control. You have nothing to apologize for. You were protecting your sister from potential danger, and there's nothing wrong with that."

"There's nothing wrong with it, but you're so angry with me you can't even look me in the eye?"

Drake growled softly and met her eyes again. "I'm not angry with you."

She surprised him by laughing. "Care to take a lie detector test?"

The corner of his mouth twitched, but he didn't let himself actually smile. "All right, so I'm a little angry. But I know it's not fair of me, and if I could use my conscious mind to turn my feelings on and off, I'd shut this one off so fast your head would spin."

"I think it's perfectly fair," Faith said, "but let's not argue about that."

Feeling the goodbye coming, Drake drew back into himself and sat up straighter. "When are you leaving for Philly?"

"I'm not."

Drake blinked, not sure he heard right. "What did you say?"

"I'm not leaving."

Much as Drake hated the idea of her leaving, he wasn't sure he could bear the thought of her staying. He might try to purge that painful memory from his brain, but he doubted he'd have much success. He'd hung on to the memory of Eamon's death for more than a century, and though the pain was less now than it had been, he knew it would never go away. If he'd been forced to face it day after day, he'd have gone mad by now.

"I want to stay," Faith said. "Not because I have any special fondness for Baltimore, and not because I've bonded with Gabriel or the Guardians, but because of you." Her voice hitched a little at that. "I don't know if you can ever forgive me, but I hope you're willing to give it a try."

There was a shimmer of tears in her eyes, and suddenly Drake felt like a bastard. He moved from the recliner to the sofa, putting an arm around her shoulders and pulling her to him. He planted a kiss on the top of her head, though what he really wanted to do was raise her face to his and devour her mouth.

"Have you ever considered that it's not you I'm having trouble forgiving, that it's myself?" he asked. "Armand might have manipulated that encounter, but he couldn't have done it without my help. I should have fed. As Gabriel tactfully pointed out to me, there's enough crime in some parts of this city that I probably could have found someone in the middle of some heinous act if I'd just stopped wallowing in self-doubt."

She snuggled closer to him on the couch, laying her palm against his chest as her head tucked into the bend of his neck. "Self-doubt is something we're both guilty of," she said. Her hand stroked his chest, and the touch sent a bolt of desire straight to his groin. Desire he tried like hell to swallow when she sighed and pushed away from him.

But she didn't go far, instead cupping his face in her hands and looking at him intently. "You're one of the good guys, Drake. You proved it when you jumped out a second-story window to keep from hurting a woman who meant absolutely nothing to you. And I knew it even before you proved it. I knew it that first night when I blurted out the truth of what Armand had asked me to do. I didn't realize I knew it, didn't recognize what *it* was, but right here," she pressed a hand to her chest, "I knew."

He swallowed a sudden, painful lump in his throat. And knew that no matter what, he couldn't let her just walk away. That might be the easy way out, might save him some future heartache. But as he'd decided tonight when he'd dismissed Padraig's temptation once and for all, the easy way wasn't always the best way.

Drake opened his arms, and Faith accepted the invitation. "I told Gabriel I was halfway in love with you already," he said, holding her tightly against his body. "I think I might have underestimated that a bit."

"Good," Faith said with a sniffle, "because I'm at least three-quarters of the way in love with you myself."

He inhaled the scent of her, then wrinkled his nose as the paint fumes marred her subtle perfume. "I'd like to take you upstairs, show you the rest of the house."

"Would the rest of the house include your bedroom?"

"Yeah, I was thinking that might be the first stop.

I'm determined to get you at least four-fifths of the way in love with me by the time the sun rises."

She laughed through the remains of her tears, pushing away from him to regard him through her damp eyelashes. "You think I'm going to admit to being hopelessly in love with you just because you give me an orgasm or two?"

He gave her his best wolfish grin. "There's only one way to find out."